A N

AN AVAILABLE MAN

a novel by

PATRIC KUH

AVAILABLE PRESS

BALLANTINE BOOKS • NEW YORK

An Available Press Book
Published by Ballantine Books

LIBRARY OF CONGRESS CATALOG CARD NUMBER: 89-92114
ISBN: 0-345-36429-5

Cover design by James R. Harris
Cover photography copyright © 1990 by Frederic L. Dodnick
Text design by Beth Tondreau Design/Jane Treuhaft

Manufactured in the United States of America

FIRST EDITION: March 1990
10 9 8 7 6 5 4 3 2 1

"I have always lived in error . . ."

—CASANOVA

PART ONE

CHAPTER 1

She didn't look like she could handle money for sex, so I thought I'd do her the service of telling her I was an artist. She could feel easier thinking her money was going toward paint and canvas. Most of the women did. Then they opened their purses without the slightest embarrassment. They were bohemian and just so Parisian. Art patrons now, in their own way.

She was dressed all in taupe. From the pumps to the big-shouldered suit and the bow in her hair. About forty-five, I thought. She sat over a demitasse at a café just off the Madeleine. I was right in front of her, waiting to cross the street. Our eyes met, and when I'd crossed and I looked again, hers were still on me. I walked into the café and sat down at a table beside her. She immediately opened her *Herald Tribune* and began to read it.

It was hot. I'd walked all the way from the house with a towel and swimming suit in a *cantine* bag. I was going to Deligny to try and get a swim in before the end of the day. It was June, and already the engines of France had been turned off to coast to the usual July and August standstill. Soon it would become a sinister city again. A procession of pulled-down shutters and tour groups. The Seine glinting like molten sheet metal, and the tour buses moving through the streets like sharks through a sunken city.

The glass panels of the café were open onto the street to enjoy even the slightest breeze. The waiter leaned on the counter with an elbow on his tray. He let me wait in case anyone else came in and he could get us both on the same trip. When no one followed me, he came over. I ordered an iced coffee.

She'd turned her back slightly to me. I was thinking that maybe I'd imagined her look and that she didn't have the slightest interest in me. I would have been glad to continue on to the pool. I would have liked the money even more. Two weeks before, I'd refused a sculptress who was renting a villa in St. Jean de Luz. She'd invited me for the summer, but I had already decided not to put myself up for adoption this time around and had turned her down. That was fine, then, in May. But now it was summer and no one was passing through and it was quiet and I had to take anything I got.

Her eyes came up from the back page. Mine were still there, and hers dipped again. The waiter brought my coffee and put down the bill and left. I'd give her some line anyway. "You know . . ." I said, and she looked up. "It's so refreshing to see a woman in this heat who can look so elegant without resorting to overkill."

It worked, because she didn't switch off. She smiled and said, "Do you hand out antacids with lines like that?" We both laughed. She could say any damned thing she pleased as long as we were talking.

"May I join you?" I asked.

"If you like."

"I would like." I stood up and took my glass over to her table. I sat down across from her. "Are you on holidays?"

"Not at all. Work. I'm a buyer."

"Of what?"

"For a chain of women's boutiques. Around L.A."

"Here for the designer shows?"

"Yes."

This was a lie. The designer shows weren't on for several weeks. Just one more of their little white lies. A little white lie was a good sign.

"And you?"

"I'm a painter."

"Oh, a painter! And you're not painting today?"

"It's too hard in this weather."

"It is hot. But I would have thought it would be just divine to paint in this weather in the City of Light."

I decided not to carry out my promise to sock the next person I heard say City of Light. In front of us a taxi trying to pull away from the curb made a motorcyclist swerve. The cyclist stopped and got off and laid his scooter under the car's wheels. The taxi now could not move. The cyclist took two chains that were wrapped around his seat and held one in each hand and started to curse the cab driver, who now got out of his cab. The cyclist swung his chains and screamed insults. Through the open panels our waiter and the barman began to shout encouragement. The cab driver backed away from the circling chains and said, *"Calme toi, calme toi."* The moment the cyclist did calm down and dropped his arms the older man lunged and grabbed one of the chains and hit him across the shoulder. That was reason enough to never calm down.

The waiter and the barman yelped with delight. My companion made a face. I hummed "I Love Paris in the Springtime" and she smiled. This time our eyes met and held. "How would you like to take a walk?" I said.

"I would love it. I think."

We strolled around the Fauchon side of the Madeleine and then down the Rue Royale to the Tuileries. In the central path the African vendors tried to sell their multicolored plastic birds. They wound up the bands on the birds' insides and sent them off on demented flights through the trees. Either they would attract passing children or be trodden on for a forced sale. We walked across the park as far as the balcony looking over the river. Floating across on the far bank, the decks of Deligny were still covered with people. I would miss my swim now. We walked back toward the Rivoli gate. In the sand along the wall groups of men were still playing *pétanque.* We watched them measuring up the small wooden ball and then throwing their metal balls toward it. They landed with a thud and raised dust. Near the players the small donkeys were being tethered together for their walk to the stables after all the rides of the day. We crossed the Rue de Rivoli to the arcades and walked up the Rue de Castiglione. I gave her my tour. I showed her the building where Chopin let out his last breath and told her about all the cannons from the Battle of Austerlitz that Napoleon had melted down into the Vendôme column. I also told her about Marcel, deep in his coat, dining at the Ritz while Big Bertha and the zeppelins bombed the city. Like all of them she enjoyed the Proust anecdotes, so I told her more. I told her about the originals for the characters. Like Boni de Castellane, who married Miss Gould. Tracing his bloodlines to Charlemagne and depending on the Kansas City–to–Chicago cattle train to pay for his white-wigged postillions. Then I told her how in the end poor Boni had to hock all his objects d'art to Daniel Guggenheim. It was all very grand standing in the Place Vendôme in the dusk talking like this, and my companion was just eating it all up, so I suggested we go up to the Café de la Paix for a drink. We rounded the corner into the Boulevard de l'Opéra and walked over to the terrace. There were still some free tables. The outside lights were on, and insects fluttered around in their yellow glow. I gave her the seat so she'd be facing the opera house and we sat. "How about some chilled *poire*?" I said.

"Is it good?"

"It's the best thing to have with this view."

"I'll have to have one, then, won't I?"

The waiter came over and I ordered two. While we waited she took a small camera from her handbag and walked across to the Métro entrance and took a picture of the Opéra. Its walls were glowing now with the last light. Then she took a picture of me sitting at the terrace. This was a good sign. She came back to the table smiling. The waiter brought two chilled brandy glasses with their cups still frosted and poured the *poire*.

"Did you get a good picture?" I asked.

"I think so. Considering the subjects." She smiled.

"Do you hand out antacids with lines like that?" I said, and she burst out laughing. She turned to look back out at the Opéra.

"It's just like a Tintoretto. Or is it Turner I'm thinking of? You know, all those soft pinks. You should paint it."

"I have."

She took a sip at her glass but said nothing. She looked out at the street.

"That's the same look you had when I first saw you," I said.

"Is it?"

"A penny for your thoughts."

"Oh, nothing."

"Nothing?"

"Last time I was here actually, years ago . . . oh, what does it matter? It's the anniversary of my divorce, actually. What am I telling you for?"

"Don't." I quickly raised my glass. "To France for always having had the courage to stick to the surface." Anything to get her away from memories.

"You're right, you're quite right. To France!" Our glasses clinked, and we sipped at the cold eau-de-vie.

"I'm sorry we didn't meet before," she said. "I'm going tomorrow. You would have been quite a guide."

"Oh well."

"Next time."

We needed an action now so we wouldn't get to talking. That could take up hours. Putting down my glass, I grazed her hand. "Not next time, this time." I said. She raised her thumb to be able to bring it closer and return the gesture. There was no more to be said now but hotel and room number. When she told me which hotel it was I just stopped myself from saying, My they must be paying clothes buyers a lot these days. It would have been just like me to ruin it all with a quip.

Walking back the way we had come, I entertained the latest

thought process. If she's as easy with me, how many has she been this easy with? Onwards, can't be taken hostage by possibilities. Please, Surgeon General, be infallible on rubbers. A block before we got to the hotel I told her I'd follow her in five minutes. I didn't have to explain why.

"You're sure?" she said.

"Yes."

She squeezed my hand and I brought her toward me for a kiss. She grabbed me behind the head suddenly and whispered in my ear. "You're such a strange turn-on."

"Oh."

"You're so reserved."

". . . ."

"And that makes me real curious."

She went into the hotel, and I walked once around the block and then followed her in. The doorman opened the door for me and smiled. As always I wondered whether it was just politeness or if they recognized me. They saw so many people it would be hard to remember. I walked straight to the elevator. The pianist was playing some Cole Porter, and people sat around having drinks, already dressed for dinner. In movies they always made such a scene about getting through, as if these places were crawling with security. Not once had I been stopped. Even now, dressed as I was for the pool, I walked right through. It was when you could hardly afford a drink in a place that you had to walk through it as if you owned it. I had long since learned that. I shared a lift with a blond family. The boys in blue blazers and the girls in frocks. Maybe some of the concierges and doormen did recognize me and were just being French. The good French, glad that while they suffered on stage at least someone overhead was getting their rocks off. The family got out, and the old lift operator looked at me. He would obviously never get used to the idea that someone in jeans and a T-shirt could be a client of his. We continued up. I was glad I'd given her the kiss so the pact was already sealed. At least we wouldn't have to go through that. I was glad I'd given her the artist story, too. Whether she believed it or not. She did look like it would be easier for her. The cruelest thing was not to allow someone a graceful way out. I had learned that, too.

CHAPTER 2

As always I was awake long before she was. A question of going public. The early sunlight came in across the tray of drinks and her cases and my clothes on the sofa. She didn't have a penthouse at the hotel or even a balcony, but she did have a large window. She'd insisted we keep it open all night and the air-conditioning off. Probably because it made her feel horny, or something equally original. I sat by it in my trousers looking out. We were up high enough for the view not to be blocked by trees. It was a good view, all the way across the Tuileries to the Left Bank. Of all the views from all the hotel rooms in Paris, from the Place Vendôme to the Rue des Beaux-Arts, it was one of my favorites. I had known the Tuileries bare in winter with the gray statues standing guard over the frozen fountains, and then when they thawed and when the buds came and in summer with crowded pathways and with children pushing sailboats off from the stone sides of the fountains. If I stayed quiet and she didn't wake up, I'd be glad to just sit and watch it all warm up.

I stretched the phone as far as the bathroom and called down to room service and asked for coffee and newspapers. I told them I'd leave the door open and not to knock.

A man in his fifties, much too old for the graveyard shift, I thought, came up with a tray of juice and coffee and three French newspapers and the *Tribune.* He put the tray down on the table in the sitting room. "Monsieur must be interested in current affairs," he said.

"Fascinated."

In case Madame would be woken he said nothing else. While he gathered the drinks trolley I went through Madame's handbag and found a tip. I sat in the sunlight and read all the papers. The *Tribune* said that the Mets were way ahead in the National League East.

The papers were all at my feet and I was just sitting looking out when I heard her behind me. She turned over, searching for a cool spot, and wound herself in the sheets. She turned again, felt again, didn't find it, and sat up, looking at me groggily and half shielding her bloated face. She glanced discreetly at the bedside table to make sure her rings and necklace were still there. They all did and they all thought that it wasn't noticed and when I saw them do it I didn't even mind anymore. She patted the covers beside her, motioning me to sit. I didn't move. "Come" she said.

"I'm fine here."

"What are you doing?"

"Nothing. Watching the poor suckers rush to work."

"Oh, I'll just sleep another half hour, then." She rolled over.

I was feeling lousy. Keeping the windows open all night was not the only thing she'd insisted on. She'd also insisted on calling me John all night. I told her my name was Francis. This seemed to have little to do with it. Also by the fifth time she'd dragged me back into bed I was beginning to doubt that she was quite as innocent as she'd seemed the evening before. I'd kept on trying to get out of bed. I thought I was going to choke or faint with the clamminess of her skin touching mine, and everytime she pulled me back she laughed as if she were doing it playfully. Hookers have it easy, I thought: bang-bang, bye-bye. These women always wanted more, to feel your arms and your lack of beer gut until they fell asleep. To murmur "come" in the mornings with their dip-shit poignancy and then to slap the sheets and expect you to rush over just to feel that knowing hand on your chest. Sure, baby, you and me, all the way.

When she did wake up she broke all the rules. I was rereading the papers for something to do and she was staring at me from the bed. The six-grain cereal she'd taken from her suitcase was eaten, and she dabbed at her mouth, pushed her tray away, and leaned back into her pillows. Of course she felt wonderful. At night she'd come, and in the morning she hadn't broken her diet. Everything had gone her way, and I hated the arrogance it gave her. "But why do you stay?" she said. We were off.

"Oh, *la vie,* inspiration." I continued the artist story.

"I know all about *la vie,* but that is no answer."

I would have preferred to stay silent than talk and risk the money, now that the job was almost over, but I felt, well, I felt nothing, I just hated the arrogance, that's all. "Not everyone's trying to sell you next season's look, *chérie.*" We were both silent. The traffic roared by below. The drivers furious at spending the summer in the city proved it by charging toward the traffic lights at Concorde. I closed my eyes and felt the sun on my face.

"I'd get you a job just like that if you came to L.A." It was a typical last-day thought. Once they found a trick they liked, they liked it even more within hand's reach. "And you really don't look like the type who likes to go hungry."

Very well, I thought, as you insist, Madame, I shall put you through your paces. "Bliss, that's why I stay."

"Bliss?"

"Yes, bliss. Because sometimes here we are granted moments of pure bliss. Or maybe because here those moments seem to come more often than in other places." I stood up and took a breath and a practiced look across the Seine. Her eyes of course followed mine. I'd let her have it all. "It's nothing much, a shade of light on a façade, a ripe peach and a glass of Sauternes down by the river." I swept my hand over the roofs of the Left Bank as if over some personal accomplishment. "Because of views like this from up here. This is the way it should be, what makes it all worthwhile and absolves anything else that might go on." It worked. I'd made a chink, and even though the sun was still coming in her very own Parisian window, she now wasn't feeling quite so ethereal herself and she shut up.

In the afternoon I took her out to Charles de Gaulle. Standing in the check-in line she asked me for my phone number. I gave it to her. She said she'd be coming back soon to buy for next season's collection. I didn't tell her she'd better get the dates right next time. She took out her wallet and opened it and I could see the hundred-dollar bills. I thought she might be having a moment's hesitation in case she might offend me, but all she handed me was a card. It just had an address and a phone number. "If you should get to L.A. first."

"Sure," I said.

Once they'd taken her luggage we had very little time and rushed toward the gate. We passed cafeterias and bars and assorted souvenir stores. We were moving through the people saying good-bye clustered around the official boarding area, fifteen feet from the security check and falling. She is playing with you, I thought. This is a cookie who cruises cafés and now is going to make you stew for not having bared your soul to her over breakfast. We were standing facing each other while cameras and handbags were fed onto the X-ray belt.

"Well," she said, smiling.

I cursed the loudspeakers for complicating my thoughts. Can she really be under the impression that it was all a shared tender moment? Jesus, do I have to wear a sign around my neck that reads HUSTLER? It's for their sake I don't spell it out.

"Well?" she repeated.

You cannot let her go. You simply cannot let her go. Do something. You can't leave, and this shit for brains probably thinks that you can't bear to part. Screw your phrases, of course you're just one more dark figure hanging around the dear ladies. Worry about it at home. Just ask for the money now, ask for the fucking money and leave.

"Well, I have your number," she was saying.

"Yes."

She was kissing me on the cheeks. She was putting her handbag on the belt and passing through the detecting door frame. She was disappearing down the corridor, being swallowed in the crowd, and I, in a final proof of my absolute assholeness, was waving after her. It was dandy, she'd just burnt me, and I, with the imprint of her patent leather loafer fresh on my teeth, was waving merrily.

Back at my apartment the red light of the answering machine was flashing with its load of news. I treated myself to a beau geste and ignored it. I went around the house throwing open all the windows. I threw off my clothes and took a half-hour cold shower with my eyes closed. Afterwards I fixed myself a stiff screwdriver. I took a chair to the window, and, balancing carefully with the glass in my hand, I climbed out onto the sloping roof. Stooping low, I walked up as far as the chimneys and sat down and looked out. I could see the outlines of people on the roofs way into the distance. I had spent many scorching days in their company. Like them, happy to inhabit a separate city above the sweltering pavements and the clogged traffic. And I, in the middle of it all, bringing my tan to a perfect tone.

Even now when I hadn't been able to spend my day up on the roof I was still in time for my favorite part of such days. As the sun begins to sink behind the roofs, the people studding them with their towels and deck chairs linger on, knowing that the richest moments are still to come. Still slightly dazed from the sun, drunk with the heat and stoned with well-being, we watch the evening light decline over the city. Then, just before night falls on the spires and domes and roofs, the strangest thing always happens—strange at least for a people whose only allegiance is gastronomic: from one roof to another they wave. They have never and will never meet, have never spoken and by then are only distant silhouettes to each other. They have only had the pleasure of a day spent in the sun, and it always touched me that somehow each felt glad that others had shared it with them. People were waving now. They were not the studied waves of people aware they are taking part in a ritual. They were casual waves, as people on deck might wave to a stranger on a pier. I was glad to acknowledge our strange complicity. I joined my wave to the others.

I could have slept up there. I toyed with the idea. At the top it was flat enough, and the heat of the day was trapped in the lead roof and would be released for hours.

"You're a lousy closet sunset watcher!" How often I'd heard Emma say that and roar laughing, showing her beautiful teeth. There, it was starting already. Just knowing that her father was around. Maybe that's what had been wrong all day. Well, he was around, and ignoring his message on the machine downstairs was not going to make him go away. It would do nothing, and this was one time where nothing would not do. I'd call him.

CHAPTER 3

I fixed myself another screwdriver and pressed the playback button on the machine. First on was the Greek in her come-up-and-see-me-sometime hiss. "Hello, François. Just double-checking that you got the arrival time right. It's the noon flight direct from Athens. *A bien toto*, kissy-kissy!" She giggled off.

Next was Cullington's Texan drawl. "Mr. Buchanan, Sid Cullington here. I'm in Vienna right now but I hope you've decided whether you'll let me buy you a drink. For Emma if for nothing else, right? I'll be at the Meurillon from about eight or nine tonight. Call me. I'm counting on you. It has to be tonight."

I called the Meurillon and told them I wanted to leave a message for Cullington. They told me he had checked in already and they could put me through. I told them that it wasn't necessary and just to give him the message. I said I'd be at the Café Dakar at ten thirty. I gave the address. The operator made me repeat it; she must have thought she'd misunderstood. I repeated where it was, and she didn't say anything. I put the phone down and lay on the bed. It was dark now, but I didn't put on any lights. A blast of hot air came up from the street and in through the window. I could hear the voices of people sitting out. I could smell the leather from the Ghanaian sandal store on the ground floor. The Portuguese concierge was frying fish in the courtyard. That way it never smelled up her house, it smelled up everyone else's. It conjured up wharfs to me. Fish sold on the pavement and sold fish wrapped in newspaper. My neighbors below had their windows open also. They were having dinner. I could hear the cutlery on the plates, so they'd probably brought the table right up to the window.

"It's like Naples," the wife said.

"It's like Algiers just before a storm," the husband said. They had been civil servants of some sort when Algeria was French. It wasn't hard to drift in the heat. I drifted. Emma. There was no way I could stop her now from prying loose and floating to the surface. I'd been meandering in the Luxembourg. It was four springs ago and the wake of a rain shower. There was a moist sky, and the pathways smelt of damp earth. She was sitting in the grove of the Fontaine Médicis reading *Le Français et la vie,* volume 2, with an English-French dictionary in her lap. The little knapsack on the chair beside her said it all.

" 'Il pleure dans mon coeur, comme il pleut sur la ville.' It weeps in my heart as it rains on the city. Verlaine. An adequate translation?" I said.

"No one likes a smart-ass, pal," she said, giving me a peek at her Texan accent.

"Just my luck, an American. So tell me your life story then." She was preparing for a year at the Sorbonne by spending the summer taking French at the Alliance Française. Every day for the next week I waited in the courtyard of the Boulevard Raspail entrance until she came bouncing down the stairs, braless, in her white ankle socks with her verb books under her arm. And every day we went down the Rue de Fleurus, where I pointed out where Gertrude and Alice had lived, and since she was a student treated her to coffee in one of the kiosks in the Luxembourg. Cullington had rented a marvelous apartment for her on the Rue de Médicis, and one day she invited me up. One wall was stacked with a stereo, she had a cigar box crammed with coke, the best view of the Luxembourg, and when the ankle socks were wrapped around my back she came in a fit of laughter.

This went on for a month. Every day I'd wait for her and we'd cross the gardens and if the weather was clear have coffee. Then go up to the apartment and make love, and afterwards, while I sunbathed on the balcony, I'd watch her lying naked crossways on the bed, sipping wine and mastering the *passé composé.*

One night after much blow and *vin rouge,* sitting outside La Palette, I finally told her how I paid the rent. By the time she'd made me swear—cross my heart, in fact—that it was true and she had chuckled herself dry, I was in love.

About two weeks later I was quite happily going from antique store to antique store on the Rue de Seine with a very elegant German woman who was in town for the weekend when Emma walked by. She was already going through the mandatory Jean Seberg stage like every other American girl in Paris and she'd cut her hair.

"You don't need people, you need scalps!" she screamed, standing in the middle of the street. I was embarrassed for the German woman, though she seemed very amused by my imbroglio and wandered off among copper bedstands until it was over.

By the end of the summer Emma had given up the apartment, the French classes, and the plans for the Sorbonne. She'd had a bridge-burning fight with Cullington, and she was living with me and without money. She started off putting an ad in the *Tribune* with all the other escorts.

"Why?" I asked.

"Spite."

". . . ."

"You would have to have grown up like me."

I sat up from the bed. Even with a bathrobe it was too hot. I threw it off. I pulled the head of the fan up as high as it would go on its pedestal and locked it into position so it pointed down at the bed. I turned it on to its top speed and lay back down. I had slept less than I thought the night before with the woman dragging me back. I was sinking into the bed now. The fan felt good, and I thought, Yeah, sure, all that Emma stuff is lovely, but get to the end. Get to the end now before you go and see Cullington. Skip the crap, skip the good times, skip the two years of good times together. Get to the end. To the week searching Paris at Christmas because she'd earned all that money and was on a heroin binge. How about that white Christmas then? Let that one float to surface, drift on that one, pal. When that model from Detroit told you where she was and took you to the Rue St. Denis. Remember the stairs blacked out and a queue of men lined up on the stairs holding candles because the light had been cut off. And above the rooms where the girls received, the shooting gallery where Emma had spent the week because all those black hookers had taken her in. Remember Emma in the corner saying, "Help me, help me!" Remember saying that you couldn't, not anymore. Remember. Remember saying you were worn down and you couldn't help her and remember that was the last time you ever saw her, and now, damned fool, you're going to see her father. How about that? She left you just like that, you haven't heard from her in two years, and her father calls and off you go. Well, how about it? Remember some more, like her holding the girl from Detroit, there against the wall of that shooting gallery. Just because she had to hold someone and it couldn't be you at that stage. Yeah, it was the girl she wanted to hold while she shivered and she did and you watched. That was the junkies' ultimatum, sign up for the voyage or get lost. Just sticking around was the unpardonable. She sure made that decision for you. She left. She didn't even come back to the house for her stuff. Just like that, just like Emma.

I got off the bed and turned on the light. Jesus, I thought, lucky for Cullington he'd gotten me at the right sort of time. And not because I was feeling I could finally face it or process it or whatever new term the shitsuckers were using. Something was wrong. Getting smarmy over asking for money at the airport was warning enough. Something had to change, no more than that. I took another cold shower.

At eleven I went out to walk the four blocks from the house to the Café Dakar. Down the block a police wagon was carrying out an I.D. control without much enthusiasm. Just procedure. Unlike the times when they cordoned off all the surrounding blocks and came through in their vans from every direction and then went building by building. The results of these operations were published the next day in the papers, together with a list of seized weapons, kilos of drugs, and illegals. Since I'd been granted my Carte de Séjour I was fearless. All the same I took a right into an alley so as not to be bothered by them. Three alleys later I rounded into an alley of bars. Signs glowed tacked onto the scarred and patched-up walls. There were cars parked all along one side, leaving only a narrow corridor. At the end of the alley Le Lys was the new hot spot. A line outside it waited patiently to slum. Across from it Le Dakar flashed. In its pink neon brilliance it could have been a fifties sign for the Alcazar or the Folies-Bergères.

Outside the door I noticed two guys leaning against a car. They were blond and had crew cuts and western boots and big-buckled belts. Cullington had arrived, it seemed. They had the windows of the car down and listened to some country-and-western sop on a tape. I said, "Howdy," and they did too. Friendly enough. I went in.

Le Dakar was always filled with the type who cater to those who frequent hot spots. (This season Le Lys was practically next door, which made it even more convenient.) Emma always called it a honky-tonk. It was no more than a large back room. Like a place to hold a country dance in. On some nights there were only a few Senegalese sitting around chewing cocoa beans and Moroccan workmen stalling over a coffee before turning in. Tonight it was full. The red lights were all on, making the place look like some cheap brothel in the East, and the wooden counter was covered with drinks and the sawdust on the floor smelled fresh. It was always a break from the rest of the places in Paris. Abadou, the owner, was shining glasses and looking over the tables. He was from Senegal and just hummed his way through the nights and kept a list of those barred. Friday, being mosque day, he was closed. I nodded across to him. He didn't see me. It was too full to spot Cullington, and I walked between the tables. There were a couple of Arab pimps and a table of laughing street boys from the Rue St.-Anne. Another table of burned-out Jamaican grass dealers and a table of Chinese smack dealers as always playing cards and then the usual assorted nondescripts. Cullington was sitting by a wall, looking around and not touching his beer. He wore a bush jacket over a white shirt. I could see different colored pills and capsules in his pocket. He'd never sounded like he had a weak heart. Seeing me coming toward him, he stood up with his hand out. "Mr. Buchanan?"

"How did you know?"

"You look American. What kind of a son of a bitch place is this anyway?"

"Emma's favorite."

"I figured so."

"And the goons?"

"They're my pilots."

"They double as bodyguards?"

"Hope you don't mind. The concierge suggested it when I asked him where the hell this place was. Drink?"

"Later maybe. What did you call me for?"

"Very well. Look, Mr. Buchanan, there are very few things that really worry a man my age. Any age, I suppose, one of them is family and—"

"You seemed to survive the two years she was here."

"You know that I didn't force her to come back. She came by herself."

"Yeah, I know that part."

He leaned across the table and pressed my forearm. "Look,

Francis, let me say my piece. The past is the past. I think that Emma needs you."

"Like a hole in the head."

"You don't realize what it is to have someone who—"

"What the hell are you talking about?"

"Very well, you want to talk business?"

"If that's what it's about."

"Good." He collected himself and took a swig from the beer. He looked glad to get back to his own known waters of supply, demand, and curve. "Emma came back to Houston and thought she could get herself together. She went to a hospital and got off all the drugs. She borrowed money from her trust fund and bought an apartment and started a clinic for Mexican women. It lasted a year before she was back on the heroin. She was happy with you, Francis. I never thought I'd say it. All that year that she was fine and running the clinic that's all she talked about."

"So what does this have to do with business?"

"Okay, here's the deal. A year ago I came back from a trip and found she'd signed herself into a Swiss nut house. I haven't seen her since. I've talked to her a few times and also to her doctor. Well, she's coming in from Geneva tomorrow to spend a few days here before heading back to Houston for the rest of the summer. Don't ask me what the hell she wants to do here, but she insists, and you know what that's like. But anyway, well, she'll be here tomorrow, and I'm willing to give you double your rate if you just go and spend some time with her. Never thought I'd be saying this to you, but there it is."

"My rate?"

"To escort."

"How do you know that?"

"Because I had a detective on you for a month after she moved in."

"That's how things get done in Texas, is it?"

"Oh, who cares, Francis! I don't want her escorted. I want her to have company. Company, damn it all. At your age you have no idea what it means. It just tears me up knowing she's alone. Nut house or not, she's alone all the time. If it goes wrong this time I just don't know what I'll do."

"Or what she'll do."

"Exactly. So how about it? We got a deal here?"

"Not yet. If she's coming in tomorrow and you're here, why don't you see her? Seeing as it just tears you up and all."

"I've got business."

"I thought this was business."

"Look, Francis, shit or get off the pot. You do or you don't want to earn some money."

"Sure, I'll give her a call. Four hundred up front, and if she wants to have some company then that's fine."

"So we have a deal?"

"How is she?"

"Brassy as ever, just as brassy as ever." Resigned as it might have been, we actually exchanged a smile.

I spotted a girl named Lisa across the room. A few nights before she'd been crying her troubles to me. She'd been trying to get some photographer to use her for an airline shoot. It was the old-faithful Trocadéro–Tour Eiffel shot, but he couldn't use her. I'd managed to say to her, "Don't get scared off," and she'd said that she wouldn't, that she was here to stay. She had the longest legs and huge fleshy lips and was nineteen. I'd watched her buy drinks with a real case of the nowhere-to-go-back-to's. She, of course, had reminded me of Emma at a certain time. Finally she'd told me that just to get by she wanted to get into escorting. I thought Cullington probably was a live one and maybe even kinky enough to want to check out what his only daughter had spent two years doing. I waved Lisa over.

"How about yourself," I said to Cullington. "Feel like some company tonight?"

"In the shape of what were you thinking?"

"The girl walking toward us."

"Mm-hmm-hmm!"

She sat down and we ordered drinks and at Cullington's insistence she started on the roundabout story made up of opportunities taken, missed, and lost which had brought her from Carson City, Nevada, to talking to him at the Café Dakar.

"Cowboy country out there, I love it!" he said.

"Yeah. My dad's a dentist."

They talked on. The place had filled up even more. When it was at its rowdiest the bar always had the feeling of being one of those little bars always on the outside edge of some European quarter. The sort of place where should you have wanted to wear a white dinner jacket you could easily imagine yourself to be back in the Bal Negre of Brassaï or a dive at the bad end of some boardwalk waiting for the ship to come in from some exotic city of fantasy. Peter Lorre would have been a regular. It had been Emma's favorite haven. Between the regulars' orange smiles from their constant cocoa-bean chewing, and the beer crates which on crowded nights doubled as tables and chairs, and the occasional knife fights, she could cut moorings and drift. She was always very particular about where she allowed herself to slip and drift. Extremely methodical in her entrances, not quite so about her exits.

"Shall we go and have a drink at my place?" I said to my companions. "You can take back some of Emma's stuff maybe."

We went out. The pilots were still standing by the car. While Cullington with much backslapping sent them back to the hotel, Lisa and I wandered down the pavement. "Isn't it thrilling, your first oil baron?" I said.

"Beats listening to Mr. Yamamoto's economic predictions." She sounded as if she'd been at it for years. "And by the way."

"Yes?"

"Who was Emma?" She'd eased right into it.

"No one. You were still throwing batons in Carson City."

"But who was she?"

"My girl."

"For want of a better expression."

"Yes."

"You're such a sap."

"Have you enough money for a cab?"

"In case he's a weirdo?"

"He's no weirdo. Just in case you don't feel right, because I'm going to sleep."

"You sound like my mother."

My clock read 3:00 A.M. when their voices woke me from the sitting room. Cullington was telling an involved story about a fishing trip that went wrong off the Cayman Islands. It was followed by much laughter, mainly on his part. I woke again a few moments later and they were both talking loudly. He'd obviously made his move and they were in full negotiations.

"So you're going to sit over there all night. I wasn't quite figuring it this way."

"That's right. You should have made it clear that's what you wanted. I'm an escort."

"Oh Christ, baby! How long have you been at this?"

"Never mind."

"Well, I'd have a lot more fun in Nevada."

"You could have it in Paris, too. You should have made it clear."

"Make it clear! Make it clear! Why didn't you make it clear you were inviting me back for conversation?"

"I didn't invite you, Francis did."

"Look, hon, I'm not adverse to a deal myself. You want double, you got it."

"No."

"Please, baby, please. Triple?"

"A hundred dollars and good night."

"For what?"

"Listening to you for three hours."

"Dream on, baby. I pay only for what I get, and so far that's nothing."

"Let's have another drink."

"That's more like it. I might just be able to persuade you still, mightn't I?"

The next time I was woken by a shriek from Lisa. I rushed into the sitting room before I'd thought better. Cullington was on top of her in the reclining chair with his bush jacket spread over her like a bear skin. He was so awkward that she was laughing at his efforts, and then he started to laugh also.

"Please, baby, please."

"The joke's over, you oaf."

"This is no joke, baby."

"You're heavy, man, get off!"

"Surrender?"

"Get lost. Get him off me, Francis."

I put my hand on his shoulder. He stopped his antics but made no move to get off her. He was panting, and when he turned around his face was much drunker than he had sounded. "So this is where the pimp mugs me."

"No, just where I tell you to get off her, to pay what you owe, and leave."

"And Emma?"

"Whether you can pay me to be with her? I should have socked you one then."

"Christ, then I won't pay you! You still do care or you wouldn't have come."

"Wrong, Cullington. Dead wrong. Life's too short. You look after her."

He wasn't smiling any longer and had stopped panting. He found his feet and stood up, unruffled himself, and addressed me. "Now let me tell you, these legs stood for three hours in water in the Philippines while the Japs fired at us. I'd think twice before pulling a fast one."

I don't mind hitting a drunk. In fact they're the only type of fights that I like to get into. The odds favor me, just have to be quick, take them completely by surprise, and then take the time to decide how much damage I wish to inflict.

"Nests of Japs all along the beachhead. Know what that feels like, sonny?"

"Just give Lisa her money."

"Let me ask you a question first. Did this sort of scene go on with Emma also?"

"Pay her and get lost, Cullington."

"Did it?"

"Never. The talk never lasted this long."

He moved. I was waiting for it, and it was sweet. Before his left was up, my fist was deep in his stomach. It was enough; he was stunned. When he straightened back up, I jabbed the heel of my hand up under his nose and then he was down on the sofa, moaning.

"Je-sus! Oh Je-sus! Damn it, man, that's a damned shame to hit an old man." His nose was bleeding down into his lip, and he wiped it off with his cuff. I didn't want it all over the sofa so I took some tissues from the mantelpiece and handed them to him. He looked up and made as if to take them but grabbed my wrist and jerked me forward. *Whack!* My head slapped the wall. He was up and standing and had me pinned above where he'd been sitting and was throwing knuckleballs into my kidneys. Just as suddenly he stopped. I thought it was some sort of gentlemanly notion to let me get off the sofa. When I turned around he had stood back and was looking very dazed. I got off the sofa and sent him three roundhouses. Almost not noticing, he made three fast blocks with his forearms. Shit, I thought, maybe the old fuck really is about to kick your ass. He just stood there swaying more and more as if with all the sudden movement the booze had gone up to his head. He looked as if he were about to fall.

"You all right?" I said.

"Sure kid it's just—"

"Well, this will help you!" I brought my elbow right up

into his stomach with such a kick that his guts should have come out his mouth. He held up for a moment, looking at me as if I were his best friend and had just shot him in the back. He managed to say, "That's not how we do it in Texas," and then he went back, doubled over, missing the chair that was waiting for him, crashed against the stereo, and grabbed on to the amp wires to hold up. I thought it was all about to come down, but he let go, and as he crumbled he reached out again, grabbed a bookshelf instead, and brought that down with him. He was out.

The concierge was screaming from the courtyard. "*Mais vous êtes pas possible vous, vraiment alors . . .*" I ran to the kitchen window and looked down. I couldn't see her, as she was probably screaming from her bedroom, which gave onto the courtyard.

"*Excusez-moi, madame, un petit contretemps.*" I closed the window. I took two beers from the fridge and went back into the sitting room. I sat down on the bean bag. I handed Lisa one of the beers. She was huddled in the corner of the sofa. She'd lost a lot of color in the last two minutes but put a good face on it.

"Some catch," I said.

"Is he all right?"

"He seems to be breathing." We looked over at him. He moved and stretched and groaned in drunk comfort.

"All I wanted . . . all I wanted . . . was a little company . . . company . . . comp . . ." His head went over to the other side and he was out again. Lisa tried to keep from laughing by drinking her beer, but I could see it coming. Once she'd started I started. We didn't stop laughing for ten minutes while we drank the beers. I stopped only when she began to find my eyes.

"What are you going to do with him?" she said.

"Leave him there. He'll bleed on the sofa."

"You aren't going to kick him out?"

"No."

"Well . . ."

". . . ."

"Guess I'll be heading home, then."

"Guess you will."

"Guess you were right about having the cab money."

"Guess I was." I stood up, and then she did. That was that over with.

"He's really quite sweet," she said, looking over at Cullington.

"Aren't we all." I went over to where he lay. There were paperbacks all over him, but at least he was on his back so I didn't have to turn him. I cleared the books away. His wallet was in an inside pocket of the jacket. It had dollars and Swiss francs, all the hot-shot credit cards, and a photograph of Emma. The way he wanted to remember her, in her late teens. Before she went wrong. She was in camouflage, kneeling, holding a rifle, and there were three wild turkeys she'd shot laid out in front of her. I took five of the fourteen hundred-dollar bills and four hundred Swiss francs. The pills from his shirt pocket were on the floor around him, and I gathered them and put them on the mantelpiece. I rolled him over. He carried his money clip in the back pocket. It was thick with five-hundred-franc notes. I took two thousand. Of course he'd realize he'd been robbed. Screw him, he'd cost me plenty of work. I stood up and held out three hundred-dollar bills to Lisa. She had said nothing all the while and now had dropped to yet another shade of paleness. There was not a hint of bravado from her now.

"Take it, he owes you," I said.

She stood rooted for a moment longer and then grabbed the money and turned toward the door. "Oh God, let me out of here!"

The light outside was already strong when I woke. Cullington was shouting into the phone. "What did the market do? . . . I don't care if he's got a goddamned zillion, he's hocked to the hilt . . . He'll drill teasers till he goes belly up . . . Has no idea . . . And I'll sue his ass . . . Five percent of the issue, he wants to get the S.E.C. in on this? . . . Yeah, well tell him we'll meet in hell first!" He slammed down the phone.

When I went into the kitchen he was back on the phone. He was sitting at the table with the coffeepot and a bottle of rotgut Calvados he'd taken from the fridge in front of him. An old newspaper and the back of two envelopes were covered in scribbled numbers. The phone was nestled under his chin as he waited. His shirt swayed on a hanger in the window, the bloodstain on the cuff now a light pink like some frantically rubbed-off lipstick. I didn't bother meeting his look, just took a cup and poured some coffee.

"The phone calls are collect, right?"

"Course. Oh, hi there, speak English, honey? Good. I forget the room numbers but I want to speak to Larry Hook. . . . Larry! Yeah, listen, reserve a spot for as close as possible, let's see, it's two o'clock now, how about fiveish. I know it's crazy but I just have to get out of here today . . . I know I wasn't at the hotel . . . something like that . . . same hangar we came in to . . . course I know it. Pick up my bags at the Meurillon, will you, and phone the office to tell them to look after it. See you boys before five then." He put the phone down and stood up with his hand out.

"Sorry about last night, amigo, I was way out of line."

"Sure, forget it."

"And thanks for sparing the face. Nose is a bit swollen, that's all. Truth is, I haven't felt this good in years."

"I know what you mean."

I went back to bed with my cup of coffee, and his play for time started. First he wanted to borrow a razor. I told him to take one. He didn't rush his shaving, and then he asked for a towel. I told him the press was at the end of the corridor. He patted his face in the door of my room and it was a cigarette that he wanted. Finally he wondered if I wouldn't drive him out to the airport. Apparently it was never too late to negotiate. I said I would. Emma would approve. If someone was this desperate you either didn't bother at all or you milked them.

It was early rush hour, and the traffic streaming out was slow. All the way out to Le Bourget we said not a word. There he directed me through a maze of hangars. We stopped at a security hut, and Cullington didn't have a pass so the guard had to phone his pilot. Cullington was nervous. He thought he'd miss his takeoff spot and drummed the dashboard.

"Don't worry, she isn't arriving today," I said. He grinned. The guard let us through, and we drove along the edge of the tarmac and onto the taxiing strip. The plane was warming up. The same two guys from the night before waited at the foot of the stairwell. Instead of boots and buckles they wore epauletted white shirts and aviator glasses. I drove right up to them. Cullington got out, and I didn't.

"You going to fly her today, sir?" one of them said.

"No, I figure not. How d'you boys make out last night?"

"Just fine, sir."

"Good, I want a full report. I'll be up in a moment." The pilots went up into the plane and Cullington came around to my window. He put his hand on my forearm. "Francis." It was some technique of his, touch your forearm and call you by your first name as if all his attention was on you. "You deserve whatever you got last night. And I still owe you four hundred dollars for making the call. Have we got a deal?"

"There was never any doubt, was there?"

"Good." He tightened his grip for an instant on my forearm. Then he opened his wallet and handed me four bills already folded. "She'll be at the Meurillon as of tomorrow." He put his hand out and we shook hands awkwardly through the window. "Good, it's a deal, then," he repeated. One of the pilots called him from the top of the stairwell.

"We'll be here all night if we don't take this spot, Mr. Cullington!" This was enough for him. He trotted up to the plane, the ground crew rolled back the stairway, the jet lurched forward and taxied away from the hangar, taking its place in the line of planes waiting for clearance. In some fit of fondness Cullington waved at me through a porthole.

I drove back through the hangars. He sure had been a live one. The two hundred I'd kept the night before and the four now was six hundred bucks. I calculated that the four hundred Swiss was about sixteen hundred French, which was about two fifty in dollars. Plus two thousand more French was about six hundred bucks more. Almost fifteen hundred bucks. Certainly enough to kick back for a few days. The last four I could just call a tip for driving him out. I had a strange feeling of relief now that he was gone. He'd happened, I'd dealt with him, and it was cool again. And then there was nothing like a few little atrocities like beating him up and robbing him to completely take away any courage I might have been able to work up to actually go and see Emma. That's how I had to begin to see anything to do with her. Throw her in with all the other daughters, bosses, dirty secrets, woes, and general jive-shit problems that they all felt so free to off-load on me. My crew.

CHAPTER 4

I was up on the Champs-Elysées the next morning having a Screwdriver at Fouquets and trying to determine the nationality of a loud family sitting at the next table. I decided they were South American. They had expensive shopping bags all around them, proving to all comers that they weren't people who went into Vuitton for a key ring. The women were laughing in that slightly hysterical way which always meant they'd just come from spending a lot of money. A well-kept mother sat with two daughters. Pop had questioned the bill in weak French, and after an exchange the waiter had stormed off with a final, *"Oh la la, ces Espagnols alors!"* Pop, crushed, returned to his drink. Poor sucker, I thought. The morning's outing had probably already cost him ten thousand dollars, and the women were still in time to giggle over their aperitifs. Even if ten thousand was nothing to him, he was still a poor sucker. Imagine trying to keep all those women happy, and then the lousy waiter hadn't even allowed him to pull off the Argentinian polo-star act.

Something was still wrong with me. I never stopped at Fouquets, not at midday anyway, never drank Screwdrivers in bars, and certainly never wondered about people like this.

I looked down the avenue. Suddenly I thought I saw Emma. I could only see the girl from the back. She had the same blond hair that fell down thick and straight as if it were liquid. She stopped at a newspaper booth. Now I couldn't see her face because of the green canvas sidings of the booth. She waited for change and turned the magazine she'd bought over in her hands. It was *Rolling Stone;* it had to be Emma. She was handed her change and her body turned as if she were going to head up toward me. I bolted and ran into the inside of the bar. I looked out through the glass partitions and the outside tables and the potted shrubs. She walked right past where I'd been sitting. It wasn't her. Boy, you had better keep a handle on yourself, I thought. Three waiters were grouped by the counter looking at me. I went back out and left the money for my drink and walked toward the car.

At the airport it continued. I'm only the proverbial "girl in the port" for them, I thought, looking up at the arrival screen. They come and go across the world, and I am no more than a pit stop. I am the keeper of the summer home where people come only to have fun but forget there's a winter also. I am a bellhop yawning in the pantry during the party of the year. This would not do. I saw that the flight was a few minutes late, and I went over to one of the bars and ordered a Screwdriver.

In front of me another set of monitors flashed arrival and departure times, and an angelic voice came over the public address calling flights. I was served my drink and looked across the concourse. I knew every type in the hall. The ingénues in their oversized T-shirts and Vuarnets come to perfect their French, the gangs of women coming to shop, and the busloads of Americans and North Africans for different reasons just waiting to get out of the place. A big-shot businessman swept across the hallway with a train of three secretaries, a medium-range one looked at him enviously, and Mr. Small Potatoes blocked it all out by digging his face deeper into his copy of *Time.* Four cops in bulletproof vests and carrying machine guns stood around the El Al counter, and down the bar from me a tour group groaned over their delayed flight and wondered whether to cancel the whole thing as it probably wouldn't be this hot again for decades. Cities in Africa, Asia, and South America kept on flashing up on the monitors before me. Emma would be at the Meurillon, Cullington had said, and the Greek always stayed there. This could be very close.

I wasn't quite checking on the exits, but it was a great relief when the arrivals screen showed that the flight from Athens had arrived. I drained my drink and stood up.

Pump it up boy, here she comes. The Greek was coming out the gate, pushing through the other passengers as no sardine seller on the Piraeus would dare. She came through flapping with magazines and a handbag and the current fat bestseller. Her passport dangled from her manicured fingers, and her wrists clattered with gold, leather, ivory, and wood bracelets. For some reason she trailed a chinchilla wrap and led a porter with a loaded chariot.

"*Bonjour, chéri!*" she yelled, spotting me. She always liked to get off a few words in French before changing back into English.

"*Bonjour.* Nice flight?"

"*Magnifique, mon grand.*" She kissed me on the back of the ear and we headed out toward the car.

"It's very hot for that wrap. We're having a heat wave," I said.

"Dear Francis, I've just had too many things stolen by baggage handlers. It just isn't on anymore."

"I saw your picture in *W*, by the way."

"*Oh, vraiment?* Was I in *that*?" As if it weren't already pasted into the scrapbook she kept of her every mention in the society magazines. While hubby—who only appeared with her in *W* at the most prestigious charity balls—slaved at the mine face, Madame led an international existence. New York and Paris were the hubs, and on each trip she traveled with the same amount of trunks as the climates she intended to hit. Each trunk labeled so it didn't have to be opened until its place on the schedule had been reached. The last time I'd seen her was in winter, and the porter had been pushing a chariot loaded with seven trunks. One full of day clothes for Paris. Another for the side trip: to check out a painting in Milan and to go to a concert with a friend. A trunk full of ski and après-ski gear which wouldn't get opened until Switzerland, where a party was being given for her. Another full of tweeds for shooting in Scotland, where she'd spend the weekend with hubby. Another full of tropical clothes for some Caribbean island where she was to be a house guest. A trunk with two ball gowns for two Parisian parties she was to attend. And finally one full of shoes, toiletries, and accessories.

As we crossed to the car she told me that this time it was just an "in and out." A dinner party in Paris, then down to Monte Carlo for a party, and then back to Greece to wait for the next batch of house guests at the island where she'd set up summer camp. While the porter loaded the trunks into the car she took an envelope from her handbag and handed it to me. I opened it. The bills were already divided by paper clips. One was pay, the second was tip, and the third miscellaneous, like cabs, tips, and restaurants. "To keep up appearances," she'd said the first time. At least she'd said it instead of the others who only implied it. I took a bill from the miscellaneous clip and handed it to the porter when he'd finished. The Greek smiled. It was easy to keep her happy. I'd been waiting for her, and we'd swept across the hall, and the car which she liked so much was waiting. In many ways she was a straight arrow.

She'd taken the top suite at the Meurillon. I went up with her. No one at the Meurillon ever questioned Madame's visitors. The owner had even left a bouquet for her and beside it one of their kid leather diaries with the Meurillon logo stamped on it. His card said that he hoped she enjoyed her stay. I gave another bill to the bellhop. Madame smelled the flowers, then read the card and threw it away. She opened the doors that gave onto the balcony and went out to sigh with delight over the view and the river.

We went to have lunch at a place just off the Place des Victoires. She'd heard about it through her free-masonry of cognoscenti. She had heard of me through this also. The place was bistro-chic, serving nothing I couldn't get at Chartier or a hundred other bistros except the company of a famous lady singer at a nearby table and Ikey Yakaso, the designer, who crossed the room to say hello to the Greek. The *patron* walked around in a pristine white chef's jacket and with his hands pursed. He looked jolly and still stunned by his own good fortune. His English crash course for his new clientele had left him with one word, "quaint." Everything he had described for us on the menu was quaint.

By the end of the first course she'd told me all the anecdotes that were worth repeating regarding the latest house guests she'd had in Greece. There was the princess who insisted on having fried eggs and bacon for breakfast. The ballet star who called up the security guard in the middle of the night because the air-conditioning was numbing his high-strung muscles and then tried to seduce him. The movie star who was tanned on one side only, and the famous writer who lived on olives and Stolichnaya and would not leave the kitchen. "*Le chic* is a wave, Francis," she was saying. "It's nothing but a wave. You have to be on the crest, the crest or nothing, because *le peuple* will soon be raining down."

"They'll be raining down?" The trick was to turn the last phrase into a question to keep the conversation going. It gave a semblance of interest, and there were no pauses.

"Of course raining down. It's like a wavelength. Fashion, chic, *bon goût*—some receive it and some simply don't."

"They don't?"

"Exactly. You know the air is jammed with airwaves. If I had my radio here I could pick up hundreds of them."

"Hundreds?"

"*Mais oui!* A wavelength, *une honde,* you're either on it or you're not."

"What do you mean you're either on it or you're not?"

"Exactly that. And at this very moment the wavelength is running like a tingling wire right across this very floor. The owner doesn't know what he's got, he thinks it's just success. To him, of course, success is a full register and not who fills it. Oh yes, for a few months the tingling wire will run across this very floor, it will be spoken of by us in the four corners of the world, then more will come—"

"The public will rain down." Between her talk of crests of waves, the masses raining down, and the hundreds of wavelengths and tingling wires, I was beginning to feel as though I was in the middle of an electrical storm.

"*Exactement, mon grand!* And we, the walking receivers, will all vamoose to greener valleys, and then those who believe themselves to be on the crest will fill the place and with time *even they* will tire of the place and all this shall return to its humble origins and *ce petit bonhomme là*"—she pointed to Monsieur le propriétaire—"will not know what has happened." I watched him standing beside his cashier with his hands still pursed. He was beaming over the room. I hoped he was thinking, You quaint dumb fucks.

"You really don't think he'll know what happened?" I said.

"Of course not. . . ." She droned on. Sometimes even repeating their last phrase didn't work. I drifted off.

I had started out as a chauffeur. One of my brain-dead ideas. That first summer six years before I had looked for any kind of work. It was hard enough for the French; for anyone else it was a true test of courage. The notice board of the American Church listed babysitters, the *Tribune* wanted international secretaries and house sitters for Neuilly. My neighborhood's employment agency consisted of row after row of waiting and depressed men. Every official asked for papers, and when they saw I had none their faces beamed in appreciation at being given the chance to say their favorite phrase—*But Monsieur, you are in an irregular situation!* with which they returned fulfilled to their nail filing. I would have told them to screw themselves right there, but it would only give them the opportunity to give me a shot of their second most favorite expression—*If you don't like it here, go home!* The days ended with me completely down, a mood where the city seemed more unforgiving than ever, and I walked along the quays back to the rooming hotel where I was staying, not wanting to catch the Métro with the crowds.

It was late October. The only job offer I had was to work the bar at a Tex-Mex restaurant wearing a T-shirt with the memorable epigram BRONCO-BUSTER-VOUS? printed on the back. It was situated a few doors down from the Dôme. This made it no easier. One day I took a listless walk in the flea market of the Porte de Clignancourt. There was a gray wet light. Among the stalls of old clothes and crockery and *pension* furniture and stolen goods I saw an old Citroën 11L complete with running boards. I had a flash of what the city should be—for some reason black gunwales sweeping through dark streets. I continued walking. Farther on I saw an old chauffeur's tunic. It was off-white with double rows of brass buttons and a high collar. Beside it was its matching cap. The car and the tunic came together in my mind. The tunic belonged to something like an Hispano-Suiza, and the 11L had once been a common car, but they did come together. I walked on for three blocks to try and talk myself out of the idea I felt coming. It was no use. It only took one look at the engine and one short ride with the owner. Most of the money I had left after my two purchases went for printing up cards. Nothing quite like a printer's order to test one's enthusiasm.

I figured on one hundred and fifty cards to one hundred hotels. Fifteen hundred cards of rich blue on aqueous gray saying "See Paris Right!" I drove around to the concierges, was friendly with them all, and had them take stacks of cards.

A month after I had bought the car I was speeding down the Quai Voltaire at dusk, my cap on, the high collar of the tunic now starched, and the brass buttons polished. Behind me sit a couple. He is in a dinner jacket and she in a silk dress with large bows on the shoulders. We're late for the opera. I look in the rearview mirror and see they're not gazing out as we pass it all. They should be, because what's speeding by outside in this light and with so little traffic around doesn't happen that often. I'd picked them up at the Plaza-Athéné, and they had enough time to go for a drive before the curtain rose. At a bar on the quays they decided to have a drink. I'd stood a short distance away, enjoying watching them on the terrace. But now we were late. Maybe I should have said something, but they didn't try to blame me. Suddenly the man slaps his breast pocket. "Christ! I've forgotten the tickets back at the hotel!"

"I'll look after that, don't worry," I say.

"Oh, can you?" his wife says, and sits up in her seat.

"Yes."

A moment later I sneak another look in the rearview mirror and see they are both now thrown back in the seat the way I want them to be, just gazing out at the passing quays and bridges. I cross the Pont de la Concorde and sweep up the Rue Royale in the fading light, then into the Boulevard des Capucines and do an illegal maneuver right into the bustle outside the Opéra.

"You're sure there'll be no problem?" the man says, needing reassurance.

I pull to a stop. "Come on," I say. We run up the steps toward the lit-up hallway. The chief doorman has seen this kind of arrival before and chuckles in his livery. I explain their problem to him. At such times it would be no help knowing the president himself, it's a character reference from a chauffeur to a doorman that will get them through. If I hadn't liked them, if they had tried to blame me for their being late, then I would have just said that there was nothing I could do, the doorman would have immediately picked up on it, and then, complain as they might, they would have been sent to a side room to wait for the intermission. Now instead of the usual checking and cross-checking of reservations and seats available from cancellations which ordinarily would take place, the head doorman takes out of his pocket a thin stub of tickets which he keeps for just such occasions and in a few moments my clients are being ushered up the curving marble stairs.

I have never had any desire to go in and sit through one of the performances. Enough for me to have pulled up among the cars and have run up the stairs and across the foyer and then to watch them run on alone up the marble staircase. I stand for a moment longer at the foot of the stairs, and then just as I picture them getting to their seats, the first bars of music reach out and upward toward the dome. For me this is the finale. I stay on for a while and have a cigarette with all the doormen who can now relax and throw away all the stubs.

The Greek snapped her fingers in front of my eyes. She did it nicely, but she did do it. "Even the echo is gone." She smiled. Yes, she wasn't paying me to space out at lunch. The thrill of being on the crest of the wave seemed to have lessened. Now she was feeling the pull of another wave. Yakaso's table had nothing left but mangled napkins, and three record executives were escorting the famous lady singer out the door. Madame was now smiling at me and, pump off, was searching for the warmth of my calf.

CHAPTER 5

The list of places she wanted to hit that afternoon could wait. We didn't have another bottle of quaint Côte Chalonnaise either. We headed back to the Meurillon and instead of the quaint *tartelettes de framboises,* she had me for dessert.

Afterwards we left the car parked in front of the hotel and decided to walk. We were having a fine time. We went all the way up to the Elysée and then turned around and came back on the other side of the Faubourg St. Honoré. As we walked it was clear that the holidays had begun. It was as if a huge mass of people had been lifted off the city. The terraces weren't crowded, and we didn't get pushed off the pavement, and as long as we stayed in the shade it was very pleasant. I went into the boutiques with her and sat in the chairs while she browsed. She told me that a great secret was to buy off the rack and then have it taken in at home. It always looked tailored and was a great money-saver. Anything she did buy she had delivered so we wouldn't have to carry any bags. When I got tired of watching her I told her I'd wait outside and went to sit at a nearby café. I sat and ordered a glass of white wine. Waiting for her I tried to remember the names of all the glasses up on the shelf behind the bar. There was the "*ballon*," the "*demi*," the "*choppe*," and the glass for pastis and the glass that looked like a tulip with a long green stem which was for Alsace wine. I couldn't remember its name. Then there were the cordials, grenadine and mint and lemon, with which people liked to flavor their beer and lemonade and pastis. A "Monaco" was pastis with a drop of Grenadine and a "Diabolo Menthe" was lemonade and mint. Lemon I couldn't remember. They were all fresh and good summer drinks, and the people drinking them all around me looked like they thought it was quite a treat to have one in the middle of the afternoon.

The Greek came out of the boutique and spotted me under the parasol and walked toward me. I stood up, which was something she loved, and I helped her sit down, and then I sat down. The waiter came over. She told me she'd have a glass of white wine, and I told the waiter—she loved this too—and then I told him he might as well bring me another while he was bringing hers.

"Oh, it would be so nice if you could come to this party tonight," she said.

"I know."

"What do you think about when you're waiting outside?"

"Nothing very much. How long it'll be until you come out."

"Oh, you sweet thing, it's not true."

"Sure it is. What else do I have to think about?"

"You don't mind tonight?"

"No. It'll be a nice night to drive."

"Maybe we'll go out afterwards. Just the two of us."

"Why not?"

After we had drunk the wine and rested we continued down the Faubourg. She wanted to go to Chanel and take a look at what they had and maybe pick up something. ("I don't want to bring out any of the big guns for a full fitting" was the exact phrase.) When we got there I sat down to the side of the central area in one of their comfortable chairs. She soon found a blouse she liked, but they only had it in very small sizes. "*Pas chez Chanel* surely. *C'est absoluement* crazy!" This bellowed phrase was a perfect creation of her own making. The assistant mumbled something, and they both disappeared back into the changing space.

The assistants were all busy showing groups of two or three women around the clothes. There were two other men, one sitting and one standing. The one sitting had a lost-boy look that only lifted each time his wife came over to do a twirl in front of him. The other, well advanced in years and porcine, cooed beside some woman admiring herself in a pants suit. A young girl was all caught up in wanting everything in the store. She wanted shoes and she wanted a handbag and she wanted a bolero top. Her mother and the assistant were smiling behind her, conscious that with that first ensemble it was a coming of age ceremony they were witnessing. The Greek was back and started charging around in another search for a blouse which she just hoped they had in her *taille.* She had four already over her arm when I heard Emma's voice. "Well, if you can't put three stitches in while I wait I'll leave it." It was her voice for sure, and this time I was on open ground.

"Well, if you insist, Madame. Half an hour," the assistant said.

"I'll wait outside." She came stalking across the floor, stared straight at me, and continued toward the door. When I followed her out she was already a few paces down the street. She was wearing the Chanel uniform in blue and white.

The modern one made from denim. She gave it everything it lacked with one foot up against a lamppost lighting a cigarette. Bacall in *To Have and Have Not.* All my loaded words for the occasion deserted me. "That's not very Faubourg St. Honoré." It didn't escape me just how ridiculous it was to say this. As if I couldn't think of anything else. I couldn't. The purity of my anger for the last two years could have driven me to poetry. This is what I came out with when faced with her. She was up to it.

"Don't be cutesy."

"Very well, I won't be cutesy. Can I start over?"

"For a start this is the Rue Cambon, and anyway I was never a very Faubourg St. Honoré sort of gal."

We were saved by the sound of sirens. A motorcycle escort screamed past us and was followed by three black cars. They were probably heading for the Elysée. We both watched them, unable to speak over the noise. "I couldn't avoid hearing you're in a great hurry to get your clothes."

"Couldn't you? I couldn't help noticing that you're not very interested in what your date's buying."

"You've been watching me?"

"Of course. She doesn't even pretend to be interested in what you think. She could at least go through the motions and ask you now and then."

"You seem to be going through a few motions yourself. Few days in Paris, visit Chanel. You look great in the uniform by the way. The denim I suppose is for younger matrons."

"Francis, shall we pretend that this never happened. That we've not seen each other?" She turned and was inside by the time I said, "Let's," to the doorman. Not such a humorous interlude after all, I thought. Feel something, damn it. The only thing you feel like doing is going in to scream after her that her father's a whoremonger. No, that makes even less sense than having followed her out here in the first place. Followed her! Yeah, like a lost puppy. Oh, a great moment all right. At least there'll be no regrets now of what could have been if you'd actually taken Cullington up. You blundered, from the start, from the asinine conversation. A lost, yapping, backbiting puppy. Jesus! If all you need is a good shakeout, she's certainly the girl to do it.

CHAPTER 6

Madame had a new walker on this trip, and she told me about him while we dressed to go out. Her usual one, a man of means himself and the kingpin of Paris walkers, was out of town for the whole summer. The stand-in was a bridge master and biographer by trade. She'd only met him twice before and didn't quite know what to expect. I was dressed before her and went into the sitting room and leafed through magazines. When she came out of the bedroom in her ball gown she did a twirl before me and as always had me do a twirl for her.

"Shall we go?" I said.

"He's waiting downstairs."

"You want me to wait here?"

"Oh, Francis dear, I'm sorry, but who knows who he'll be dishing it with tomorrow if he saw us together."

She went downstairs and took the walker to the bar. I waited five minutes and then took the elevator down. I kept my cap off while I crossed toward the door in case the walker would see me. The staff were too busy to notice me, and even if they had they'd probably only add it to the list of outrageous outfits they had seen. When the Greek came out with the walker I was holding the door of the car. The walker thought this was a charming concept and asked for my card. I said I'd forgotten them. He'd made no connection between us. Someday, once he'd been tested on the all-important exam, discretion, maybe the Greek would tell him. It would make a good racy story for after dinner. I could already hear her telling it.

We drove up to the Avenue Foch. She took the invitation from her purse to tell me the building number. She didn't have to because I'd already spotted the cars. There was a large black Cadillac with embassy plates parked halfway up on the grass to let the other cars through. Two Secret Service men stood by it. I thought it must be the ambassador. I parked between two stretch Mercedes and got out to hold the door. Madame had to gather her dress and decide whether she'd been crazy to bring the chinchilla stole, so I just stood there. There was a security guard at the front gate with his arms folded. He talked with two other chauffeurs and two bodyguards. The Secret Service men kept their distance. I noticed there was another in the hallway. This looked like quite a party. Across the avenue, a meat rack of hookers fanned themselves with magazines while being perused by all the drivers coming down from the Arc de Triomphe. Two more cars pulled up with guests, and with their presence suddenly the poufs of the dress were no longer a problem, and she told the walker and he got out and then helped her out of the car. Now at least two couples had witnessed her arrival. Me in my white tunic and cap holding the door of the polished old car. They undoubtedly thought it oh so original on her part. Just like the time she'd invited the cream of society to eat a spit-roasted lamb, retsina, and baklava in a *salon privé* of the Meurillon. It had been very successful. The picture in the social pages had showed her with a "big gun of fashion" on her arm. This arrival too they would think just too chic for words. She nudged me with her elbow as she passed me. She was already having a good time. I watched her laughing with the other guests as they walked into the lit-up building.

It would be at least three hours before she came out. I drove across to the Place Victor Hugo and parked there. I didn't want to listen to the chauffeurs' and bodyguards' stories anymore. I also wanted to take off my tunic. It was too hot. I thought of going to have a drink, but I'd have to carry the stole. I didn't even want to touch the fur. I crossed the street to a corner grocery store and bought a liter bottle of beer and came back to the car. I sat in the front passenger seat with the door open and my feet out on the pavement.

A question: How long could I get by on spite? Not very long. Hadn't Emma proved that? But if not spite, then what? At one time I would have been thrilled to be sitting on the Place Victor Hugo waiting for the Greek. At one time also I could have just pictured my alternatives, like the bar of the Friday 5:18 to Westchester, and be doubly glad for what I had. A position of sneering was at least a holdable position. Let them go to their soirées and fundraisers and fashion shows and spas and galas. Let them handle their guilt about their bread and lose sleep over the help, I'd always be glad to stay home and drink their Champagne. At least I always had been.

Too harsh? No, quite necessary. In those moments when I realized I was nothing but their latest vanity case, a set of silk-lined compartments, escort, arm to lean on, audience, pocketful of toot if they wanted, shoulder to cry on, mouth and dick. Necessary in those hours when I realized just how long ago I'd said, "This isn't that bad after all." Necessary also in those hours when any other way of paying the rent seemed better. Any job, out at five o'clock, close your own door behind you, your own bottle of wine to sit over, and do no more than watch the evening news.

No, there still was no rush to change any of it. The rich might not know what they wanted, but they sure knew what was good enough. And if at times that turned out to be me, it still seemed enough of a paycheck. There would be time enough to wash up and vegetate in California with half the people I knew. Get a few friends together and sit around the backyard drinking beers and telling war stories. I knew at some stage there'd be no more Paris la-de-da and then I'd be sorry.

I still had two hours to go before the Greek came out. I sat on and drank the beer and waited.

We drove the walker back to his house. They were both quite drunk. He kept on repeating a story about how when you put the silver serving utensils back into a soufflé it would collapse immediately. Then she got her chance to repeat how much she looked forward to seeing him in Greece before the end of the summer. We got to the Place du Palais-Bourbon, where he lived, and he kissed the Greek's hand and got out. I drove off and put on a tape of nocturnes. She liked as much as I did to ride around at night with that music on.

When we got to the Meurillon she almost collapsed into the arms of the doorman. She took my arm and we walked into the foyer. She was wobbling on her heels, and she only did that when she was very drunk. Two old couples of Americans were all lit up, and one of them was waving a photograph around, passing it from the concierge to the bellhops. They all smiled politely. I asked for the key at the desk, but by the time I'd turned around the Greek had joined in the fun. One of the men had his arm around her; his shirt under the chandelier looked like the strobe lights of a discothèque in hell. The Greek was holding the photograph. "Francis, you must see *this!*" She handed me the snapshot. It was the same two men except as young GI's in pressed uniforms. They had their arms around each other and stood in front of the *obélisque* at Concorde.

"Long, long time," the one who had his arm around the Greek slurred.

"You are the heroes of our age, monsieurs," the Greek said.

"Long, long time."

"Oh, I could cry. You are the heroes."

"Liberated Paris."

"I insist that we have a drink." At this the two women and one of the men disappeared, but the one who'd been doing the talking was not going to miss the opportunity, and the three of us went into the bar and found a corner niche and ordered. When the drinks arrived, the old man started on the beaches of Normandy and began to make his way through orchards and yards full of chickens to the moment when the photograph was taken.

Emma walked in. She didn't see us because we were to the right of the door. She was dressed in jeans and a light blouse and drunk as hell. She marched up to the bar and ordered. She looked at the bar stool but thought better of risking it and remained standing. Her drink was put before her, and she signed a chit. Beside me the old man was flushing out a village. Did the Greek know what sound a retreating Panzer Division made? She did not but was on the edge of her seat wanting to know. Emma turned around and, elbows on the bar, heel on the footrail, took up her saloon stance. She looked down into the surface of her tumbler with her eyebrows cocked as always in that "Oh well, there you have it" look. Then she saw me and my entourage. I didn't look away. I thought, Oh Emma why am I here with these people? Liven it all up for me. Laugh with me over this. We who have laughed over a hundred mise-en-scènes like this and an equal amount of less than sublime moments, please, please laugh with me over this. Give me a smile, just a lousy smile. The snipers were on the roofs, the volleys of gunfire cracked through the streets, the glasses on the table were Allied positions and the ashtrays were German. Emma took another sip, just enough to get her upstairs, and walked out past us with a polite "Bon soir, Monsieurdames." Not even with someone to pretend she wasn't alone.

When the glasses had conquered the ashtrays and the old man had given the Greek one last hug and gone I told her that I wanted to stay on for a drink by myself. "Are you sure?" she said.

"Yes, quite sure. I'll just be a minute." I gave her the key and she went up and I ordered another drink and was thinking just how comforting an old barman and a well-kept bar were. I stayed on until the bar was empty. I did the right thing and asked for the chit so he could close out his register, but I'd be damned if I was going to rush it to make his life any easier. I was thinking, Don't think about Emma. If you think about Emma, you'll never go upstairs. If you don't go upstairs, you'll never see the Greek again, and that would be bad business. Think about the barmen.

They were both at the end of the bar, talking straight out toward the room so it looked like they weren't. The young assistant was very excited. He was talking about his new Vespa and the girl waiting outside for him. She worked at the Samaritaine and was getting very pissed off at the hours he had to work. The old barman laughed and told some story of his own courtship. Then he decided it was time to do the bottle inventory. The young guy asked if just this once the old man could do it for him. The old man shrugged and said, *"A chacun son boulot"*—to each his own work. The assistant said nothing and started counting bottles.

I thought, Hell, of course it was tough, but you were right to tell him. He might as well learn as soon as possible that it's all a crock of shit anyway, and in the crock of shit, to each his own work. Well, this is mine tonight, old guy, to keep the bar open and keep you shining cocktail shakers and sparkling glasses in that white jacket of yours. I should really go out to wherever that girl is waiting. I'll tell her too. Hell, I'll scream it out for anyone passing by—to each his own crock of shit. I'll tell her to stop complaining, and when he does finally come out from counting bottles to ride that new Vespa through the summer night and hold his shirt and rub her breasts against his back and be glad for the love that she has. Jesus, man! Look how you get. Stealing glances at Emma. What next? Spin the bottle? As if she were some fucking vision of innocence or something. At least she had the decency to walk straight out without some schmaltzy look backward. Could take a lesson from her. Oh yes, Mr. Barman, that's the comedy. To each his own work, to each his own motions to go through, to get through. Have a few of my own waiting upstairs, but as Descartes said, Once you've got the rhythm it's a cinch. We could all at least go through the motions in the crock of shit. Coming, madame. I'll just drain this glass, Mr. Barman, and the place is yours.

Resolve, for no good reason, was by far the nicest thing about being loaded. I went upstairs. She'd left the door open. The clothes and shoes she'd bought were strewn around the room. She was in the bathroom, and she gave me the first volley from there. "Well, did she come back?"

I could have kicked myself for not bringing up a drink. I didn't want to sit through this without one. "Who's that?"

"The Virgin Mary. And I didn't miss it at Chanel either, you know."

"Can't a guy have a drink by himself?"

"But of course, on his own money."

"Call downstairs and have it deducted from your fucking bill."

She came out of the bathroom in a floor-length dressing gown. "Oh, Francis, you know I don't care."

"Then what is it you're talking about?"

"I don't know. That you're both so young. It makes me feel . . . like shit actually."

". . . ."

"Don't you dare look at me like that! *Je suis jalouse, jalouse, jalouse!* I am old, and I pay, pay, pay! I pay for it. For you. I have to buy it! Did you agree to meet tomorrow so you can tell her what a slut I am?"

"Let's go to sleep."

"I am a slut, aren't I?"

"Course not."

"Don't be timid, you can tell me. I pay for it. What's a slut if not that?"

"I'm tired. Why don't we just fuck?"

"But I am a slut?"

"Very well, you're a slut."

"Hiss it at me, throw it at me. Slut! Slut! Slut!"

"What is this, you want to talk dirty or something?"

"Oh ouiii, baby, ouiii!"

". . . ."

"I'm naughty, aren't I? I should be slapped." This one was far from over.

"Not tonight."

"You never minded before."

"Yeah, well not tonight."

"Oh yeah? I'm a naughty rich slut, and I count you among my posessions. Now you surely feel like hitting me, don't you?"

"No, I think it's dumb, that's all."

"Aha! Dumb. Shout it out. Dumb slut, and give me a good one across the face."

"Sorry, I'm taking a shower."

"Have I told you to get up? I've told you to hit me, and quick while you're in the full flush of anger."

"Get lost."

"Shut up, you idiot, tell me I'm dumb and a slut."

"No."

"Do as you're told, you filthy little prostitute!"

I hit her hard across the face. She shrieked and toppled, burying her face in the leather sofa. *"Malakka! Malakka!"* she screamed in Greek, forgetting herself completely. "You fool! What am I going to do with this bruise? And in Monte

Carlo! Oh no, oh my god!" She ran to the bedroom and called down to room service for a bucket of ice. "No! No fucking Champagne," she shouted into the receiver. "Just ice."

When the night service wheeled in a bucket of ice, I told him to take it straight into the bedroom. The waiter kept his eyes on the carpet on the way out. She filled a hand towel with ice and lay on the bed with her face covered, muttering under her breath. I went out to the balcony and sat in one of the chairs. When she came out to get me there was only a slight bump over her right eye. She leaned her forehead toward me as if she wanted it kissed. I did, and she smiled sheepishly. She took my hand and led me toward the bedroom. The almond oil for her massage was already on the side table. She turned to me and the sheepish smile turned into an open one and I saw she was holding an unrolled condom in her mouth. She mumbled how she'd been wanting to try this.

CHAPTER 7

Before dawn the Greek jumped out of bed and ran to the bathroom to check on the bruise. There wasn't one, and she ran back into bed and showered me with kisses. Time for a quickie, to send flowers to the previous night's hosts, and to call down for a maid and tissues. When the maid came up they both ran around the room stuffing tissue into the ball gown and all the garments she'd bought and then packing them all neatly. Then she moved all the furniture over against a wall. She plugged in her traveling tape deck and put on her purple spandex leotard and stood in the empty space, waiting for the tape to start. Soon after "Kick-up-kick-down-kick your butt-feel that burn" was being intoned, the Greek was grunting and wheezing and the fluorescent sequins of the suit glared in the morning sun.

I sat on the balcony with a towel around my waist, watching her. It was the day of departure, and I knew how to stay out of the way. It was always the same long wait until airport time. When the tape finished, she ran back into the bathroom and reappeared in a terry-cloth robe. She turned the tape machine to some FM station to hear the day's gold prices. She finished the carrot juice (which she'd insisted to room service that they could indeed make), and she started on her breakfast salad.

I rested my eyes on a book she'd brought from Greece as a present for her hosts in Monte Carlo. It was a coffee-table book full of color plates of ancient Greek art. Headless, armless, hard-eyed, and throwing disks into terra-cotta infinities. The phone rang behind me, and she picked it up and said, "Send him up." There was a knock at the door, and the hairdresser cruised in. Another American in the great expatriate tradition. He sat the Greek down on a stool in the bathroom and soon was buzzing around her head, fluffing the hair and dishing the dirt. I faced out toward the river and tried to resubmerge myself in the plates of the book. It was no use. The door was open, and I could hear everything they said. The hairdresser was holding forth. "Because at this stage, my dear, the scalpel junkie has really gotten the best of the poor girl. I'm sure she has a lift a year, I mean just look closely next time you see her, she's as tight as Saran Wrap."

"Who does she go to?"

"Oh, some trashy boob man in New York. Pity for her I know a guy right here in Paris does fanny tucks to just die for. But anyway she passes through a lot these days, she finally got the old man to agree to a divorce. Can you imagine the packet that cost her? She was always the one with the dough. It must have been real love once, though. I mean, she turned Gentile to marry him. You did know that *of course*?"

"That's old hat," the Greek chuckled.

"You're lying through your teeth, dearest. But anyway, keep still, dear, she passes through here a lot these days, and every time I just can't keep a straight face. Oh yes, my dear, *you* can laugh, but *I've* got to look at the scars every time I do her hair."

"And what do you say about me when I'm not around?"

"Only sweet things, dearie. You have a neck to go to war for."

"To get back to *notre amie.* I think you'll only be seeing her in the shop from now on, because she bought a house on the Place des Vosges. Not bad either, I believe. Of course you knew that?"

"For months."

"You did not."

"Did so, but anyway, Place des Vosges or not, I just blush to tell you the sort she hangs around with since she shook off the old man. I quite expect the morals brigade to cart her off one of these days. I mean it's practically baby snatching . . . I mean . . ." A pause where he must have remembered that I was sitting somewhere within earshot. "Oh well, I suppose they might as well send a van for us all." He tried to laugh it off and lowered his voice. "I just have to compliment you on your taste. He's the same one as last time, isn't he?"

"Sshh!"

"Now don't get flustered *chérie,* I know you have to get a plane, I'll have these curlers out in no time."

The first time I'd heard myself discussed as a dish or a pet I had felt terribly offended, but we all know *of course* that if offense has a shape, it's the shape of a funnel, broad to start off with and very narrow at the end. Now, sitting in the sun, the towel around me and the money looked after, it was not easy to take such an elevated tone. Today looked like it was just going to be another canceled day and it felt great. In five years, I thought, I must have canceled more than three hundred and sixty-five days, if I added those winter days when the cooking oil was solid above the stove in the mornings and whole clumps of months lived on coasting engines and all the spring and summer days I had been glad to just kick back in. I didn't know what defined a canceled day, as opposed to wasted ones and lazy and hung-over ones. There was something more active to it. A decision was needed. And every time I did make the decision, I was overcome with the same delicious sensation. Delicious for the relief it produced, to momentarily feel invested with a certain power, to disdain from beginning, to be able to stamp days like invoices: doesn't count, ignore, void.

I stood up from my chaise longue and stretched my arms out in a deep yawn. Paris again glowed below me. I could not allow myself to slip into last night's mood again. Maybe just now and again, as a treat. The sort of conversation going on behind me no longer amused me, but it didn't bother me either. I was not near nor was I distant; this was it. As Emma's eyes said, Oh well, there you have it. I took a step out on the balcony to watch the river and the Left Bank for a while. I looked down.

Emma was stretched out on her own chaise longue on the balcony below me. Third time in less than a day. It would seem that Paris in July was nothing more than a village. She wore a one-piece swimsuit and a hair band and a pair of very dark sunglasses. She had a Walkman on and beside her a book open on its face and a full tumbler in the shade of her body. My heart had made its tiny skip before I'd been able to grab it. She looked up. "What the hell are *you* doing up there?" she said. I covered my lips with a finger and nodded toward the inside of the room. I mouthed, Room number? She wrote 654 in large numbers on the inside flap of her book.

Without hesitating, I noticed. I threw my clothes on and stuck my head into the bathroom. The Greek sat in front of the mirrors. The hairdresser was telling her how he'd given up sex while washing out the faintest trace of dye. I told her I was going for a walk so as not to be in the way while she finished packing. She thought it a good idea.

In the lift down I decided I would be as flippant as necessary. I would not compliment her this time by being tongue-tied. I would go in on a wing of glibness and say any damned thing that came into my mind. I got out of the lift and walked down the corridor looking for the room. The door was ajar. I stood for a moment and clenched and released both fists. Wing of glibness, remember. I pushed the door. The room was as strewn with clothes as the one I'd just come from. She was on the balcony and waved at me.

"Hello, I brought a note," I said.

"Haloo there, the powers that be must want us to meet."

"They must."

"Grab a chair."

"I saw you at the bar last night."

"So that's where I was!"

"You certainly were."

"Picture of primness and poise?"

"In your inimitable style."

"So my reputation's intact. I'll fix you a drink and we can further reminisce. Gin is what I have. I suppose that'll do?"

"Gin will be fine, plenty of tonic. I have to drive to the airport."

She went inside the room to mix the drinks and shouted from there. "Aren't I the lucky girl, though, to have you drop in. Light up, I have some real torpedoes in the cigarette pack.

I'm being a very good girl really, keeping away from everything." She reappeared, grinning, carrying two glasses full to the brim. "How has it been, Francis?"

"Success to success."

"I've had a meteoric rise myself." She handed me one of the glasses, sat down, and lit one of the prerolled joints. "Well, cheers anyway, to celebrate the age when we're at the peak of our powers." She gulped. "Any great thoughts up on the balcony?"

"As few as possible."

"Anything new?"

"I've become a jewel thief," I said.

"You forgot the coils of rope and to blacken your face and wear a black turtleneck. Bad start."

"Take a deep drag on that smoke and then I'll be a lithe jewel thief and you'll be a young heiress. I'll provide violins in the background and have the lights dimmed over the city."

"Such a torrid atmosphere, and so early in the day. I knew I shouldn't have let you come down. I shall really have to be the young heiress and call the house dick."

"I am the house dick."

She laughed out loud, showing her beautiful teeth and the clean cool cavity of her mouth. The things I was noticing already. The phone started ringing. "Oh fuck, guess who this is? Don't make a sound." In one gulp she finished her drink and sucked in half the joint and then she picked up the phone. "Hello? . . . Oh, hello, Daddy . . . No, it could have been Dr. Amudsen . . . Who else would I be expecting? . . . I was just out the door on my way to the Louvre . . . Very warm . . . Day after tomorrow hopefully . . . Thanks for calling . . . Bye." She put the phone down.

"That sounded like a voice from on high," I said.

"It was."

"How is he?"

"Who knows? Don't worry, he canceled the contract on your ass." She lay back and closed her eyes. "Mmm! Good sun, good weed, drink, and tolerable company." She cocked an eye open. "Talking of voices from on high."

"I know, I'd better get going."

"Before you do, Francis dear. You know I hate to put you in the position, but everywhere I tried yesterday wasn't there anymore. Can you score a little something for me?"

"Only coke."

"Just a little smack to get me home. Pretty please with sugar on it?"

"I have so much to thank your smack habit for!"

"That's the boy, get up on the pulpit with the rest of them!"

"You know the city, you used to live here once, I seem to recall."

"I tried yesterday, I told you. I can't get sidetracked or I'll never get home. I just got out of a happy farm, dear, and I really would prefer not to start on messy moves."

"Though you will, of course, if forced."

"You have to agree, this grass business is for the birds."

"Only if you'll come to the pool with me later."

"A *date*! Goodness, what next?"

I stood up before anything else could happen. "I'll be back from the airport by the time you've finished lunch. Have a Salade Niçoise, they were always your favorite here, weren't they?" She grinned at this and I walked toward the door. She came behind me.

"Francis . . . Isn't it nice that we can actually talk to each other?"

"I know. Isn't it nice that you didn't leave this morning?"

"Isn't it, though?"

A short while later I'd brought the car around to the front of the hotel. I leaned against it with the other chauffeurs waiting for Madame to come out. She did a great exit coming down the stairs counting the trunks that the retinue of bellhops carried. They loaded them into the trunk and the back seat and I tipped them from the roll. She got into the front and I closed the door after her. As I went around to my door I stopped behind the trunk and looked up. Among the flowers and shrubs of her balcony Emma was looking down at me. I waved and she waved back. I hopped into the car. There was nothing less than a spring to my step.

CHAPTER 8

I dumped the Greek at the airport as quickly as I could afford to. Once she'd checked in we had to have a drink, but I managed to get out after one. She told me she'd be back in late September and we kissed and I left her. I went to the bank on the main concourse and changed all of Cullington's money into francs. I was going to need as much cash as possible.

Back at the house the concierge was sitting outside in the shade of the doorway making a face of general disapproval. I counted out three thousand francs and gave them to her. She said it was hot, and I agreed. She had just finished washing the hallway with some pine-smelling detergent, and in the heat it was terribly cloying and I ran up the stairs.

No, you're not excited, I thought. Into the family-size thermos I threw a glass of ice cubes, seven of orange juice, and four of vodka. I closed the lid and gave it a shake and threw it into the shoulder bag. I moved quickly. Glasses? Check. Nivea? check. New thirty-factor sun block for nose? Check. Swimming suit? Check. I chose from the stack of bath towels stolen from hotels and took the one on top, George V. I opened the sunglass drawer. Wraparounds, aviators, nerd, tortoiseshell pseudos, Riviera 1950, neo-nerd, reflectors, and campy aviators. I took the classic Ray-Bans, certain that they weren't Emmas. The last thing I wanted was for her to know I'd kept all her stuff. Everything except for those Art Nouveau cocktail glasses which one bad night I'd taken and smashed one by one against the sitting-room wall. It had given me a week-long high. Now I just had to score. There was no one at my corner, it was too early, and I wasn't going to wait for them to show up. I didn't want the hassle of Les Halles. I decided to go down to the Meurillon and get it right near there. It would cost me, but that didn't matter. Cullington was paying.

Tip for the cognoscenti: Looking for a real Dr. Feelgood without having to stray too far from your favorite part of Paris? There's a dealer from Mauritius who goes by the name of La Peste and who struts around the Rue Castiglione and St. Honoré selling to assorted bankers, tired boutique workers, their jaded clients, and matrons stranded away from good ol' Doc with a nonrenewable prescription. He only stops his rounds when stopped, and usually takes you to a café and sits down with you. It is impossible to know that behind the pinstripes and Hermès ties and briefcase he's a loaded arsenal.

I caught up with him on the Rue du Mont-Thabor concluding a deal with a bellhop who hadn't even bothered to get out of his uniform. It was probably to resell it to a guest. When he finished, La Peste got into the car and we circled the block. I scored three grams of coke and ten Ecstasies. He said, "Everyone's on this. Not all at once on a weekend sort of number but a snip for breakfast during the week." Then he talked me into a vial of some dark substance. It looked like the hash oil that had always made me sick in high school. "I sell it as opium, but, *entre nous,* I have no idea what it is."

"You sell opium?"

"Of course. They get a thrill just saying the word." I didn't even ask for heroin. He wouldn't carry it anyway. It wasn't a bell ringer for his clientele. I let him out in front of the Loti. "Aren't you taking a holiday?" I asked.

"Never in summer. I love it here. January I'm going to Kenya again to see the animals. The children love it."

I called Emma up from the foyer. First she asked me if I'd bought anything, and when I told her I had she told me she wouldn't be ready for another half hour. After all that rushing she wasn't going to reciprocate. I should have guessed she wouldn't rush down for the stuff. Like a pill-popper who cavalierly flicks one off from a handful before devouring all the rest, a junkie's daintiness.

At the bar the pair from the night before weren't on duty and I sat and ordered a beer. I had been carried away, and this was a call to order. She was right. When I let my ends fly like this more often than not I got them back in a granny knot. Emma had been known to do this. I looked out over my territory. Japs, Arabs, and more blond families. Outside two cabs pulled up together. The old doorman wasn't around, and two bellhops unpacked the two cars and loaded their trolleys. Two couples came through the door together, both followed by their luggage. One of the trolleys was loaded with the whole Vuitton collection, the other with two cases. It was a bad mistake, and the concierge would certainly be speaking with the bellhops. They had obviously not only missed out on Vuitton etiquette, but they hadn't even grasped the most basic understanding of front-door duty, that each person had to be allowed, where possible, to make his entrance believing themselves to be the grandest person who ever graced the building. But how could they imagine that this was one of the foundations that *le grand monde* was built on? And what did they care anyway? They'd get five francs for their efforts.

One day, despairing with the upscale sleaze that congregates in foyers, I had dared myself to go into the Meurillon through the service entrance. There had been no security desk, and I'd walked right through into the corridor. I walked along, avoiding the rushing waiters and delivery men. The noise in the corridor was deafening. Passing the kitchen, I saw the dishwashers scraping huge copper pots. Behind me a man screamed to get out of the way and rushed past me with the hind quarter of a cow on his shoulder. The cloth that was supposed to protect him had slipped, and the blood of the meat drenched his shirt and rubbed against the back of his neck.

It was as hot as the stoke room of a ship. Massive wires and pipes ran along the walls and meshed overhead, separating off into smaller corridors. A man wearing a thick plastic apron pushed a trolley loaded with burnished silver. There was the rumble of huge washing machines. Unconcerned whether I was a new employee, a salesman, an inspector, or a curious guest, no one stopped me.

There were chefs holding up suppliant eyes to portraits of Carême and despairing at having to make vegetarian meals for dogs. Maîtres d'hotel, comfortable in their chosen apostolate, chasing their understudies onto the floor and shouting, Show time! There might even be men, I thought, old now, cleaning a chandelier maybe, who once, in starched tunics of their own, had driven the hotel's car to pick up liner passengers at Cherbourg. I passed the laundry and heard a faint humming. A laundry maid was holding a strip of sheet to her lips and almost weeping a rock star's name. Behind her the other laundry maids danced under exit signs and held up to their shoulders ball gowns which had been sent down for a button. A team of teasing apprentices wore dinner jackets and, falling about, swayed and half hummed "La Vie en Rose." It was just what I had needed to see. A question of balance. I knew it was the last time I'd come down.

Instead of going back out the way I'd come in I wanted to get back to the foyer through the building. I walked through another maze of corridors. When I got to a swinging door with a brass plate at foot level I kicked it and went into a ballroom which was being prepared for a banquet. Men in overalls rolled round table tops across the parquet floor while others set up a rostrum and speakers. None of them paid any attention to my passage. The morning sun streamed in the large French windows. I walked across the room towards the far door until I reached the beam of sunlight, then stopped, not long enough to be noticed, and swung around to face myself in one of the wall-high gilded mirrors. Yes, it was grand, and I was still a fool for it all, and I continued out to the foyer strangely renewed.

On the deck below us at the pool the bodies were one greasy mass, and an ultramarine glare moved across it. Thick books, which they all seemed to have brought, proved useful headrests and shelves for keys and cigarettes and lotions. I tried to read the titles, but my eyes wouldn't focus. Another tour boat passed and I heard the same garbled message that this was the oldest swimming pool in Paris.

Two topless women beside us were babbling while one braided the other's hair. I would have liked to see Emma's small breasts too. I leaned across her shining body with the thermos. I let her finish her drink before refilling the glass. She sat up on her towel and reached into my jacket for the envelope of Ecstasies. She split one into halves in the palm of her hand and handed me mine. "Time for the other half, don't you think?" she said. We drank them down and lay back, eyes closed behind our sunglasses and with the coolness of the drinks resting on our bellies. "Well, the moment has come, Francis, tell me all about it."

"I did this morning."

"More."

"What?"

"Anything, something to go with this buzz."

"Local color?"

"Perfect."

"I was born and bred in the Twelfth Arrondissement. My father was a humble wine merchant. We lived over a courtyard. He was a master in the art of buying Algerian wine by the barrel and selling French wine by the bottle. As we lived in the Porte de Bercy, it was known affectionately as Côtes de Bercy, and the aftereffects were known not so affectionately as the Bercy fever. Am I on the right track?"

"Why not? But it has to have a point."

"I'll find one. To anyone who had a standing order I was the delivery boy. Childhood then was an endless visit to old ladies with red noses and red eyes."

"What where they like?"

"Well, they always liked me because I used to bring them the wine before I left for school. If it was my father who was delivering he would only get around to it in that awkward hour between the *digestif* of lunch and dinner's aperitif. On my way back from school—"

"Swinging your leather satchel as you went."

"They'd call me down from their windows where they'd been waiting for me to pass, and I'd have to go and bring them another bottle. Real guzzlers."

". . . ."

". . . ."

"Is that it?"

"That is it."

"And the point?"

"The point is that I've always been a very welcome delivery boy."

"And the American accent?"

"Another Berlitz miracle story."

"Why don't you ever tell the truth?"

"Because it's so boring."

"Is it?"

"It is without you. Why did you leave so suddenly, Emma?"

"Because with you I was on till the last stop. I had to put the brakes on."

"Whatever it might look like from the country club in Houston, I am not a damned soul."

"No, but you are a fuck-up."

"Is that how they teach you to talk at the nuthouse?"

"I'm sorry, but under it all I was afraid of turning into one."

"Well, what are you now?"

". . . ."

I opened my eyes sometime later. Someone was humming nearby. I was sweating. My glass was empty and so was the thermos, though the last time I'd poured it seemed half full. Emma was completely still beside me. The doors of the changing booths were banging open and shut below us. I could hear the attendant now rushing up and down his corridor receiving chips and handing back hangers. At the deep end of the pool someone bellyflopped from the diving board and sounded like a depth charge. Emma had her eyes open and faced straight up into the sky. How much time had passed? Our feet were shaded by the shadow that had spread across us like a gossamer sheet that had slipped off. There was the gushing sound of many showers.

"Francis?"

"Yes?"

"Just checking. Didn't want you going further into autopilot."

"A sputnik."

"Orbiting. Did you enjoy your snooze. You looked sweat. Wow, rubber mouth already. You looked sweet."

"Good."

"Hope you don't have plans for tonight. The old brain's been working, and I have plans for us."

"Good."

"Flash this one up then. First we'll go recharge our batteries on some food. Judging by the light we still have time, and

I want a sunset tour of Paris. By then it'll be time for a little drink on some terrace on the Boulevard St.-Germain, watch the strollers a while, and then go to dinner at some big old *brasserie.* Somewhere we've never been, don't you think?"

"Approved."

"And naturally you're invited. Only one thing, though."

"What's that?"

"You have to promise not to stop till I do."

"Did I ever?"

"No, I can say that much."

"Oh Emma, I still love you."

"Can it, boy. Go get dressed."

It was the perfect time to walk out into the evening and cross the quay with the stream of people leaving the pool. It was still very warm, and there were few cars around. We drove. Children played in the paths at the lower end of the Champs-Elysées. At the Grand Palais I took a left onto the Pont Alexandre III, and as we crossed, it panned out into a vista of the Esplanade des Invalides crowned with the tomb of the Emperor himself. I was on my tour, and Emma was in the car with me. It had been a long time since I'd taken the ride, cruising and in no hurry. I crossed the river again and drove all the way down the Right Bank. We circled Bastille and took the Rue St.-Antoine. At St. Paul, under the plane trees, was a roundabout with children holding on to the rising and falling horses. At the Place de l'Hôtel-de-Ville roller skaters with Walkmen. The lampposts were already lit and the fountains gushing. Down the Rue de Rivoli at Châtelet crowds waited outside the Café Sarah Bernhardt and the Théâtre de la Ville. All the café terraces were crowded, and we were back on the quays. "It's so pink, so peaceful," Emma said. "I'd like to pour molten amber over such a moment. Why weren't you a great success?"

"I don't know. I was no more expensive than renting a cab by the day. Never overestimate people. Anyway, it rains much more often than you get this light."

"I feel giddy."

"It's the heat. It will all start melting soon. Notre-Dame like a wedding cake in the sun. Quay by quay into the river. The Quai Voltaire and then the Quai d'Orsay. The filing cabinets of the ministry will bob downstream carrying centuries of protocol and the dreams of dead diplomats."

"In this light it seems as if time stands still."

"You just said that."

"Did I? Oops, next I'll be mixing my metaphors. Just think, though, all these buildings have been drinking up this light for so long."

"So?"

"So I don't know. If they could talk they'd say something like 'Hang in there folks. It's all worth it.' Not giving a brilliant example of rhetoric, am I? But it makes sense to me. In this light it all makes sense."

"Do you really think you're a fuck-up?"

"I seem to have crossed out most other possibilities. I know one thing for sure, this shit's good. I haven't been this earnest since I was fourteen and reading Emily Dickinson. We'd better go and have a drinky-pooh before we throw up from the sweetness of it all."

I drove across the Bastille again and up the Faubourg St.-Antoine. We sat at an empty terrace bordering the Marché d'Aligre and ordered beers. The market was long over. Two old women were going through stacks of rotten vegetables, and three small boys played football between the trees on the pavement. One was a goalkeeper, guarding the space between two of the trees. Another dribbled the ball, and a third panned with an imaginary television camera and shouted out a running commentary. The dribbler finally got past the goalkeeper and after so much effort disdainfully pushed the ball through. Then he knelt on the pavement with his arms out, rejoicing with the thousands of massed fans in the treetops. The cameraman knelt down beside him for the emotional shot. Emma's eyes welled up. "Oh hell, why am I being like this. Is it the booze or the toke or the light?"

The waiter was taking in the tables and chairs around us. He came over and asked us to drink up. "Saved just in time," she said. "Soppiness is not on tonight's schedule. Had enough of that last night. We wouldn't be coming down, would we? Time to go and powder my nose and renew my enthusiasm for the cause."

"Don't be shocked by the bathroom in a place like this. Should you have forgotten," I said. She didn't acknowledge it. She just stood up and held out her hand for the coke and the Ecstasies, and I handed the pouches to her.

While I waited I wondered why I was carrying her load for the night. It could have been one of her delicacies, which she sometimes had surprised me with. Like hesitating to pour her own wine when a man was at the table or always eating peaches with a knife and fork because she hated the juice running down her chin or spending her last francs on having a favorite blouse dry-cleaned. It could also be simply that my carrying it excused her for the night. Or maybe I just had to face that she'd reached the stage in her transformation where she had to test those she came in contact with. It was a habit I was sure that was instilled at finishing school. I could speak, as it were, from experience. The first semesters at Madame's finishing school for young ladies were reserved for credits such as, How to seat your guests and How to arrange flowers. I was quite sure that before Madame let her girls out she made certain that they'd taken the more advanced credits, such as, How to spot a bum on the make, and How to know who's ripping you off at any given moment. These credits were probably mandatory, and once taken Madame felt quite comfortable sending her girls off knowing that in years ahead whatever boundaries they might blur or persona they would affect, they would never forget them.

If those that they will come in contact with are household staff, caterers, masseurs, manicurists, museum curators, and professional raisers of funds, it will not be hard to single out those who might be taking advantage of the friendship they have so graciously bestowed. But what of those who believe themselves, well, racy? How do they face up to the overwhelming questions?

Take cocaine, for example. The daring ones who'll take some, seeing as they are in Paris and all, can never quite get rid of visions that the entire narcotics squad is trailing them. They ask me to carry it and then toward the end of the night they ask for the pouch back. This is just to see how much is left. I hand it back. The knowing ones will do it by touch, a tiny gesture, pressing with two fingers and never taking their eyes off me or stalling the conversation. The neophytes will go to the bathroom (the scene usually takes place in a nightclub) and open it there and check. The cocaine itself is certainly of no importance, just Madame's voice booming down through the years in its more updated version. If there is less than they expected I am either taking more than my fair share or cutting from theirs into my own stock. When they come out they will never show their disappointment in their face but it is now in the file as a black star and, whether it takes an evening or years, the moment they feel we've reached our quota our record is reviewed and we're banished among the despicable who've taken advantage of their friendship. Having now put their affairs in order they can start a new file on someone else. This is a mean way of living, and they are the only ones that suffer—we, of course, just move on to our next victim.

"Hello? Anyone home?" Emma was waving her hand in front of my face.

"Oh, hi."

"Where did you go to?"

"Just spacing."

She handed me back both pouches. "Do you realize it's almost midnight?"

"No, no I didn't."

"Well, let's go to the newest, cheesiest place."

"What category?"

"Sort of expense-account *damné.*"

"I have just the place."

CHAPTER 9

Inside La Boue a group of Japanese businessmen seemed to have hired out a whole escort agency. I recognized several of the faces from around. There was a sprinkling of Americans and even some French. A group of Arabs had taken over three tables by the crowded dance floor and were standing on them bursting every balloon they could reach. From the top of the steps leading down into the room Emma spotted a man alone. He sat on a far banquette with a drink before him. "Watch me cruise this guy," she said. We went down the steps and crossed the room toward him. He was dressed in a white shirt and slacks and espadrilles. "Bit early for San Fermin, Jake" was her opening remark.

"Who are you?"

"From the beginning? Very well, my folks are called Sunroof and Blue Rinse Moon. I took Math without Tears at Monterey Community College, flunked it, and it's been downhill ever since. This is my sidekick. Oh, and red handkerchiefs are de rigueur."

"Where?"

"Pamplona, dear, Pamplona."

"De rigueur? That's the new group from Italy, isn't it?"

He cracked up at this. He'd gotten his joke in and we were sitting beside him and he was ordering a bottle of J and B.

It was the policy of La Boue to gross out their patrons with a collection of photographs the owners had bought from a picture editor at one of the wire services. They were all the photographs that had come through the wire that were too gory for any newspaper to print. The bloodbath above our table consisted of a cult suicide in Indonesia, five bodies hanging from cords with their eyes and tongues just about to pop out. A suicide on the New York subway. The head neatly sliced, separated from the neck by a gleaming rail and no drag at all. The face of a paramedic flashbulb burned in the foreground, and in the background the luminous plaque of the RR train, stopped and shining down the tunnel like the beacon that the poor sucker had obviously not found.

"Kinky, isn't it?" the man in white said.

"Fin de siècle, I'd say, actually," Emma said. "You could get those into a Mexican murder weekly, they'll show anything."

"Do I detect a Texas accent?"

"I wouldn't know."

"Oh yes, there's a teeny-weeny Texas accent somewhere in there."

"Oh for God's sake leave Texas out of it tonight."

"Christ! Sorry, hon, I didn't mean—"

"Forget it." She stood up and suddenly pushed her way toward the middle of the dance floor shouting for silence. The DJ must have thought that there was some fresh amusement for the collected sybarites, because the music was turned down and with it the background which had given the balloon bursters their courage. The room fell silent. Now that she'd gotten its attention she just stood there. Beautiful and drunk she looked more vulnerable than ever in the spotlight and the silence.

The man in white leaned toward me. "Are you going to let your friend ridicule herself? Is she with you?"

"No, I'm just company."

"Well, she is my kind of girl."

"Go to it."

"Think I will." He stood up and walked down the three steps to the dance floor and joined Emma in the spotlight. They put their arms around each other and they were handed a microphone and without a pause they launched into the only song they were sure the other knew. "Oh, say, can you see . . . ?" The room did manage to stay silent until they ran out of lyrics, but the moment they did the music started blaring again. They came back toward the table. "Oh baby, you're too much!" the man said.

"Sure, I'll have another whiskey. Was that touching or what?"

"Champagne?"

"Divine, dearest."

While he snapped his fingers and screamed "Dom P! Dom P!" at a tired-looking waiter Emma turned to me. "Barff!" she said sotto voce.

"You took the words right out of my mouth."

"Just what I needed, though."

The waiter, only because he was probably on a percentage, deigned to take the order, and the man in white turned back toward us. "Whatever made you do that, baby?"

"Oh, I love it when you call me 'baby'! I haven't a clue what made me do that. It was all suddenly too much. Too, too much. Don't you know what I mean?"

"I sure do, baby, I sure do."

"Good. Well. Here we are. A hot Paris night. Oh boy I'm tired. No, I'm not tired, I'm weary. Today I caught myself passing the Eiffel Tower without looking up. I go, wow, Cindy, you don't even turn to look at the Eiffel Tower anymore! I mean that's the very first thing I did when I arrived here. I rushed right over to it and I went all the way up, just with the weekend bag, which is all I brought with me from Texarkana. What a view, *mon Dieu*! Now I don't even look up at it when I pass. I'm sorry, I don't mean to bore y'all."

"Oh, baby, that's all right," the man in white said with some genuine concern.

"You're too kind. I'll get a grip on myself. Let me put my head on your shoulder. There. My phone rang two times less this week than last. Has my modeling career peaked? Will I ever have another session? Is my agent tired of me? Every *maquilliste* tells me my skin is shot. Miss Applepie's lifestyle ruins her skin. Is it shot, baby?"

"Oh no, you've got wonderful—"

"Oh baby, thank you, now I know I'll hold out. Whatever happens, I'll hold out till that *Vogue* cover." The big move, arms up around his neck, damsel in distress voice, like Scarlet on uppers, she began to sing (to the tune of "Give Me That Old Time Religion"), "Give Me That *Vogue* Cover, Baby." She finished and hugged his neck. "Oh baby, kill me, destroy me, but get me that *Vogue* cover to mark my passage through the land of the living." It was perfect. The right amount of self-mocking humor for him to believe it. Her head was on his shoulder.

"There now, babe. Cheer up, I'll take you shopping tomorrow," the man in white said. I could miss this. I stood up. It was one loop too many. So what that she could still cut it? Or had it all been for my benefit? I went in to the bathroom and locked myself into one of the booths. I was grinding my teeth from the drugs and telling myself not to blow out of proportion exactly how hurt I was. Then I wondered whether I had any right to be hurt and decided that in all fairness I had not. I decided also that I was tripping pretty heavily because I couldn't stay standing, and I sat down on the bowl. It got heavier. Of course I had a right to be hurt. For three weeks our first winter we'd lived on onions boiled in milk. We would eat the onions first and then drink the warm milk. Every night we went out to a string of these trashy clubs, nodded to the doormen, and worked the room separately until dawn. Pure hit and run. When we woke, the previous night's adventures were recalled and laughed over for hours, and our laughter primed us for the night to come. Was that not the two of us? Now it wasn't even a memory anymore, just more damned reality. Of course I could be angry. Suddenly I said, "Stop it!" and I left the booth. I went over to the sink and slapped water on my face. That was a damned-fool thing to do, now I was in front of a mirror. I was aware of other people around me, but it didn't matter. I was tripping and in front of a mirror. How big is the universe? I remembered asking as a child. It has no size, I was told. It doesn't begin and it doesn't end. Would it be terribly presumptuous for me to say I felt a vague terror in that reply? I thought, the best thing about drugs is the perspective they give on the edge of real and imaginary abysses. Jesus! This stuff is bad, get out of here. Wait one minute, just one minute, you have one more thing to say to this mirror. Yes, I have renounced. Yes, I have resigned and I have jumped ship but I shall not despair. I shall take the other option: I *have* taken the other option: I coast. What to do when you've given up on life's chocolate medals? Coast or die, cop out or sell out, that's the choice. At least, Emma, at least I think I haven't sold out. There, that's what I've been wanting to say. Now get out of here.

When I came back out, they were still sitting talking on the banquette. They didn't notice me. I watched him take the bottle from the ice bucket. He poured the last glass for Emma, drained the rest by the neck, and smacked his lips. "God, that's good! The elixir of life, Cindy. I'd know it among a million Champagnes!" I walked around the opposite end of the dance floor so they wouldn't see me, and I walked up the steps and went to wait outside.

Two hours later I was still outside La Boue. I sat on the hood of a car. A lot of the dancers had come out, but not Emma. I was getting tired. Down the street I could hear the grinding of a garbage truck. The African workers were coming toward me on both pavements, rolling the bins from in front of the buildings toward the truck. Recently I'd read in the paper that one of these men, from Mauritania, had caught his sleeve in the grinder and before the driver could pull the emergency stop the man had been dragged in. That sure was a bad deal. From the bush to being mangled to death on the Rue François-1er. I went over to the garbagemen, shouting above the roar that I was the manager of La Boue, and asked them all to come and have a drink and a dance. The French driver didn't want anything to do with this irregular request, but the others, who were doing the heavy work, were delighted.

Already dancing to the music, they crowded down the stairs. One of the bouncers made a move, but I told him they were the sheikh's guests. He said, Hu! and looked at their green jumpsuits and orange caps, which seemed very fashionable, and decided he'd better go and check. By the time he came back they were bounding around the floor getting their pictures taken with the Japanese, Arabs, and blond girls.

Emma knew this was the high point of the evening, and once the men had been kicked out (they laughed all the way back to their truck) she appeared at the door with a full glass hidden under her jacket. The man in white rushed after her. I hopped off the trunk of the car and walked away down the street toward where we were parked. I didn't want to see his face. "Just a nightcap, babe. Look, look at that white Benz, that's me. Isn't she beautiful? Bulletproof, too, can't be too careful. Come on, we'll have fun. Come and have a last drink, we'll go shopping tomorrow. Don't leave me now, don't be a spoilsport, let your friend go, he's a big boy." Emma kept on walking. He fell silent. When we reached the car he screamed after us, "Bitch!"

We drove as far as the market on the Rue Montorgueil. I knew it would be open. It was difficult to find a space to park because of all the rigs of produce that were unloading. When we did find a space we left the car and walked through the market. The fishmongers cleaned gills and green entrails into plastic tubs, and women in shop coats stacked peaches and eggs with harp players' wrist movements. All the forklift drivers had cigarettes on their lips, yellow corn-paper ones, and their fumes and the smell of coffee coming out the bar doors carried a hint, if not of freshness, at least of a new day.

We went into one of the cafés. Behind the lace curtain the place was crammed deep at the counter. The fare was Calvados, coffee, and *tartines,* which the owner's wife buttered and sent on saucers flying down the zinc counter. The talk was of the European Cup qualifying rounds and lottery winners. The look was early morning roustabouts, blood-spattered aprons, rubber boots, and guffaws.

I came back from the counter carrying *crèmes* and two small Calvados and a plate of croissants. Emma sat by a quiet wood-burning stove talking to two girls at the next table. They told her they were from the Indre where they lived on a goat farm and were in Paris working in their uncle's *crémerie.* It was just up the street, and we should come and look at what they had. Their hands were still pink and soft from washing down the marble cheese counters and unwrapping the *fromage blanc* from its gauze and the butter cakes from their straw casing. Emma said maybe we'd go later and gave them a bracelet each. Once they'd gone she wondered if it might have been patronizing.

"Just give it or don't!" I snapped.

"Wow! So I'm sorry I had a good time tonight."

"It's not that."

"You didn't feel sorry for that schmuck at the club, did you?"

"No. I don't know what it is."

"Will it be hot today?"

"Hotter."

"Wouldn't you like to get out of Paris for a while?"

"Love it. Invite me somewhere with all this money you have now."

When we finished we drove the few blocks to the gardens of the Palais-Royal. I showed her an old trick. We each took two of the green metal chairs and placed them inside the fountain. The water reached high on the legs but not as far as the seat. We each stepped onto our first chair then took the backs of the other ones and lifted them further into the water. We stepped onto the second ones and repeated this until we'd reached the center of the fountain. We sat on the shoulders of the chairs with our feet on the seats. Surrounded by water we faced up through the gardens toward the colonnades.

She squatted and drew her hand through the water. "Hot as soup," she said.

We sat, no second winds in the morning doldrums, and all air pockets exhausted. The first light broke along the treetops.

CHAPTER 10

It would be a day to cancel. A beautiful boring day. It was early afternoon, and I woke fully dressed on my bed. I stumbled along the corridor to check any damage. Emma was in the sitting room crashed out on the sofa. The window was wide open, and a breeze gave a slight billow to the curtains. She cocked an eye open. "How are you?" I said.

"Stop asking questions."

"You're sick."

"*Mal du siècle.*"

We said it together: "Kidneys à la Beefeater today!" It was an old line.

"I'm going to need a jump start," she said. The pouches were still in my jacket pocket. I took her the jacket to go through, and I went back to sleep.

She was at the end of the corridor when I woke up next. The door of the bathroom was open, and she was dabbing her face in front of the mirror. She was dressed in tights and a bra. Roxy Music was blasting "Both Ends Burning" from the sitting room. I shouted, "Hello!" but she didn't hear me. I went into the kitchen. There was nothing in the fridge except beers and the rotgut Calvados and two reels of film I was keeping for someone and three old carrots. She was going through the crates of her stuff which had been stacked in the corridor. They were open on the floor, and the table was covered in all her old jewelry. I took a beer and sat down. She slid into the kitchen in a blouse and leather mini. "Sorry about the mess," she said. She took a beer from the fridge and rattled through the jewels and gulped the beer. "You kept absolutely everything!"

"There you have it."

She took a copper necklace and held it up around her neck. She put it back down; she'd never liked it. She stuck a thumb into the waistband of her skirt. "See that? It still fits!" She sat down and glanced over the pairs of shoes and chose a pair of black stilletos. "Not bad at all. I ripped them off. I think Charles Jourdan lent them for a show once." She did a twirl on the balls of her stilletos.

"Beautiful," I said.

"Who asked you?"

We brought our right hands up and slapped them together in a high-five. "Let's go, Mets!" we intoned together. It was stupid, but it always had been a tradition before we went out on our separate dates. I went down to the corner to buy food, feeling all the glow of a well-known routine.

An hour later I lay on the sofa, one eye on a tennis game and the other on Emma going through more cases on the floor. On a tray beside me lay a baguette half torn at, Brie, and red wine. She showed me her portfolio, the three magazine covers she'd managed to do, and the pull-out sections she'd been in. A box of papier-mâché masks she'd made and tried to sell in front of Beaubourg one Christmas for some quick money. Smiling because she knew what was in it, she pulled out a brown paper package. Inside was a stack of five hundred cards: SEE PARIS RIGHT. "Throw them away, for God's sake," I said. She put them back into the crate.

Before we went out she changed into something more comfortable—her old cream corduroys with the nap worn thin at the knees and deck shoes and a loose shirt tied in a knot at the belly. All her old hanging-out clothes. We walked all the way to Père Lachaise, because she said she'd never seen it. At the front gate we bought a map to find the important graves. An orange held up three burning incense sticks at Jim Morrison's. No one was near Oscar Wilde's. Emma sketched it in a notebook. When she'd finished we continued in the shade of the paths. There were wilted flowers and cats and the knowledge that somewhere maybe lovers were using its hidden recesses. We passed plastic-covered portraits on tombs and Empire mausoleums built to immortalize the standing in society of someone long forgotten, the marble dulled and the names sprouting moss and lichen. Emma sketched the angels with grime in their locks and round folds of their flesh. We heard a hymn and followed it through the paths. It led to Chopin's grave. It was covered in red flowers and solidarity banners. A small group knelt before it saying the rosary in Polish. They didn't notice us standing behind them. I am touched, I thought. I can feel my throat tingle over this. I am a fool, and still hung over. I haven't the courage to hug this woman right now, and I will never do anything either big or as small and beautiful as the last twinkling note of a nocturne.

We caught the Métro down to the river. We got off at Sully-Morland and crossed over to the Ile St.-Louis. We were walking down the Rue St.-Louis-en-l'Ile to get a cone of chocolate ice cream at Berthillon.

"Emma?"

"Yes, dear?"

"Can I spill the beans?"

"In double time."

"I have always wanted to be a boulevardier in spats, a trilby, and a lavender waistcoat. There! It is out."

"You're perky."

"Within the bounds of reason."

"That should be good enough. This Ecstasy does have a strange kickback." This was her department. Constantly monitoring the trip until it had petered out. The buzz, the rush, the thanksgiving procession in slow motion, and now this, how to cope with the kickback. The kickback of Ecstasy was like a glass house which we were each locked into for the day. We lapsed into silence. Being at different stages for the return trip was too volatile to risk.

There was a line in front of Berthillon, and Emma didn't want to wait. We walked on to the end of the street and crossed over on the Pont St.-Louis to the Ile de la Cité. We went into the park under the flying buttresses of Notre-Dame and found an empty bench and sat down. Emma spoke. "As a matter of fact, you're not the only one who kept stuff. I kept the key to the apartment."

"Were you just going to be in the house someday when I came home?"

"It crossed my mind."

"Since you're being so honest, did you come here to see me?"

"Yes."

"I knew it!"

"I came to get you out of this."

"What?"

"Oh, hell, Francis, you're going down."

"Whoa there just one—"

"I expected to find you in better shape."

"This does sound strange coming from you."

"You're going down."

"Stop saying that! I'm exactly the same as ever."

"Except older."

"So what's going down about that?"

"That you're still at it, Francis, that's what." She opened her handbag and unzipped a pocket in the back. There was a passport and other papers. She took an airline ticket from her purse and handed it to me, open. It had my name on it and was one-way to Houston. "I came to give you this. I was hoping . . ."

". . . ."

"You let me go down once, Francis."

"I thought you'd touch bottom."

"Let me tell you, the salutary effects of that are overrated."

"They are?"

"Yes, they are! You just love sudden-death situations."

"Only way I get to play the hero."

"Well, I'm playing it today. You're not going down. Come to Houston with me."

I held the ticket and we sat in silence. Something else had to be said before I accepted it. I didn't know what it was. I knew the old demon was coming up on me: force the issue to find out what it is. I gave the ticket back. She didn't take it. I placed it in her lap. Looking straight ahead I spoke.

"Good-bye, Emma." She didn't turn toward me. In the parking lot behind us there was the beeping warning of tour buses reversing.

"Why?" she said.

"That's how we get, we fuck-ups."

"That hurt you."

"Perhaps. My lack of aim is still true, though."

"And me?"

"You shat your pants when you saw the view. You stay at the Meurillon and sleep on a sofa in the ghetto. I had to sit through your coming-of-age ceremonies. That's my bad luck. Every rich girl has to go through pretending she isn't, but not again. You're not one of us, Emma. You're not. You can't have it all. You were playing hooky, the whole thing. I'm cheap and crass and I still live on my wits and I resent your plane tickets and your presence and you can't just cruise into my life to tell me that I'm hanging on by the skin of my teeth!"

"*Caramba!*" she said.

". . . ."

"Have we had our fit now?"

"Get lost."

"Why?"

"Because I'm more trouble than you can handle."

"Oh, sock it to me, baby!" It was out of faith in herself that she said this. Last ditch for a laugh. Her own old friend, to the gallows *con brio.* I should have stood up right then and walked off toward the Pont St.-Michel in some final shot. We still hadn't looked at each other. Neither of us moved, and after a moment tears were running down her face. I heard her and I had to stand up and breathe in and out to stop myself from kissing her at that moment. It was to make your stomach heave. I was the only solace I still knew how to give.

It couldn't be in the apartment. We agreed this could be crushing. But Emma insisted that it did have to be in the same area. We took a cab as far as the Place Clichy. There were certain other necessities. We stopped at a pharmacy and I went in for condoms. Right by the counter was a display of Roger et Gallet. A thrill maybe would calm me down, I thought. They sold so many condoms that they kept them under the counter so the assistant didn't have to turn. I scanned the shelf behind him and asked for some athlete's-foot powder. He turned, and I slid a small bottle of aftershave into my pocket. He handed me the powder. I said it wasn't the one I wanted. I paid for the condoms and left. Big time.

"I'm sorry, Francis," Emma said outside.

"Not at all. So much for the element of surprise, though." We continued walking. Emma went into a corner grocery for wine and paper cups. "I never go anywhere without my glasses," she joked. We walked on. At a souvenir store she stopped and bought all her presents for the staff in Houston. She came back out with a bag full of sweatshirts and key rings and mugs with Eiffel Towers and "I Love Paris" motifs.

We took a street that sloped up toward the Sacré-Coeur. It was lined with pee-in-the-sink hotels, Brazilian transvestites, and tattoo parlors with their walls pasted with sample drawings. We chose Le Grand Hôtel de Paris. On the wall beside the front door the usual engraved black mirror: *"Eau Chaude—Tous Conforts Modernes."* A stubbly-faced Algerian signed us in and gave us two hand towels with the key. As we walked up the stairs to the top floor Emma said she loved it.

It was the same sort of room as in all cheap Paris hotels. A double bed that creaked. Two mirrors, one above the sink and the other screwed to the door of the dressing closet. A desk and plywood chair. A carafe and a glass and a blackened Cinzano ashtray. The towels were worn and the bed covers threadbare from the thousands who had passed through. It was at the back of the building and looked onto a small square.

From the grocery bag she took two bottles of white wine and paper cups and a bottle opener. She let the water run until it was cool and then let the sink fill and placed one of the bottles in it. She opened the other and filled two cups. I sat on the bed, and she handed me one. She drained her own and refilled it. She came back toward me and opened my shirt. Her face moved all about my chest, and it felt cool in the spots where her lips covered. She stood back and again gulped at her glass. "Ravish me," she said.

"Oh baby."

"You would love to cut me out of my Chanel uniform now."

"I would."

She went back to the table. From the bottom of the grocery bag she took a pair of scissors. She tore off the wrapping and brought them over to me.

"That's not the uniform," I said.

"You'll have to imagine it. Just cut me loose."

"It's ridiculous."

"I thought you were a little weirder than that. Just a little more interesting."

I took the scissors.

She took her corduroys and her blouse off and stood in front of me in her bra and panties. "Oh, cut me loose from it all, Francis."

I went around her and cut the back strap of her bra first, then the center band between her breasts. Using the scissors as tongs, I nipped the shoulder bands and then slid each halfway down her arms. I slid the bottom blade along the small of her back through the tiny clump of blond down I knew so well, down the back of her panties and down between her buttocks as far as the waistband would let me. I brought the blades together and cut. I looked at her. Her eyes were closed. The front of her panties was damp. I snipped the band in the front and went inch by inch, afraid to hurt her, until both cuts met. I slid both halves down her legs. I put the scissors on the floor, and we lay down on the bed. Her cream trousers were over the back of the chair. The sun had hit the lead roof all day, and I was already in a sweat. Emma straddled my ankles and began to undo my fly.

Afterwards we lay and I watched her watching the ceiling. "And that was a freebie, ma'am!" I whispered.

"Oh sweet Jesus thank you, he does love me!"

". . . ."

"Will you come to Houston?"

"Was there ever any doubt?"

She smiled without taking her eyes off the ceiling. I stayed watching her. I wondered where she'd trailed off to. A shabby hotel, a bottle of wine and two paper cups beside us. A wisp of Gauloise smoke curling over us, and wine and the fading taste of body in our mouths. The cries of children in the little square below us, the toll of an Angelus bell, and purple dusk coming down on the City of Light. I wanted to share adventures with her again and add them to a list we could watch grow. As it once had been, to know each other's jokes and tack a hundred scenes onto a single line. As much lovers as accomplices, comrades as in camaraderie and, yes, company. All the rest was balls.

PART TWO

CHAPTER 11

Emma was up first. Long before dawn I saw her at the open window. It got light very early. She went down the corridor to shower. She came back wearing my shirt. She'd dried herself off with her blouse because she didn't want to use the towels. She hung her blouse on a nail in the window frame. She went downstairs for coffee. While she was gone I got out of bed and gargled and washed so I'd be fresh when she came back up. She brought two *crèmes* in tall tumblers and wrapped croissants which were squashed because she'd had them under her arm. When she handed me my *crème* I put it on the bedside table and brought her down to kiss her. Then she went back to her position by the window and I watched her dunk her croissant and read *Liberation* and smoke some cigarettes.

I washed at the sink, and when I'd finished, Emma changed shirts again and said hers felt all warm because it had been in the sun for some while. She washed the tumblers, and we went downstairs. The Algerian was in the booth reading the Arab newspaper. I paid him, and we went out and over to the café where Emma had been earlier. The owner looked pleased that he had trusted her with the tumblers. We had two more demitasses sitting outside on the terrace.

We walked around the hotel to the square. It was empty still, and we crossed it to the Métro. It was straight to Concorde on the Mairie d'Issy line, so she wouldn't have to change. I told her she'd reach the Meurillon before I'd walked home, and left her at the turnstile. I walked toward the house. When I got there I packed quickly. I locked all the windows and made sure the gas was off. I put the three bolts on the door and went downstairs to make sure the car was parked safely. I left the keys with the concierge in case it had to be moved. I told her that the *tabac* owner wouldn't mind moving it. He was always telling me the good days it reminded him of. She might even ask him to start it now and then so the battery wouldn't wear down.

I got on the Métro. There was a lot of room on the train because it was summer, and I had no problem with my suitcase. I felt like clicking my heels in a little airy hop. It was a mood to whistle to. The last time I'd felt this way was the day I had left New York. It was my most important departure. For one year since I'd dropped out of Columbia I'd been working nights proofreading documents for Salomon Brothers. For the three months before I left I lived on Rolaids and Pepto-Bismol. I had crippling stomach cramps. A gastroenterologist checked my test results then looked at me kindly and said, You must be under a lot of stress. I wanted second opinions on that one. I went to see three. They concurred. Stress? The end of the tether, really, and here our otherwise very comprehensive health plan failed me. One morning when I got off work I watched myself walk to the bank. I heard myself say to the teller, "I want to close my account, and I want it all in traveler's checks." A vertiginous phrase. After the bank I went to a travel agent. "I want a ticket to . . . Paris. Why not? But today. It doesn't have to be Paris, but it has to be today." I was like a suitcase that gets put on the wrong flight. Except only the suitcase knows it's empty so it doesn't matter where it ends up. At the time it was the only way to go. I ran back to my apartment (by then I was afraid I might chicken out on the concept) and packed a few things. I gave the keys to the super and told him to take what he wanted. I caught the train to the plane. At the time it was the grandest exit I could come up with. I was leaving with some sense of finality. I called no one. It was too final. I was twenty-three, I had a ticket and five thousand dollars in traveler's checks, and I was gone.

The Métro now rattled along, and I remembered how six years before, the stomach cramps had ceased with the flashing on of the seat-belt sign. I should have known that sometimes a period of feeling lousy shouldn't be referred to as such but rather as a watershed. I gripped the overhead rail and thought, A change, newness, such beautiful words.

On the coffee table of the room at the Meurillon: Emma's Walkman with speakers attached blasting an Ian Dury tape, burnt tinfoil from free-basing the opium ("What ever it was, it's down the hatch now"—Emma), the plane tickets, an ashtray full of roaches and half-smoked cigarettes, the A.A. red book and a well-thumbed copy of *Gestalt Therapy,* a half-empty bottle of Beefeaters and two full ones, tonics, lemon and ice, and the two glasses we were bringing to our lips.

"A fine still life, don't you think?" Emma said. "If I were seventeen it might be amusing."

"And if you were fifty-seven I'd give you a standing ovation."

"Oh, killing! God, I hate packing. I wish I could just dump it all in and worry about it when I get there."

"Do."

"There you go, already leading me astray. Maybe I'm a schizo. Apparently, to use A.A. jargon, it's too overwhelming for them to concentrate on more than one thing at once."

"Maybe you are. We'll find the word yet for whatever it is your problem is."

"You've brought a suit of some kind, haven't you? I'll bet he's gone and organized a dinner for our very first night. I think being in front of witnesses is the only way he can talk to me at this stage."

"Witnesses to what?"

"Paternal staying power."

"Is it very formal?"

"Not really. Once you've gotten past the five-generations-in-Texas bit you could be eating beans on the trail for all he cares. First of all, though, after hating you for so long, he'll want to check out what all the fuss was about."

"He really said nothing when you told him I was coming?"

"What does he *have* to say? I'm the one place he doesn't have the controlling shares. You'll put the gin in your case, won't you? It would be just like him to have locked the bar on me, and he'll have bribed whoever unpacks for me to take it away."

"Gin yes, but I'm not going through customs with anything else."

"Oh sure. I was going to offer to anyway. Drive-through borders are the only ones that freak me out."

"Good." I took all the drugs from my jacket and put them on the coffee table. Emma took her vanity case off a chair and emptied it onto the glass surface also. She took one of the Ecstasies and handed me half. "Just to get a little up," she said. Then she emptied a jar of aspirins onto the lid of the case and put the Ecstasies into the empty jar. She covered them with a swab of cotton wool and replaced all the aspirins on top. Extra traveling-length lines of coke were cut on the cover of *Gestalt* and the rest wrapped tight. She took the linen jacket that she was going to wear and rolled down one of the sleeves. She placed the bundle near the end of the sleeve, made one tight fold over it and then rolled it up loosely like the other sleeve. The little hash she had left she took out of the aluminum foil it was wrapped in ("You never know what these machines will pick up") and wrapped it in a sheet of hotel stationery. She dropped it into a slit in the silk lining of the case. Then she threw everything back in a jumble of paperbacks, atomizers, passport, tampons, tickets, and Walkman. She proposed a toast to methodical work.

We had two more drinks and sat in the sun for a while listening to the other side of the tape. Then we threw everything into her case and went downstairs. I loaded the cab while she looked after the bill. During the blur to the airport she said, "I feel good. There's only one way to get onto one of these flights, and that's just the way we are now."

Halfway across the Atlantic we topped off on Ecstasy and had the giggles for an hour. We laughed at the movie, with and without sound, how we'd packed her case, the garbagemen at La Boue, and our snoring neighbor. When he woke up and found out he'd missed the meal he asked for it in such a way that Emma, sensing kin, pitched in with a sympathetic "I hate this airline!" In a few minutes she'd found out he was a man who spent half his life on planes. As I put my head onto the pillow, she was talking him into drawing up a list of the world's ten best and worst airlines with accompanying vignettes. It was sure to take up the rest of the flight.

CHAPTER 12

The descent into Houston: flat scrubland first, then endless suburbs fed by endless freeways, pools in the backyards, baseball diamonds, the Astrodome, and the smoked glass of downtown reflecting the huge sky and the huge built-up plain all around it.

The heat swallowed us once we'd left the air-conditioned arrival hall. "Jesus Christ!" I said, crossing over to the taxi rank.

"Don't be taking the Lord's name in vain. That'll make you very unpopular with the people at the house."

We drove on the freeway through the swollen evening, listening to ads for a furniture clearance store on the radio. The catch line to the ad was "Save You Money!" and every time the announcer said it, our driver, from Lagos, Nigeria, practiced his Americanisms by yelling, "All right!" Between the towering billboards I looked out at pizza parlors and parking lots crammed with Wagoneers crammed with children, with giveaway balloons tied to their door handles. Then I looked out at endless rows of houses with FOR SALE and FOR RENT signs driven into their front lawns.

"What are you thinking?" Emma said.

"How long it's been since I was in an automatic."

"Oh pu-lease."

"Okay, why is everyone getting rid of their house?"

"Because oil's at eighteen dollars or something. At that price they stream out of here. If it wasn't for oil and the port there'd be no city here at all. I mean, who the hell wants to live in a swamp?"

"Your daddy."

"Each one to his addiction."

When we got to the huge metal gate of the house, Emma told the driver to just honk. He honked. The intercom picked up the sound, and an overhead camera swiveled. Emma stuck her hand out the window and waved at it, a motion detector clicked in with a red flashing light, and the gate opened. We drove up a tree-lined avenue. When the house came into view the driver yelped, "Whooee! This is what I love about this country."

"What's that?" I said.

"Here you at least get a shot at it."

I thought the wheel of a taxicab was as good a place as any to try to define the pros and cons of a country. He seemed almost disappointed when Emma told him not to pull up under the front portico. We drove across the gravel and past a recessed helipad into a huge backyard. Cullington was in fatigues and cowboy boots standing over five German shepherds sitting in five tubs being sudsed up by five Mexican gardeners. The dogs jumped out of their tubs and ran toward us, biting at the wheels. The driver said to us, "Get your bags yourself!"

"Get those goddamned fucking dogs back here!" Cullington screamed at the gardeners. They came after the dogs, but the dogs were circling the car. Cullington came up to the car and shooed them all away himself. "See, honey, everyone's expecting you, even these mutts. Go on, get lost, you damned mongrels. They won't wet you."

Emma got out. "Hello, baby," Cullington said. They hugged. I got out and went around the car to them. A butler was paying for the cab already.

"This is my friend Francis," Emma said.

"Well, it's nice to meet you," Cullington said, and we shook hands. "Honey, why didn't you tell me when you were coming? Lester would have gone to get you." There was a wail from the back door and two fat old women in uniforms led a charge in our direction. They were armed with handkerchiefs held tight in their fists, and they were followed by three younger maids. Emma was passed from bosom to bosom of the older women and cheek to cheek of the younger ones. I stood back beside the old butler and watched Cullington watching the scene. He didn't try to make eye contact with me. There'd be time for that. "Tessy Baker, I don't believe I've seen you this excited in thirty years," he said to the main wailer. A younger maid was holding a box of tissues up for her.

"Hush now, Mr. Cullington! Lawd ha' mercy, don't this child deserve a decent homecomin'?" she said.

Cullington didn't reply—he just smiled and shook his head. After a moment of just watching and smiling he spoke to the butler beside me. "Lester, please take Mr. Francis's luggage over to the cottage. We've put you over in the guest cottage, Francis. Figure you'll be more comfortable over there and all. And baby, you're up in your room, of course."

"Not the guest room?"

"Now baby, please don't get like that. This is your home. How was every little thing?"

"Oh, I simply adore cocktail hour in St. Moritz."

A chuckle escaped from him, and for just a moment he looked at her with pure adoration. Emma cut it off. "But that's enough small talk, isn't it, Daddy? Why don't you go and take Francis for 'the walk' in the garden while I go and give out some presents?"

"Sounds just fine to me."

"What time do the dinner guests arrive?"

"Seven thirty."

"You'll excuse me if I skip doing the centerpieces. I'm out of practice."

Cullington went into the house for a phone, and Lester took my suitcase across the courtyard and toward the other end of the garden. I was introduced to all the women around Emma and then quickly ignored. I stood next to Emma while she was brought up to date on all the news. Anna's daughter, who of course she had to remember because she used to work for the Booths down on the boulevard, now worked for NASA, and Mother Smith had gone back to Shreveport because her momma was sick, and the Carter boy who was always around the house crashed a speedboat in Galveston but thank the lawd was all right.

Cullington came out brandishing his phone. He waved it at me. "What do you think of this?" It was a cellular phone in a steer-horn case with a silver stud in the shape of Texas on the back and digits with rhinestone facings. "I got it from all the secretaries at the office. Isn't it just the sweetest thing?"

We walked out of the courtyard and in through manicured shrubs to the garden paths. "Well, I see you bit off the big one. Congratulations. I really have to thank you. How did she behave in Paris?" The phone began beeping in his hand. "Oops! Excuse me, Coach, I've been waiting for this call all day. Yep? . . . Speed boy! I thought it would be you. Phone didn't work on the plane. . . . Shit! Abu Dhabi, that sure is a happening place. Just love going over there. All that booze and girls drive a boy mad. Suppose that's why you work for me and not I for you. So what's the story? . . . Yeah, well maybe that's what he says now, Speed, but I knew that bastard when his idea of petrochemicals was making acrylic carpets. . . . Yeah, well *I* couldn't give a damn if he was the head of the Federal fucking Reserve, he's bluffing and I'm calling it. That bastard can put damned near a quarter of a million barrels of crude through there every day. . . . Yeah, well his hotsy-totsy New York lawyers can kiss my ass. You tell him if he fucks with me on this one I'll sue his ass for every mile of pipe he ever put down or ever hoped to put down! Got it? . . . Yeah, in those words. Even his sonofabitch lawyers can understand that. . . . Get back to me, Speed boy, whatever the time." He took the phone from his ear and chuckled. "Sorry, Francis, that's one of my boys in a shoot-out over in Saudi with a fella from Dallas." He shook his head, not unlike the cab driver. "Sonofabitch! I've got him over the barrel this time. Damn I'm good! Where were we, Coach?"

"Whether I'd be your inside man on Emma. No."

"Course not. I was only asking how she behaved out of concern. I appreciate you saying it straight out, too. You do understand why I said she needed someone, though?"

"You said she needed *me.*"

"Well, whatever."

"For company."

"Yeah, for company. And while we're talking straight, why don't we nail down salary to get it out of the way. How much were you thinking of?"

"Actually, I wasn't thinking."

"Oh come on, you're not going to leave it on the table, are you?"

"Why not?"

"Because that would be plain dumb, actually."

"Cullington, we had a fight over this a few days ago."

"Yeah, but then we came to a deal. Come on, Coach boy, you're missing work in Paris, and that's all there is to it. I'm only reimbursing you, so don't read so much into it."

". . . ."

"I'm sorry if I'm too forward about this, but in business, things must be as clear as possible. *Hablando se entiende la gente,* as we say in Juarez."

"Get it out of your head that you and I are in business."

"I know. I'm sorry. I'm a one-trick pony. How much?"

"Two hundred a day."

"Fine. If you're happy, I am. Paid weekly in cash. Is that all right?"

"Yes."

"Shit, though, it sure is good to see you. She's vulnerable, Emma. She's a . . . a . . . maverick, damn it all. She's told you all about the nuthouse, I suppose. She's the one who signed herself in to it. I think it's a plain dumb idea. She should be here. There's nothing gaga about that girl, she just hasn't found a shoe to fit her size. But then who has?"

"That seems to bag it."

"Very well, so we've got it clear."

"That I'm on salary."

"If that's how you want to put it. Anyway, we've got it clear." We had reached the pool, and the gardeners were now busy taking in all the royal-blue cushions and mattresses from the furniture. They carried them over to a shed behind some bushes. "Every night they go in, and every morning they come out, and no one ever uses the pool." He spoke as if it were the first time he'd realized this.

"I'll go for a swim," I said.

"You will? Oh, good!" He shouted at one of the gardeners. "Florencio! *Déjame una silla para el hombre, por favor!* You're a pretty neat guy, even if you do go around beating up on old men."

We walked back toward the house through an aisle of classical statues. The dogs trailed their tails behind us. "So we got that nailed down," he repeated, "and now you're going swimming. Good." The meeting was now summed up and ticked off somewhere among asses to be sued and tankers racing futures prices. He looked up from the gravel path at me. He was smiling. He looked around at the perfect flower beds, the rococo fountain, the illuminated lawn, and then around at all the statues holding scrolls and harps, bare-chested and with winged helmets. "Such bullshit, eh?" he said surprisingly.

CHAPTER 13

It was a mission-style bungalow. Inside, it was like an extremely large suite. Everything was covered in a racehorse design in tan and cream. The wallpaper was the same as the bed covers and the lining of the chairs and the settee and the curtains. A polished dresser held a selection of silver clothes brushes, and on the bedside table was a bowl of fruit and an insulated silver water pitcher with two crystal glasses on a doily. Just so.

A maid came out of the dressing closet. She was young and Mexican. I hadn't noticed her at Emma's homecoming. She wore a neat seersucker dress and was carrying my suit and shoes. "Hello. Welcome to Houston," she said.

"Thank you."

"I've unpacked. Emma asked me to."

"I see."

"I left the bottles in the closet."

"She can trust you?"

"If she sent me, right? My name is Lupe."

"Mine is Francis."

"Mr. Francis."

"Of course."

"There are glasses in the bathroom. I brought over some mixers. I put them in the little fridge there." She walked over to a small fridge and bent from the waist the way a woman does who wants you to notice how cute her ass is. "There's the tonic and lemons."

"If you brought them over, why are you looking?"

"I'm showing you."

"I see."

She laughed, almost blushing, I thought. "I'm taking your suit and shoes to touch them up. Will that be all, Mr. Francis?"

"Yes, thank you."

I changed into my swimming suit and took a towel. It was almost dark as I walked back across the lawn. The pool was lit, and instead of one cushion they had all been put back to allow me to choose. I jumped in immediately to avoid the insects. I did laps until my shoulders were tight.

When I got back the bed was turned down and the suit was hanging in the closet. My shoes were underneath. They shone. One whole wall of the room held photographs of Emma at different ages. There were horses in all of them. In one Cullington was holding her up on one as a baby. In another she wore a checked shirt and chaps and held a spotted horse. In another she rode bareback in a bikini top with a white-toothed smile and proud of her budding chest. After I looked at them I sat across the room and turned the pages of a book of paintings of famous racehorses.

I was dressing when I heard the screen door rattle and then a knock on the door and it opened. "It's me," Emma said, and crossed straight to the dressing closet. She came out with one of the bottles. I brought the glasses from a shelf in the bathroom. Emma mixed the drinks. "Tired?" she said.

"I'll manage."

"Good. Well, here's to a long life, and may you die in Ireland." We knocked glasses. "Lupe figures you're all right, you'll be glad to hear." She walked back into the sitting room. She was wearing the ensemble she'd bought in Paris. She sat down in a rattan armchair with her legs slung over an armrest. "I'm not going to dinner."

"You can call me worried."

"That's great."

I finished putting on my tie and shoes sitting on the bed.

"He's used to it," Emma continued.

"And the guests?"

"It's a young set for our benefit. No high cotton."

"So?"

"So they'll be on the chain gang for ten more years before they can do anything for him."

"Yeah, but you're the one that's not going."

"Oh shut up. What the hell do I care what they think?"

"Certainly not less than I do."

"It goes without saying."

"Yeah, so I hope you don't think you're upsetting me."

"But you do understand, don't you?"

"What's that?"

"My position. Half of them are people I've grown up with. I really couldn't bear to hear myself say, 'Gee, you look so cute.' "

"You say you don't want to go, and I say fine. Let's take off these duds and go drinking with Lupe, since she's such a good friend of yours."

"But you have to understand. It's a trap. They're suitors

now. It's a barrage of suitors. He doesn't care anymore who they are, he just wants to—"

"Get you nailed down."

"Get the rock on my finger. This is just step one in the big plan. I swallow this and next I'll be shopping for the fall wardrobe with the girls. I'll be sitting around the Bayou Club, yuck! The only reason I'd go there is to see the people who work there who've known me—looked after me, I should say—since I was a girl."

"Let's go to dinner there."

"I swallow this and soon I'll be going out with a different guy every night. God, I've seen them all drive up in their cars. As expensive as possible, of course, in case I might think that they weren't quite of my class and all. Then they take me out to expensive dinners. Five nights a week I've been to Tony's. Thank the Lord for discreet captains not to spoil it all for the lambkins. Shit, it's not as if half the nice boys in town and way beyond wouldn't give their right arms to get a shot at me. A good looker and loaded and only daughter of El Gran Sid. Two years of that. It's only natural I ended up in the happy farm."

"I know."

She'd finished her drink. I still had mine. She went back to the small fridge. "No, you don't know, actually. You have no idea just how pathetic I feel. The real reason I don't want to go is that I'm embarrassed to see them."

"Oh, come on. You give them something to talk about."

"Yeah, but I'm not moving forward. You should have seen me last time I came back."

"From Paris?"

"From the hospital after Paris. I was spouting all sorts of

stuff. I told them they could keep their arts-committees crap, and I started a well-woman center for Mexican women. Did I tell you?"

"No."

"Diet and family planning and all that. Basically, once I'd had a year's fun with it I went gaga again and left it. It's just too pathetic, Francis, and the worst thing is that it's still there, but guess who's funding it now? El Gran Sid himself. You think that one doesn't hit home?"

"It's hard to picture him paying the bills for that."

"It's hard to picture him doing a lot of things, and he'd die before saying he did any of them."

"Well, it's not pathetic, Emma."

"Yeah, and I'm Florence Nightingale. Let's have another drink."

"Before going over."

"Oh, it's all so easy when someone knows you. Love the regimental tie, by the way, Hussars or Scots Guards?"

After another drink we crossed over toward the house. In the front yard the cars were already parked. We hadn't reached the house when we heard a voice coming through the bushes. "Come here to me, child!" Emma smiled. There was a path between the bushes, and we followed it. At the end of the path was a small house with a porch. Tessy, who had led the welcoming charge, was sitting with another old woman. They both wore church hats. "Come here, child, that I see you better."

"What are you doing here, Tessy? Thought you'd be in preparing this dinner."

"Honey child, I'm too old now for all that fussin', you know that. Your poppa go get outside help now for big dinners.

Well, they ain't really outside help, they old Harvey's folk. You remember old Harvey, don't you?"

"I haven't been away ten years. Course I remember Harvey."

"I know, baby, I know. This here's Miss Bruce. She just gone brought me some eggs, some real country eggs, lawd ha' mercy, and a coon. A real nice one, too. I'd show it to y'all only I just got one of them gardening boys put it over in the ice box yonder."

"Nice to meet you, Miss Bruce," Emma said. "This here's Francis." We shook hands.

"Lawd yes," Tessy continued, "I seen shindigs here. Many's the time we'd be finished with the dishes and come out and talk a moment and the morning light would come right up on us."

"Which is when I'd come rolling up the drive," Emma said.

"Now, child, don't go talking to *me* like that. There ain't nothin' wrong with you, and folk know better than to talk that way in front of me! Now, child, step up into the light till I see what you're wearin'." Emma stepped up right in front of Tessy. "Ooh lawd! Honey child, ain't you just the prettiest! Ain't she though, Miss Bruce?"

"You sure ain't lyin', Mother Baker, you sure ain't lyin'."

"Thank you. How's the house, Tessy?"

"Ooh baby, the house! Your poppa gone and done me right. Lawd ha' mercy. Ooh yeah, that man gone and rebuilt the whole thing. And I sure told him not to. I said, 'No need to go to all that trouble, Mr. C, I ain't long for this world anyhow, thank the lawd.' He said, 'Hush now,'—you know the way he always be growlin'. He said, 'Hush there, Tessy

Baker, one of the women around here's gonna get hitched, and you need a nice-looking place to receive company.' Lawd, that man's bad, bad, bad, baby!"

"Well, Tessy honey, if I stand here any longer this mascara's going to start running."

"And that sure would be a shame, honey. I sure didn't mean to keep y'all from your guests. Both of you look so fine there. Just come here a moment, babe. Let me give you a kiss before you go." Emma went back up the few steps to the porch, and Tessy put her heavy arms around her. Her eyes, lost in the folds of her cheeks, were shedding their tears.

"Now Tessy, don't you start me also," Emma said.

"Oh, child, pay me no mind. It's just happiness, child. To think I brought you home from the hospital when you could sit right in my hand." She pulled a handkerchief from the sleeve of her frock. "Don't mind me, child. It's just plain happiness."

We walked over to the house and went in the back door. The kitchen was full of a whole new set of people, and again Emma was passed from breast to breast. When this was finished we went into a back room with a metal stairwell going down to the wine cellar. We went down into a butler's pantry. Lester was getting his serving dishes out and telling an assistant how each guest liked their drinks.

Emma stopped at the door of the cellar. "Shall I play the drooling nut or just be a bit spacey and roll my eyes in their sockets?"

"Ready?" I said.

"Hit it."

I opened the door for her, and the eighteen people in the room turned around. Cullington in a dinner jacket and black slippers was standing in an alcove talking on the phone. He had his back to us.

A young woman in an alligator-skin bolero and with bows in her hair rushed across the room. "Oh, Emma, you look so cute!" she said.

"Catherine!"

"How ya been? Can't wait to hear it all."

"I don't think you mean that." There was a chuckle. "Since we're only a small group, let me make a general introduction. This is Francis. He's a well-known architectural historian in Paris, should anyone be curious. We might just be able to convince him to accept some Texas hospitality for a while." They all clapped to this. Emma was swept off.

The first man who approached me brought a Champagne flute and a saucer of canapés. "Hope you don't mind the informality," he said. "This is Texas—we don't stand much by protocol. Name's Trey Clinton. Glad to meet you, Francis. Guess you've already noticed something?"

"That it's almost a stag party?"

"Knew you'd get it. Told you we didn't put much by etiquette. This is Texas."

"So you said."

"Ahahaha! Actually it's very 'summer in Texas,' this sort of gathering. Man's got to put his time in here in the summer. Can't be frightened off by a little heat, now can we? The fair sex goes off, but a guy's got to stay on deck. Gotta keep on working so the girls can go off and spend it. Gotta keep the girls happy, know what I mean?"

"I figure."

"Ahahaha! Matter of fact, Louise, my wife, is in Paris right now. Yep, just been getting her credit card bills this week.

Glad to see she doesn't believe in cutting corners."

"What is it she's doing?"

"Some damned cooking course or other. I think it's just an excuse to be there for a while. Supposedly when she comes back she'll know three or four menus that she can turn out when we entertain. Not for me to point out that our very good cook's yearly salary is less than this little trip. Gotta keep them happy!"

One of the four women present came up to us. "Name's Annie. How do you do, Francis? And Trey Clinton, don't be complaining. We make no fuss when you boys go off fishing in Nova Scotia or on shoots. I hear you're planning on bagging another polar soon. How much does that cost—fifteen, twenty thou? And without stuffing it too. You go up in a chopper with a couple of M-16s and nuke that baby, ain't that the truth?"

"No, it actually ain't the truth!"

"Well, it's hardly the call of the wild, now is it?"

"Oh man, Annie! Why must you always complicate everything? Gotta go, Francis, this girl gets me mad. I'm going right over to John and tell him he'd better send you on a mission of mercy to Bloomingdale's. Ahahaha! Catch ya later, Francis."

"Great."

"We actually aren't idiots, Francis. That boy's been pulling my ponytails for over twenty years. So! Anyway, you're an architectural historian. That must be fascinating in a place like Paris."

"It is."

"Course even little ol' Houston is interesting when you've got the knowledge."

"I'm sure."

"Fact is that I'd like to start a conservation or preservation—whichever it is—society here. There must be plenty of things to save here. I organized the museum ball last year and I was on opera the year before, so they won't be coming around for a while and a girl's got to keep herself busy. Course I'd ask Emma to join me, she'd be the perfect person, but I can just see her laughing in my face. She is an original, isn't she?"

"She's an original?"

"Well, yes, I mean . . ."

While Annie droned on I glanced over her shoulder and shared a moment with Emma. She was between conversations; our eyes met and she rolled hers to the ceiling and held up a glass of sparkling water in mock pride. She was swept off by another group. I thought, We are accomplices now.

During the meal, a young heart surgeon, who Annie told me was 'a real up-and-comer in the Methodist' and whose picture she'd seen in the paper running from a helicopter with a heart in an icebox, gave a fifteen-minute summation of why he still believed aluminum rifle scopes were better than graphite ones.

A young wildcatter, Annie told me, "one of the few left," insisted that the case of Lynch-Bages he'd brought be opened. His futures had just arrived, and he wanted to compare it to the Latour and Palmer we were drinking. If it proved to be as good—as apparently it was less expensive—it could then be considered a scoop, possibly a world-class deal, and certainly a story with which to garnish some other table.

Cullington took two phone calls.

The woman who was selling tables for the museum ball

grew flustered that they weren't going like hotcakes. ("Though once we've had our fun, would any of us actually not go?"—Trey) Somehow she blurted out the price—$10,000—which caused Cullington to blare down from the end of the table, "For that sort of money you should at least not have to go!" This was greeted with polite laughter, particularly by the woman selling them, knowing that here was someone who could actually carry out such a threat, if only for the image of an empty table in front of the band all night and to have a story to soothe one of his desperadoes trapped in some far-off shoot-out.

A young stockbroker began a phrase with "I was having breakfast the other day at '21' with the head of Lazard Frères . . ."

Trey spoke to me on his favorite subject. I thought I'd never forget the way his mouth exploded on the plosive in the word *billionaires.* "You see, Francis, we're not stuck up at all. Honestly not stuck up. It's very subtle, because there are so many who are dishonestly not stuck up. We are, what most of us of course wouldn't dream of imagining, it would be un-Texan, '*pas fait,*' as you might say, but we are, and possibly it is ironical, I think so certainly, but we are, and I say it not as some Texas parvenu but as someone whose grandmother once took three floors of the Ritz in Madrid for a wedding group. We are some of the very last really aristocratic people left. We have the naturalness of real aristocrats, and just as importantly we have the means. Others, if they are lucky, only have one or the other."

Toward the end of the meal I was swirling a glass of thirty-year-old Château d'Yquem and had completely forgotten the snideness with which I had begun the evening. I had just finished discussing plans for a bicycling tour of Provence in the spring with Trey and his wife and was improvising to Annie on the similarities in the transepts of Notre-Dame de Paris and Notre-Dame de Chartres when suddenly the lights went out. One whole wall of bottles was rolled to the side by Lester, and a giant video screen appeared behind it. With the controls in his hand, Cullington treated us to two replays of the Santa Anita stakes two years previously, with Emma smiling beside him in the winners' enclosure and holding the bouquet. Then a race at Belmont and again the winners' enclosure, though this time no Emma—it was only one year before. Finally, back twelve years to the Kentucky Derby, and as the horse tore into the home stretch Cullington zapped into slow motion and Lester, on cue, pressed on the soundtrack to *Chariots of Fire* all the way to the finish line. No one spoke until after the enclosure: Cullington and a fifteen-year-old Emma, touched, silhouettes in the light from the screen.

The lights came back on and Lester passed between us with a humidor of Montecristos. ("The only un-American activity I'll ever commit!"—Trey.) Cullington himself poured for everyone either "perfectly chilled Framboise or the best damned Chartreuse you've ever had." When he finished he handed both bottles back to Lester. He held his cigar up to his ear, rolled it in his fingers, and smiled. He nicked the tip with his teeth and lit it very slowly and deliberately. Everyone was looking at him. I felt it coming by the silence. He kept his eyes on the glowing tip, then he let them wander over the labeled bins, the sepia prints of oil derricks, and the cashmere shawls Lester was now handing out to the women. "Thank you, Lester," he said, and Lester left the room, closing the door behind him for the first time in the evening.

Cullington finally stretched his look all the way down the length of the table to the mistress of the house. Her stare was waiting, but it was Annie who spoke up. "Remember the time you flew us all up to the Super Bowl, Mr. Cullington?"

I decided she deserved a monument at every crossroads in the country.

"Don't believe I do, Annie, right now. Fact is, I was thinking how we've hardly talked oil tonight. I'm sure glad. It's the most boring talk. Yep, sure am glad we could keep off it while our guest Francis is here. Wouldn't you agree, Emma darlin'?"

"Uh-huh."

"In a way, though, at the risk of boring our guest, I do wish we'd talked some, just to remind you, darlin', just how boring it all really is."

Emma stood up and took a tumbler and filled it with Framboise. She came back to the table and sat down and looked back up the table toward her father. "Circle the wagons, boys, here we go."

Cullington chuckled. "You know what you love about it? The adventure, because you're so adventurous, but there is no adventure to it anymore."

"Don't start on the romance of wildcatting. We never did—we always came in with the big guns."

Cullington ignored her. "It's the tomboy in you, the hell-for-leather, risk-it-all-every-time haughtiness. Honey, it ain't that, it's shitheads on WATS lines on the fiftieth floor sweating it out over a fifth of a cent per barrel on a convoy of tankers. The days of spit-and-shake agreements are long gone."

"They never existed. Spindletop was crawling with lawyers. Anyway, have I said anything?"

"No, honey. No, you haven't. I just worry that you'll forget the reality of it again. I just wanted you to know that it's slit-throat alley, and it's no place for a woman."

"I thought we'd done with this conversation five years ago."

"Yes, we had. I just wanted to make sure. All I ever asked of you was to enjoy it all."

"Well, I certainly haven't disappointed you there."

A barely suppressed chuckle went around the table, full of envy for her cavalier spirit.

"No, honey. No, you haven't. Enjoyed you have, though maybe not that happily sometimes."

"Oh no, I would have been much happier joining the Junior fucking League, or breeding, or pretending I had to work, or going to live in an ashram and giving it all away."

"Now honey, I—"

"Or maybe I should have had a museum or hospital built after you. Let's see what else? I mean, how many choices did I have?"

"Now honey, I never said . . . Look, all I want to know and what I mean to say is—"

"All I want to know is who first said, 'I'd rather be a known drunk than an anonymous alcoholic.' It kills me that I didn't think of it." She stood up. "Come on, Francis, let's get out of here."

"I don't think he's going anywhere. I shouldn't think so, anyway."

Only for a moment did Emma stay at the door, looking at

me. Then she said, "What a pity," and stormed out.

All eyes now were on me to see if I would follow. My own were lost in a bin of assorted bottles.

Annie said, "It's the heat."

Trey said, "Shouldn't have had that last bottle, I suppose."

Cullington said, "Someone's got to feel nostalgic about the oil business, and that's a woman's role. That's all I was trying to say. A rancher's wife and daughter should feel that way about cattle and a lumberman's about lumber. Christ though, she's got it more than all of us. I know she's got it—she feels the thrill. You boys have been to business school too long to have it. Whatever the hell the Mercantile and the Arabs are doing, out there the roughnecks are still bolting lengths of drill. She's got that in the blood. How else could she be? Granddaddy made one good deal in East Texas, shook the right hand in the half-light of some saloon, talked the right farmer into selling his mineral rights. Just once, but the right once, and that's all that was needed. Jesus, she has the haughtiness. She reminds me of my grandfather, right over there in that picture. They were on a mission, goddamn it. They knew there's no occupation more important than oil. The owners of the arteries of this land. What the hell is more important than getting cheap and constant energy to the industry of this country? It's practically holy, a crusade to keep the whole big show on the road or it will clonk to a standstill. Those were the men she could have felt close to, American and visionary. Oil was cars, and cars was America. Now it's MBA land; now you could be selling fridges. Just look at those pictures, look at the faces—just a couple of gusher-drenched roughnecks, but look at those smiles, look at the lakes of oil behind them and their clothes stuck to their bodies. Why the hell wouldn't they be smiling like fools, knowing what they'd just done? After all those years crossing Texas and Arkansas and the Louisiana bayous, their hands still cracked from Dust Bowl winters. They couldn't imagine what the future held, and Emma couldn't give a damn about it. She's closer to them than all of us put together. Before families spread out like hornets in formation swarming in on the golden crock, before five hundred got to suck on one tit, and before women went shopping for Picassos, and before prep schools in New England and polo and stud farms and Newport and hangars full of airplanes and Swiss finishing schools and graduation to Swiss nuthouses. Yes! before all that there were spit-and-shake agreements in places like Smackover and Magnolia and Bear Creek and North Carterville and wells that started it all, which none of you probably know about, like the Daisy Bradford No. 3 and the Elenor Hope 1, the Lathrop 1, the Keystone field and Humble and all those men covered in mud waiting for the black column to burst the crown blocks. My girl, my only sweet girl. Maybe I was wrong. I told her she couldn't play in the big game, and now she won't play at all. Excuse me, y'all." He stood up, for the first time looking every one of his years, and left the room.

In his well-practiced two-step, Lester came back in.

"Don't worry about us, Lester," Trey said. "We can let ourselves out."

I followed Cullington up the cast-iron stairs. In the kitchen everything from dinner had been cleaned and put away. The security guard sat in a booth off the storeroom with three monitors and a portable television in front of him. He nodded. "He's in the vestibule, or whatever the hell it's called."

I went down a corridor lined with hunting trophies. I could

hear only my own footsteps on the marble. Then another corridor lined with paintings lit with single beams that cropped them neatly. I saw him outlined against some Impressionist master. He looked at me and then away, out through the portico. He began to shout. "Lester! Lester!" It bounced around the marble. I heard a quick nervous step. Lester was coming down the same wing I had just come down. In the lit courtyard all the cars were leaving.

Lester arrived. "Yes, sir, she's gone. Tore out of here."

"I know you're tired, Lester—"

"Is Mr. Francis coming with me?"

"Thank you, Lester. Yes, he is. Get a car and give Mr. Francis the list of bars and drive him till he finds her."

"What's the rush, Cullington? She's only been gone thirty minutes," I said.

"But it could be three hours before you find her," Cullington said. He turned his back to us and slowly began to walk up the staircase. "But it could be three hours before you find her," he repeated, as if to himself.

Lester and I walked back down the corridor toward the kitchen and the garage. Without stopping or turning he said, "Where we're heading you'd better not go dressed like that."

CHAPTER 14

Lester took one of the staff cars and waited for me in the courtyard while I changed. When I got in he handed me a typewritten sheet of paper. "She's probably in one of those, Mr. Francis."

"First, let's drop the 'Mr.' It makes me nervous. Second, why don't we just leave her be? She's got to come back."

"Oh no . . . Francis, it's always better when we go and find her. Not too soon, of course, but by the time we've found her it won't be. Believe me, she's always been very glad to see us come."

We headed down the drive. The dogs barked and snapped at the wheels. They came from among the trees and bushes with their teeth milky white in the headlights. Had I been driving, I wouldn't have resisted a quick swerve to belt one back to its Maker. Lester pressed the zapper clipped to the sun visor and the gate opened.

He had taken the one car with air-conditioning problems. We found out two blocks from the house, after much fiddling with the dashboard and oh-lawding. "Oh lawd, sorry, Mr. Francis."

"What the fuck does the Lord have to do with it?"

"Plenty."

"Sorry, Lester it's just—"

"I know, boy, I know."

It was bad. I'm a fine one all right, I thought. Sweating like a pig, errand boy for Cullington, taking it out on dogs and an old man. I kept my face close up to the open window.

Much thought had been put into the list, because the places, according to Lester, were in order of appearance when coming from the house. I could just see a secretary in her success suit waiting for Cullington to bark his orders for the day, and these being to find out whether the Homeboy, Dee-rails, or Casa Jimenez came first. This picture made me feel better.

It was the Homeboy. Lester pulled up across the street from it. Before he could make a U-turn into the parking lot two hookers had their faces in the window, handbags dangling and their arms glistening in the heat. "Hi there! Little company, boys?" the one in my window said, choking me with Listerine and Peach Brandy.

"No thanks," I said. Lester crossed into the parking lot and stopped behind a line of large motorbikes. He didn't move, so I said, "I'll go in if you prefer." He didn't answer, so I got out.

I was in the doorway of the bar when one of the women called from across the street, "Yo baby! Sorry, didn't know you boys just wanted to suck some cock!"

From the doorway I looked back at Lester, hoping that somehow he'd blocked that out. He looked like he was attempting to sit at the wheel looking straight at the lights of a diner. Maybe he had blocked it out.

Inside, my eyes scanned the room. It was like passing all

its contents through a sieve. There were men in black leather chaps and T-shirts at the bar. There were groups playing pool and drinking pitchers of beer. In the back garden there were men in each other's arms and others standing around as if at some polite cocktail party. There were quite a few girls, but no Emma. On the way out I stopped by the barman. "Seen a girl here, long blond hair, bit drunk maybe?"

"Plenty."

"One who doesn't look like she should be here."

"They all do. What about you, big boy, having a drink?"

"No thanks."

"Okay, you're looking for Emma, then? I didn't know she was back."

"She is."

"Did Lester retire?"

"No, he's waiting outside."

"Oh he is? I just have to go and say hello." He shouted to the men at the bar, "Anyone caught pouring their own draft is out! Tex, you're in charge." From behind his studded jacket Tex smiled and cracked his knuckles. All the others laughed.

Outside, the two hookers were now sitting on the car, making faces at Lester through the windshield.

The barman shouted, "Get outa here!"

"What's wrong, sonny, haven't gotten any lately?"

"Lousy douche bags! Get the fuck outa here!"

"Hey, *un momento,* faggot. You own the pavement now, or what?"

This short scene was brought to a close by the flashing red and blue of a silenced police siren. It cruised down the curb from bar lot to fast food, liquor store to oriental massage. A face appeared at the window. "Y'all break it up here before I get out, scum." The women climbed off and coolly continued their stroll in the opposite direction from the squad car.

"Sorry about that, Lester," the barman said. "Gotta get back in now. I ain't seen her, but give her my best."

"How's your momma doing anyway, boy? You give her my best too, hear?"

We pulled out of the parking lot. Lester turned the radio on to a gospel station. "You don't mind, do you?" he said.

"Course not."

He shook his head. "Damned shame. That boy come from church folk too."

When we weren't on freeways we were on side streets, stopping to yield at every corner. We didn't speak. Lester didn't have to look at the list of bars; every time he just pulled up to the next one. At every bar it was the same. He'd pull up as closely as he could to the door, then turn up the hymn or the preacher, whichever was on at the time, and I got out. Inside it was also the same. The same scanning of faces and the same blur of details. A punk bar where a boy in a torn T-shirt was banging his head against a post. A transvestite bar with many silicone breasts and wigs and dancers rubbing a pole in the middle of the dance floor. A salsa place with dudes out front where I was frisked at the door. Inside it was bathed in crème de menthe lights and sharp-looking couples danced to a band. I had a double margarita and listened to the music and watched the women, all hips, sprinkle the dance floor with talc when it got sticky. Then a lip-sync club on Aretha night and a bar of lesbians in cowboy boots who crowded around a stripper, stuffing dollars in her g-string. A country-music bar with bleach blondes, spikes, rhinestone-studded denims, and an electric violin somewhere in the music. Then the door of a Chinese supermarket, where Lester told me to knock. A grid opened. "You wan'?"

"I want a girl. Long hair. Emma."

"Gil lon her? Gil lon her? Emma? . . . Ah tha gil! Oh, she no here. Lon tie no see!" Behind the rotten teeth framed in the door I could hear the dice being thrown.

We were two-thirds down the list, going deeper, over train tracks and along a wired-off lot of stacked wrecks. We came to the front lot of a shingled cabin with battered pickups and assorted low-riders parked out front. A patch of light came from the half-open door, followed by an accordion and a voice wailing, *"Entre cantina y cantina!"* I stayed in the doorway and checked it out. Counter full of Mexicans, dust-covered boots resting on stools. The walls covered with pictures of Mexican stars taken from magazines. I was handed an open briefcase. It was lined in velvet and held a selection of lockets and chain bracelets that read "Love Always" and *"Amor Siempre."* I put it on the table nearest me and went into the room. Most of the tables had bottles of liquor in paper bags, like a real wine-and-beer-license place. I walked past a pool table to a dance floor. There was a record cabin off to the side lit by a bedside light. Emma and Lupe had their arms around each other. Emma was crying. Lupe saw me through the glass and nodded to me to go back to the bar.

I sat at the bar, in the light of an old color television tuned to a phone-in shopping channel. Lupe came up to the bar and went behind it. She smiled at me and took some empties off the counter. She put a beer with cut-up limes and a salt cellar in front of me, then came back around the bar and started taking empties off all the tables. I drank two beers, and then

I heard someone say, "Emma." I turned around and saw that her name was up on a blackboard of people waiting to play pool. She appeared and racked the balls up. The man who'd called her name broke. On her third shot she sank the eight ball by mistake and lost. She did an "Oh well, there you have it" with her eyebrows and shook hands. The man held up a quarter, showing that the next game was on him. She pointed at the blackboard, where there were other names. He laughed that they could wait. She laughed and disentangled herself and came toward the bar. She greeted everyone. *"Ayii Mamita chula! Todo chevere?"*

Some smiled at her, others ignored her, and others shook their heads. *"Si todo chevere Emma."*

"You know what *chevere* is?" she said to me.

"No."

"*Chevere* is cool, man, cool and hunky-dory. You see, there actually is more to life than cruising the Rue Cambon."

"You look right at home."

"You'd better believe it. Who brought you anyway?"

"Lester."

"Oh Lester, Lester. I see Lester waiting outside my school. My one image of him forever, waiting for me to come out, every single day asleep at the wheel under the trees."

"Well, I'm sure he'll be glad to know it. Now it won't have been a completely wasted evening."

"As a matter of fact, he probably would like to know."

"And he can understand all those complicated problems of yours and all the bars we've just been in, and he can put a HANDLE WITH CARE sign on you and head back home in peace."

"Well, I did tell him not to send Lester anymore."

"And who the hell else do you think gives a damn about what happens to you?"

"You're right, of course, as always. But let me deal with him before I get to you." She drained my beer and went to a sink behind stacked beer crates. She washed her face and straightened her clothes, and we went out. The radio was blaring, "Lord, yes! Hallelujah, Lord, I believe!" around the parking lot. Lester must have known by the wait that I had found her. He was leaning against the car as if ready for some sort of action. He came toward us when he saw us.

"I am found, Lester, I am found," Emma said and hugged him.

"Yes, baby, thank the Lord."

"Thank you, Lester."

"Don't be crying, baby."

"I'm all right. You go home. I'll be all right with Francis."

"Well, you call me if there's any problem, hear?" Out of his butler's jacket I could see how strong he was. Cullington knew what he was doing when he sent Lester out. The sort of teetotaling old black who would never have an inch of fat and was probably not bad with his fists either when absolutely necessary.

He pulled out of the lot and we went back into the cantina. Nearly everyone was up and dancing to a ballad. She caught my smile and took it as a good enough starting point. "You could at least not think about it."

"What?"

"I can hear the cash registers from here. Isn't it the easiest money you've ever earned? And don't think for a moment I'm going to tell him to call the deal off. I rather like the idea of having you as an employee. You'll have to get used to these wetback places, though. You missed it when your friend Trey told me he paid his ranch hands six bucks a day."

"Meet me at the barricades, amigos!"

"Look, I'm the one who's supposed to be bawling you out for being such a slimeball, so shut the fuck up."

"I'm ready."

"I said shut the fuck up, because *I* am talking to *you* now! One, so that you're not under any illusions, I've always been happier on the down escalator, and that's the only reason I asked you to come. Two, you have grown to be pathetic. You are now a bore and a shit, and you just stand there and take it. For three hundred or five hundred or whatever I think he got a damned good bargain. Leave, pal, get up and leave. No one is keeping you. But you don't even have the balls for that. For all your posing, you're the most bought person around."

She went back to the dance floor and twirled alone to the accordion of a *ranchera.* Then she asked a man to dance. He was drinking with a group of men, and he stood up sheepishly to show that he was a sport. She pulled him toward the dance floor. They stamped their feet and lifted dust from the planks. The man waved his straw cowboy hat and Emma yelled, "Aii-yii-yii!" The man she'd been playing pool with still had the table, and he asked her to play. The balls were already racked up, and she broke, and by a complete fluke she sank the eight ball first. She punched the air in delight and invited him into the bathroom for a snort. Then she invited Lupe. They came back to the bar together. Lupe lined up two tequila shots and beer chasers on the counter. The lime wedges were already cut, and she put them on a napkin. Emma suddenly threw her arms around me and brushed her face up to my neck. Damp met damp.

"I'm sorry, Emma," I said.

"Oh, Francis, Francis. *I'm* sorry. Spineless is how I love you!"

". . . ."

"It's true. But what am *I* to do? My problem's the headliner here."

"I don't know. I really don't know."

"Two years to think about it and you still don't know. Great." She pinched some salt, shot her tequila, sucked a lime wedge, sucked in half her draft, and shuddered. "Well, at least let's be nice to each other," she said. "And that's an order."

The cantina closed its doors at two in the morning, and then for two more hours Lupe kept on serving. The door was locked, and anyone who went out was out. At four she began asking everyone to drink up. They left at intervals, two cars at a time so as not to attract attention. The jukebox was silent, and through the plank walls we could hear the adioses and the roar of the souped-up crates and with every exit from the lot the crash of the nose as it hit the roadway from the pavement.

The moment Emma's hands touched the wheel she gave a very practiced impression of sobriety that lasted in silence all the way to the house. The security guard must have seen us on the monitor. He was standing at the entrance to the courtyard keeping all the dogs around him. Before we'd gotten out of the car he'd disappeared back into the house so as not to give us the impression we were being watched.

Inside the bungalow Emma turned on the night-light by the door. She took a container of insect repellent from under the bathroom sink and sprayed the screen door and the sides of the windows and the flats of the air conditioner. I fell face-first onto the bed and listened to her mixing the drinks. Outside the window, under the plantain trees, I could hear the dogs pawing at the earth to find a cooler spot to rest on. "They always go there," she said. "They like the smell of themselves where they've been." She came over to the bed with the drinks and put them on the table. "Is that a loaded phrase or what?" She sat on the bed. There was a whistle from the house, and the dogs all stalked back across the yard to the guard. With my head on the side I could see him standing under the portico.

"He does the rounds?" I said.

"Once every hour, never at the same time. Pure Marlowe." She kicked her shoes off and lay down beside me, an ashtray resting on her belly. In a moment our feet were touching. I drew the backs of my fingers up along her cheek. I moved closer. "Don't please."

"Why?"

"I can't get messy again."

I stretched over her and took my drink. Her eyes were closed, and a cigarette was burning almost down to her fingers. I put it out in the ashtray and put the ashtray on the table.

She said, "I must have been about eight," and stopped. It was said with much intent. After a sip she continued. "It was a party night. I was up in my room, and Mary, Tessy's sister, was combing my hair and putting silk ribbons around my ponytails. We walked down the stairs and past all the mirrors to the library. Mary led me in. My father said, 'Here's the Queen of the Night,' and took me in his arms all around the room to meet everyone. Lester was mixing drinks and smiling at me from a corner. Then dinner must have started and Mary took me into the kitchen. It was full of waiters, and Tessy's right in the middle of it unmolding . . . tomato aspics. Of course, she was worried because they'd been out in the heat too long. I looked out the window. There was a line of the latest, biggest Cadillacs. I cornered Mitch, the youngest waiter, and said, 'How'd you like to take one of them for a ride?' He said, 'Oh no, Miz Emma.' I said, 'The keys are still in them, you know?' We left out the back gate. He drove very carefully, because he didn't want to be stopped. All the way he just kept slapping his thigh and laughing. Mitch was Lester's youngest son. Jesus! Don't tell me the whole thing doesn't suck—there are pieces of him still coming down in Vietnam. Finally we got to the Fifth Quarter or the Heights or wherever it was and everyone was just hanging out in the heat. Fanning themselves on the porches and outside the pool halls and bars and on the steps. Why? Why always that image? All the faces black and wet and kind, I suppose. I sat in my frock in the front seat and Mitch just curb-crawled and everyone came up to him to check the car out and he was giving fives out the window with all of them. He stopped the car and we went up to a porch where all these old women were sitting out. Mitch said, 'This is Mr. Cullington's daughter.' They all patted my head and said, 'Child, child, what you doin' down here? Lawd, ain't she beautiful! Go fetch this child a Coke from the icebox. What you doin' down here, baby, this is the wrong side of the tracks.' "

She thought I was asleep. I heard her put her shoes on and stumble back across to the house. I still had my face in the pillows. I wondered whether it had been a story at all. But if not that, then what? Some kind of excuse?

CHAPTER 15

I woke to the sound of Cullington shouting, "Go! Come!" and "Good boy!" Looking through the screen, beyond where the guard had been a few hours before, I was relieved to see he was shouting at a young dog. It was retrieving something Cullington kept on throwing. I thought of not going to report on my mission, but I didn't want to start calculating my moves with him. I showered and changed into my bathing suit and a bathrobe. I took a towel and walked across the lawn.

The estate was in full mobilization. A large black man drove around in a lawnmower. He wore a pith helmet and already had a large purple stain seeping across the back of his work shirt. Two of the Mexican gardeners were at work in the flower beds lining the security fence. Two more worked in the shade of a truck loaded with rolls of lawn. They sprinkled the earth they were preparing to unroll it on. In the middle of it all, Cullington stood in slippers and a nightshirt. He was throwing a duck, which from the sound it made was frozen. As he threw it the whole nightshirt swung around, but—doubtless to the pride of some Jermyn Street shirtmaker—the phone never fell out of its monogrammed pocket. The duck landed in the middle of some bushes. The dog sniffed for it but couldn't find it and looked back. Cullington slapped his right thigh with his right hand and the dog retraced its steps. It found the duck and came toward us wagging its tail. Cullington turned around and feinted at me. "Morning."

"Good morning."

The dog licked my leg with its hot tongue.

"Stop it! Down, Ya-mani!" The dog cowered. Cullington picked the duck up off the grass. "They start to smell bad pretty soon if you don't freeze them. Plastic's no good. They have to smell it, then it will never leave them. It's like pussy. Know what I mean?" He studied the duck in his hand. "Guess this one's getting sort of funky. Hey, Eusebio." A gardener's head shot around. *"Ve y tráeme otro pato de la* freezer, *por favor.* Something like that. Right, Francis? How'd you sleep?"

"Fine."

"Good, good. Where did you find her?"

"A cantina."

"Why the hell does she always go to those damned 'can' places?"

" 'Can'?"

"Oh that's Texan. Messi-can, Afri-can, Puerto Ri-can."

"It would be much better if she got wasted at the club."

"Yeah, well I hope it wasn't too much trouble. First night back I wasn't expecting it, to tell you the truth."

A massive flock of blackbirds had settled in the large patch of open earth the gardeners were preparing for the lawn. They feasted on the freshly unearthed worms and bugs. The gardeners sprayed them with the hoses, but there were too many and they only lifted from one spot and landed on another.

"Fuck a duck, wish I had a gun," Cullington said. The gardener who'd gone for the duck brought one back, but Cullington had lost interest and told him to take it back to the freezer before it thawed any more. "Well, I see you're going swimming, Francis. Good. Myself, I've got to go and earn the bacon. Y'all enjoy now, hear!" He crossed back to the house, with the dog wagging its tail behind him.

All the cushions were out at the pool. I took the sun for ten minutes. By then I was running with sweat. I dived in, determined to lose myself in laps. The inside of the pool was painted dark blue, which made it look cooler than the usual color. Y'all enjoy, I heard again as I crawled toward the other end. I knew he meant, Let's see how long you can keep my only sweet little girl under control. Let's see how long you can keep the pace. Fat bastard. Still can't get a somersault turn. *Bang!* I heard a shot. I treaded water, looking in the direction it had come from. Cullington's sporty Aston-Martin sped down the drive. He waved out the window at me with a pistol in his hand. He was beaming. Behind him a curtain of black wings and a thunder of caws rose toward the trees. What could I do but wave back?

When I was dressed I crossed over to the kitchen door. Tessy was there, and a younger maid was reading in a corner. Lupe, in a pink seersucker uniform, was leaning against a set of drawers. Tessy cut okra and kept her eye on the confessions of an anorexic from Cleveland on the television. Emma stood behind her, dressed in blue denim and with both hands resting on Tessy's massive shoulders. "Oh, there y'ar," Tessy said. "Mawnin', Mr. Francis. Breakfast's set up in the conservatory."

"The conservatory? He can have it in here," Emma said.

"But Lester's gone and set it all up for you there."

"You know I don't have breakfast, and what's Lester doing up anyway?"

"He's workin' child, that's where he be, and just because you don't care for breakfast that don't mean Mr. Francis don't. It'll only take a moment to fix."

"That's all right. Thank you, Tessy. I'll just take some coffee," I said.

"Well, that's a shame," Tessy said.

"Why don't you just sit down. Lupe, will you get Mr. Francis a cup of coffee so we don't have to spend the whole day on the subject," Emma said. There was a play between them which I had missed. Lupe didn't get me the coffee. I took a cup from the rack and poured it myself from the percolator. Tessy let it be known that she thought it was a damned shame that I had to get my own coffee. Then she yelled at the young maid who was reading not to forget the corn bread in the oven. Then she turned back to her okra and the talk show. "Y'all have that over yonder, Mr. Francis—eatin' and purgin'?"

"I guess."

"Ooh Lawd ha' mercy, that sure ain't good!" There was a break for commercials and she remembered a story that she'd meant to catch Emma up on. "Ooh baby, we had the finest service when Alberta passed on. That man flew right back. I got one of them secretaries to phone him the news, and he gone and flown back and drove straight up to the Ebenezer just to recite the Twenty-Third Psalm. Baby, he sure did read it fine, too. Lawd, you know how Alberta made him promise all those years that when her time came he'd be the one to read it. What a voice. I never will forget. The Lawd is my shepherd, I shall not want, he maketh me to lie down in green pastures, Yea, though I walk through the valley of the shadow of death, yet shall I fear no ill."

"Amen, Tessy. Amen!" the maid who'd been silent in the corner said.

"Tessy Baker, I do believe you have visions of yourself as the dove of peace in this house," Emma said.

"Now baby, *what* do you mean by that?"

"Aren't you done singing Daddy's praises? That's what I mean."

"Oo child, don't you think for a moment you're too old for me to take a hand to. I been workin' for that man ten years more than you been alive. I seen him court your momma, and I seen the Lawd take her back. I brought you up with these two hands, and I cannot see why you won't give him some happiness. You're all he's got. Lawd ha' mercy, everything that man has, and you're all he cares about. You shoulda seen the way he moped all last year, never mind before, the things you done to him. Don't forget, this is my home too, baby. I'm old, and I've given my life fo' y'all. All I can say is that thank the Lawd black folk don't come as plain dumb as me any-more. I still deserve more than to watch it all fall apart now when the Lawd's got half a mind to call me back any day. It ain't right, baby, it just ain't right, and you know it!" The handkerchief was out, and Tessy was crying again. Lupe went out. Tessy hid her face behind the okra, and Emma buried her face in the wiry gray hair. "I'm sorry, baby," Tessy said. "You know how it is sometimes, word just follows word."

Emma decided we were going to the ranch for the day. We wouldn't get there until the evening, and we could spend the night there. We took a Suburban with a walk-up shooting deck welded to the roof. The first stop was a liquor store in a mall far enough from the house not to be spotted. I waited in the truck with the windows up and the air-conditioning on. Emma came out waving a bottle of Cuervo Especial and two bottles of Spanish Champagne that were on special. "Dom P! Dom P!" she mouthed. The shop boy carried two six-packs of Mexican beer and a bag of ice. They put all the bottles in the ice chest in the back. Emma took the ice from the boy and dropped it on the ground to break up the cubes. Then she emptied them over the bottles. She climbed into the driver's seat and opened two beers with the back of a spoon she'd taken from the house. ("He's hidden all the bottle openers. I just know it.") She kept her bottle between her knees and reached for an envelope in the map compartment. "Little toot?" she said.

"Not particularly."

"I'll just take a snip. It's a long trip."

I watched the cars roll into the parking lot of the Safeway across the street. The parents and kids all plopped out of their cars and almost ran for the cool recesses of the market. A sign in the window said that there was a special on turkey wings while 97,000 pounds lasted. Emma was done in a series of quick movements, not trying to hide, the only way to do it in public. She checked her nose in the rearview mirror, checked that the radar detector behind the sun visor was on, and put on her sunglasses. "Well, at least I'm keeping away from the real stuff." I shrugged disinterest and she pulled out of the lot and headed for 610.

She gave an answer of sorts to my shrug during the trip to the ranch. She was telling me about three detectives her father had put on her when the clinic for Mexican women had started to go wrong, and how they'd had to take it in eight-hour shifts to keep up. The highway was sinister and deserted. She was doing ninety-five in the middle lane when a car trying to cross on an open intersection stalled, taking up the two central lanes. She at least didn't slam on the brakes, but she didn't change lanes either. The face of the woman we were closing in on was a zoom-in on terror. This is not the way I'm going, I thought, but my arms wouldn't go up to grab the wheel. The stalled car lurched forward out of our lane and we raced past. Fifteen seconds in all. "Wouldn't be feeling too smart right now if I'd tried to pass in front of her," Emma said.

"Or if she'd stayed put."

"She looked much too dumb for that." A mile further along: "Don't worry, junkies don't take the deep six. That's the one payoff."

We pulled into a yard and in the settling dust spotted three men in Bud Light caps studying trailer wheels. "How ya been keeping, Bill?"

"Long time since we saw you, Miss Emma."

"I've been studying in Switzerland."

"So your daddy said. Mighty fine, mighty fine."

"This here's Francis. A friend from Paris."

"Glad to meet ya, Francis."

"Daddy said you had a mare who had a cesarean."

"Sure did, and she's doing mighty fine now. Y'all want to see her?"

"Course we do." We walked across the yard to the stables.

The mare was in the first stall. When she saw us come in she backed into her feeding bin. She had a wide bandage wrapped around her belly, and some blood was caked dry where it had seeped between the layers. Emma went up slowly and rubbed the mare between the eyes. "There, there, baby. What's her name, Bill?"

"Xanadu."

"Daddy must have been feeling swell."

"Guess he was."

"Couldn't save the foal?"

"Bad deal all the way."

Emma tried to get closer, but the mare backed and stared out at the three of us. Bill led us out of the stables and across to a hangar. The crop duster and the chopper and the team of three-wheel motorbikes all had "Carrascal" written on their sides. It was the name of the ranch. "Know how to ride one?" Emma said.

"Better than a horse, I figure. Is this where the racehorses are?"

"Oh no, this is the token Brahman ranch. The racehorses are in Kentucky. Now, these things aren't like two-wheelers, you know. The balance is all different."

"I'll figure it out."

"I hope so. I'm a take-no-prisoners sort of rider."

"That's a surprise," I said. Even Bill thought this was funny. The bikes didn't need a kick start, and he shouted above the roar for us to have a good time. We drove out through the hangar onto an airstrip.

Emma made me circle a few times before we went any further. "Race you out to the end of the strip!" she said.

"Give me a head start."

"Chi-cken! I'll count to ten. No more."

I took off, tearing up the strip, but she passed me halfway. At the end of the strip she continued on a dirt track. Where the ground got rough she stood up off the seat with her feet on the rests. Soon I had mastered this one too. We drove through wide-eyed Brahman cattle. They hardly moved out of our way. After an hour we came down a ridge and stopped on the flat bank of a bayou. A black family was fishing there. The father sat on a cooler with a rod in his hands. Three small children beside him held canes with lengths of string. They'd watched us come down the rise until we were right beside them.

"Any luck?" Emma said.

"None so far," the man said, and the children shook their heads in agreement. Emma picked up a rifle that was leaning against a tree. "Never know what might be passin'," the man said. "Hope you won't be tellin' ol' Bill we're here."

"No, I won't. Don't worry."

"Thank you," the man said.

Emma lifted the rifle to her cheek and panned it over the water. "Nice weight. Any gators?"

"Just seen one across by them reeds. It just went down."

"Got to come back up, don't you figure?" she winked at the children, and they all nodded back in agreement. "Mind if we take a shot?"

"Shoot away. Less gators the better," the man said.

Emma's eyes scanned the dark surface of the water. It didn't take her long. She pointed far right, away from the bank and the reeds to a copse of trees and brambles growing out of the water. I followed her finger and found the nostrils and snout and hooded eyes just breaking the flatness. "Want to try it, Franky?"

"Sure."

"But don't hit it."

"I wouldn't know how to."

"Well, don't hit it by accident."

"So why fire at it?"

"To scare it. To let them know I'm back. One of them ate a dog of mine once. Daddy wanted to electrocute the whole damned lake, but I talked him into letting me take them one by one." She positioned the rifle for me so my cheek rested correctly, and then she stood back, watching with the children. I fired and thought my shoulder was torn off. Emma and the children fell back against the tree, they were laughing so hard. We thanked them for the use of the gun and wished them good luck, and Emma reassured them she wouldn't tell Billy of their poaching. We took off toward the ranch house.

She rode ahead of me and I rode in the dust she lifted until she stopped to let me catch up. The rest of the way was almost flat and straight, and I didn't have to watch the ground too closely and could watch her. I was glad Texas was flat and straight so I could watch her, and I was glad the roar of the engines didn't let us talk. She took her bike straight up whatever small ridges presented themselves, and, laughing, with her hair tucked into the back of her shirt, she ate up the track. The cloud of red earth we left behind was like so many exploding sandbags, I thought.

Bill had left a note that there was iced tea in the fridge, and his wife had put vegetables on the wooden counter and in the sink. The tea was in a large pitcher with tea bags and fresh mint floating in it. We drank it in plastic tumblers on the porch and chewed ice looking out at the evening. Dinner was a joint effort. The vegetables were still covered in earth from the garden. Emma filled a sink with water and washed them all in the same water so as not to waste it. First the lettuce, laying the leaves on paper towels, then small tomatoes and baby zucchini. She mixed the lettuce with sliced yellow tomatoes. I found all the ingredients for a vinaigrette and made it with Dijon mustard so it would be thick. Emma said cilantro was good in a salad and through the window she showed me where it grew against a shed wall. I went out and picked some and washed it and chopped it and sprinkled it on the salad. She took a bag of chorizo from the freezer and put it in a skillet to cook. I cracked a half-dozen eggs into a bowl, and at the last moment she emptied them into the skillet and scrambled it all together.

We ate on stools at the kitchen counter and drank our way through the Coronas and half the tequila. By the end of the meal we had a full bowl of sucked lime quarters. She told me that as a girl she used to spend weeks at a time out at the ranch with Cullington. When she fell silent I told her I loved her, and she smiled. I told her I intended to become an apprentice rancher so the two of us could spend a lot of time at Carrascal. She laughed.

We gathered up the dishes and cleared the counter. I told her that I'd wash them. She went over to a storage room just off the kitchen. She began to take down trunks and boxes. It was all stuff that had been caught between houses on rushed trips. When I had washed and dried the dishes I went over to her. She was getting further into the trunks, and she didn't hear me at the door. She looked like she was enjoying it so I left her to it.

I walked down the roadway toward the only other light. The outlines of the trees rang with the chirping of crickets. Billy was chugging a beer and picking at a bowl of nachos with his wife and watching the Astros. He offered me a beer and told me how Cullington hardly came down anymore. This was just fine by him. He showed me the chart of how he timed calf births. Then he took me out behind the house where he had two calves that were sick. He shouted back in to his wife, asking if she'd fed them. She shouted that she had. He showed me the bottle they fed them with, which looked like a large baby bottle. We went back inside and had another beer, and he filled me in on the fates of the Astros, the Rockets, and the Oilers. His wife asked if I would share a Lean Cuisine lasagna with them. It would just take her a moment to zap another. She patted Billy's stomach and said that it was the only thing she'd let him eat these days. I thanked them and said I'd just eaten. He gave me three videocassettes of the high spots from the last three World Series. I turned down his offer of a drive back up to the house, and I walked back through the darkness.

Emma was now surrounded by all the stuff she'd taken from the trunks. She flung a cowboy shirt over at me, the kind with three pearl buttons on the cuffs. She asked me to put it on, and I did. "Will you kiss me, cowboy, only once?"

"However I want and as long as I want?"

"Deal."

While we kissed she held me by the wrists and thumbed the buttons. "What was that all about?" I said.

"A memory."

"Madame Saccharine."

"I *have* been away."

"Or out of it."

"For a long time."

"Is Pop in it?"

"Sort of."

"Spare me. One more and I'll feel spoiled."

"It's really about how I lost my cherry."

"Start talking."

"Just a guy, at the proverbial prep school. We were going to go on and study—"

"—geology."

"Did I tell you?"

"Only that part."

"Well, *el capitán* wanted to take the guy for his little walk in the garden, so he sent a plane up to Boston to pick us up. Bad start—the guy didn't know whether to say wow! or to just say nothing. My god, the things one learns to pick up on, isn't it awful? Anyway, it was night when we got in, and the runway was all lit up. He had a lady friend up for the weekend to put us at our ease or something, and they were waiting. My guy got off the plane in his blazer and kissed the woman's hand, and that was that."

"Why?"

"Well, it looks a bit ridiculous in an eighteen-year-old."

"He was doing his best."

"Oh, for god's sake, do you want to hear the story?"

"Yes."

"Well, by the end of the first day even the bimbo was saying, 'Where's what's-his-name?' The end came when we were taken out to shoot one morning. We took a chopper out, and the gun boys made a fire and tortillas and all that stuff for breakfast. We were sitting around the fire and first he tried to get a business conversation going with Daddy. You can imagine how far that went, six in the morning with a high school senior, on a shoot. But that was nothing. He next took a tortilla from one of the gun boys without thanking him and then he wiped the bottle off before taking his swig. I mean, they're all 'cans' and niggers to him, but that you do not do. He got up to kick the mud from his boots, and I just closed my eyes on the whole scene. God, all I wanted in those days was to go wait tables in some hip café."

"Spare me the part on how hard it is to be rich."

". . . ."

". . . ."

"You are vicious and ruthless. You know that?"

Without realizing it my hand formed a fist, and I brought it down with all my strength onto the kitchen counter. "I am not, Emma. I am not. I am playing a role, and I am trapped. I was happy today."

"Talking of saccharine."

She went back into the storeroom, and I went into the sitting room. I stuck one of the tapes into the video recorder. I had the bottle of tequila and a mirror and blade and sat in front of the screen. During the second tape I went back into the kitchen. She was still going through the trunks, and she wouldn't acknowledge me. I came back.

On the third tape a rookie was up. It was the ninth inning of a tied game. Some grand old man of pitching had two strikes on him. The announcer said, "This boy's in the chair, whether it's AC or DC, he's going to get it." The phrase could have nailed me. The grand old man threw his knuckleball, and the rookie sent it to left field for a stand-up double. "Wowwee, that had mustard on it!" the announcer shouted. Yeah, you can sit right here, announcer, I thought, and held my index finger up to the screen.

I stood up. "All right, boys," I said to the screen. "No second-guessing *this* game in the clubhouse!" I turned and went back into the storeroom. Emma was asleep now with the contents of the boxes all around her. I picked up a photo album made and bound by some expensive New York studio. It was of Emma as a deb. Then I looked at an old nature study album with leaves and twigs falling from between the pages. I put it back down with all the other stuff and stumbled back into the kitchen. I opened and closed the fridge. I sat on one of the stools where we'd eaten and held on to the cutting board. I wanted to talk. I wanted to phone someone. I went back on the stool. I landed on a plastic bin. I was on my hands and knees reading the labels on a shelf. I pulled myself up on the shelf, and I had them all right in front of me. Cheez-It, Bonnie Hubbard Garbanzos, Progresso Tomato Soup, Campbell's, Log Cabin Syrup, a twelve-pack of twelve-ounce Buds. Some kind of home.

CHAPTER 16

We sat in the bar of the country club. Around us families pecked halfheartedly at their club sandwiches and fought. Lunch had been a succession of women in headbands and men just off the tennis courts, some with small children on their shoulders and most dangling the keys to German cars. Dangling them with a certain sense of urgency, I noticed. They seemed glad to see Emma, but though "Let's get together" and "Let's do lunch" had been repeated often enough, no one had cared to make the statement any more concrete. Emma was troubled, and these were people who'd known it since the sandbox.

I didn't want to be presented again. My specialty was not being taken for a woman's lover when I was. Now I was being taken for Emma's when I wasn't, and the joke was on me.

That's how I was feeling, starting at the ranch once the coke had worn off toward dawn, and I had been looking at my right hand for some time. It was swollen around the knuckles and purple with internal bleeding. When I woke Emma to show her, she insisted that any setting that might be needed should be done in the medical center back in Houston. The drive up was hell. Emma became a mine of stories about hands that had to be rebroken because they'd been set wrong in the first place, and I had to sit through them with no coke left. Not even, just this once, for medicinal purposes.

When we reached the hospital I wasn't even considered a serious emergency. The nurse in the outpatients' room told us to get in line, but a call from Emma to some important doctor in the place got us past all that. He, of course, was a hunting buddy of Cullington's. He came down and got an Indian intern to look after us. Hardly was he gone when a phone was handed to me and Cullington was on the line. While the intern tried to move my knuckles and clicked his tongue, Cullington chuckled and offered to talk me through it and told me how fond of me he was becoming. That's how I was feeling—the patsy; any jokes going were on me.

I looked down at the crumbs of my own club sandwich. Then I looked across at Emma. She was drawing a map for me on a bar napkin. It gave directions for getting from the Galleria, which apparently even I would be able to find, to the cantina.

"Don't get lost now, Champ." She patted my bandaged hand—two broken knuckles.

"Let's get out of here," I said.

We left the bar and went out into the front hallway. More people nodded at Emma, but she only nodded back and smiled at them—she didn't stop. We each gave our tickets to the parking attendant, and we stood at the door of the club waiting for our cars to be brought round. Below us, outside the wrought-iron gates, I watched a charter bus unload a group of people with cameras. A man in a polyester suit carrying a clipboard was their guide. He yelled, "This one sold for six big ones. Yabetya! Six million pesitos!" He pointed at a huge house, and the people on the tour all took shots of the mansion and then of themselves standing against the gates with the mansion in the background.

"Why can't I go with you?" I asked Emma.

"You can come as far as the apartment to get some clothes, but not to my aunts. That you're not allowed."

"Allowed? What apartment?"

"The one I had until I relapsed. You don't want to spend the day with my cousins and aunts, do you?"

"You want to? I don't know why you're going at all."

"Procedure."

"Is that nuthouse jargon?"

"Oh no, nuthouse jargon is stuff like achievement, cunning, compulsive, denial, craving, unmanageable, self-esteem, powerless to shortcomings, hit bottom, surrender, complete defeat, hostile, judgmental—sound like anyone you know? Miss Denial herself." A woman suddenly swerved away from us. She'd been coming toward Emma smiling until she got within earshot. Emma winked at me.

"Why have you come back at all? I don't understand."

"Lordylord, does this rarefied air make you nervous or what? It's very simple why I came back. After a year in the bin I have to be careful not to make a messy first move. I thought this wasn't too messy."

"I don't know what it is, but I know I don't want to showboat you around this place, and I don't want to be an item with you for the benefit of your acquaintances."

"Now champ, after dinner with my aunts I'll go and show my face at the local narco meeting, and the last testimony should be over by eleven, and then I'll meet you at the cantina."

"Do whatever you want."

"Hot, huh? I told you it's hell. It's like living under water—thick and green and still water."

The town car she'd chosen from her father's garage was finally brought up. The attendant hopped out. "Thank ya, Miz Cullington. Nice to see ya again."

She thanked him and tipped him and turned back to me. "But you'll get to love it. Bye now!"

I watched the attendant taking his time in bringing up the car I'd chosen for the day, a waxed red Fairlane convertible. Home from the hospital, Cullington had helped me take the roof down. He was still chuckling at my bandaged hand. ("As long as it doesn't do more than twelve to the gallon, I can take to any car!")

The attendant stopped in front of me and got out. "Nice wheels!" he said.

I agreed.

It wasn't long before I decided I should have taken another car—one with a roof and air-conditioning. To keep cool I kept my foot on the gas and bombed along on the outside lane. I had gotten used to stick shifts; automatics propelled you. I felt like being propelled, and I was, all afternoon, around the loops, ramps, and beltways of the city, comfortable behind the pull of the engine and the fuel marker bouncing in green.

I tuned the radio to a light FM station. The stress-free music they promised appealed to me. I thought I'd drive out to see NASA, but when I stopped to look at the map Cullington had given me it looked too far away. I decided that I didn't want to see anything in particular anyway. I wanted to drive. It had always made me feel that somehow I was in transit.

Toward mid-afternoon I pulled off the freeway into the lot of a bar shaped like a boat. It had a satellite dish on the roof. The parking lot was made of crushed oyster shells. Inside, the bar counter was in the shape of bulwarks. Mexicans in baseball caps were shucking furiously. I ordered a dozen oysters and a beer. I was given fourteen beauties, equally shaped and as translucent as tears. My porthole gave onto the freeway, so I ate facing the bar and watching the Astros up in the corner.

The bar filled up. It looked like the sort of place people stopped off at on their way home from work. They all seemed to know each other. Some of the men didn't even have to order their drinks. I had two more beers and shot some tequila.

Back outside I noticed a miniature golf course across the parking lot. What the hell, I thought. I paid for a putter and a ball. I was doing fine until the sixth hole. It was placed right on top of a mound. I kept missing it, and every time I did the ball either rolled back toward me or down the other side. I was never any closer. I tried several times. Finally I just whacked the ball away. It bounced off the cement banking and over the wall onto the freeway. From his booth the manager called me on the PA. "Careful there, hole six!" I took the putter back to him and said, "Forget it." I paid two dollars for the ball.

I was back on the freeway. My stress-free station was threatening that if I didn't use a certain weed killer my lawn would keep on growing while I worked, slept, and played. Then a siren was flashing behind me and a nasal loudspeaker was saying, "Pull over, red Fairlane." I pulled over to the right and there was a face in my window telling me to get out. Standing on the shoulder of southbound 610 I counted odd numbers backwards from ninety-nine to seventy-three. Then I stood on one foot with my arms held out and looked straight up at the sky. I didn't fall over, so the cop made me explain my French license. When I had done so he asked me to explain the ownership of the car. This had to be radioed into the precinct and checked. I watched the traffic until the precinct called back that everything was all right. I was given a pink citation anyway. "But I'm not drunk," I said.

"You're not drunk enough, Frenchy. That's for hogging two lanes."

"But—"

"You going to give me trouble?"

"No." The thought did cross my mind of going on a spree and giving the car back to Cullington with a ticket from every cop in Houston.

"Nice wheels, by the way," he said. "No Renault bullshit in that baby!"

Being careful with my lane position, I decided I'd better head for the Galleria.

I didn't bother exploring the Galleria. I found a bar on the top floor, and from my table on the balcony I could look down at all the levels of shoppers going from one store to another. The main floor held a large skating rink. Once I'd ordered a margarita on the rocks with salt I looked down at a group of little girls in ballet poufs who were practicing an ice version of *Swan Lake.* Before the drink arrived I took the opportunity to answer a question. Could you ever live back in this country? No. If I felt this way after several hours at the wheel of a Fairlane with Ray-Bans and FM stations and bombing between canyons of car dealerships and food franchises, then from every other position it would be worse. Worse? More distant. The afternoon's experiment was over. My drink arrived.

When I ordered a second one I made sure to specify a double this time and with less ice. They put so much ice in the drinks it was reason enough to get turned off the whole continent. *Swan Lake* gave way to an ice sweeper, and that gave way to a Shirley Temple look-alike contest. Black, white, and brown little girls in frocks and golden ringlets warmed up by skating around. When they bobbed too much they skated over to their mothers in the audience who straightened the locks. After they'd cleared the ice "Polly Wolly Doo" came on, and a large crowd converged around the rink. The first contestant did a tap routine and was applauded. The judges reminded the competitors not to kick up too much ice. Points would be deducted.

There would have to be extraordinary reasons to stay in the country, I thought. Circumstances as special as Emma. Then it would be just dandy to live in Houston. We would buy a Wagoneer. Emma would make no messy moves. I would learn to shoot as a first step to becoming a favorite son-in-law. I could even open an account at Abercrombie and Fitch. Cullington would find a cushy job for me in a back corner of his company. I would have an impressive card printed up, and I would bestow it with abandon. I would be tolerated by my co-workers, but tolerated would be enough—it would be mutual. Emma would think in terms of wallpaper patterns. I would leave the office early—who could say anything to me?—and we would enjoy our quota of cocktails in long-drawn-out evenings by the pool. We might even become favorites at the Galleria for the sheer volume of our purchases. It would be just that, a controlled environment. We would have put ourselves away in mothballs, and together we would love every moment of it.

I could also stop sneering, I thought. That also might be a good start. Houston, France, a freeway is a freeway. The thing is, you've spent the afternoon on it, and the real thing is that once again you've been told to wait outside. Nothing new, except this time it's Emma who's told you to wait outside. Yeah, just like all the others, except this time it's Emma who's said it. Why don't you stop sneering for a moment to find out how crushed you really are by this? Crushed? Yes, crushed. On the one hand is Emma. On the other, well, loneliness. God, a little loneliness, could it be so simple? What else? Is it so incredible that you don't want to be left alone for trips for clothes or aunts or NA meetings? You came here when asked, you even thought you could be of some help, and then you're just told to wait outside. Is it so incredible to be crushed?

It was six in the afternoon, my drink was ruined, and I had nothing to do. Recording a song in a ten-minute booth wouldn't do it, nor would wandering in scented-candle boutiques or sipping Chablis in a croissanterie. Not even a good burger and a long-neck beer and some R and B would do it now, even if it had been available at the Galleria. It was all ruined.

I took out my country club napkin. The Galleria was a big "G" on it, and the streets were well marked and straight. It would be easy to find the cantina from where I was. I hoped Lupe was off. Yes, Lupe might be off. Lupe probably was only on when Emma was around. If Emma thought I'd take a "You wait outside" from her, I'd show her.

It was still too early for the clients of the cantina, and the parking lot was empty. The jukebox was faithfully blaring out a *ranchera.* Empty as it was inside, I could see the place was no more than a collection of vinyl-backed chairs, chrome-and-wood tables, and the pool table with it's banks pocked with cigarette burns. At the end of the bar I spotted a man lining a wall of the dance floor with mirrored tiles. He tore off the back paper of each one and aligned it carefully with the others so there was no gap. He thought he was alone. While I watched he put up six tiles, and three of them came off and broke on the ground. When the seventh fell and splintered he stepped down from the stool and looked at the mess and laughed drunkenly. *"La chingada!"* he said and turned. As he left he doffed his straw hat quite majestically. It wasn't at me. I heard a laugh behind me. Lupe had been watching us both. She stood in the doorway of the back room holding a curtain to the side. There were beer crates stacked beside her, and behind her I could see the sink where Emma had prepared herself before going out to see Lester. She had a towel around her hair, and her brown skin shone where the frock didn't cover her. It would have jolted anyone.

"What happened to your hand?"

"Oh, I fell ice skating."

"Ice skating?"

"Don't have much else to do."

"Awww! Mr. Francis been left all on his own?"

"There you have it."

"Let's go out back. Anyone who comes this early can call for it."

"Could we take a few beers?"

"There's plenty back here."

She led me through the crates of empties and through the back metal door into an overgrown lot. Six porches of flaking and warped planks gave onto it, and a beat-up Chevy was up on blocks, and three men drank beers beside it. They nodded at us, and we went up to one of the porches. An old woman dressed in black got up. We were not introduced, and she shuffled back inside. I sat on a beach chair. Lupe came out with beers and a hairbrush and sat beside me in another beach chair. She called over to a girl who was washing a doll in a basin, and the girl stood up and ran over to us.

"Do you mind if I take the towel off? It won't look very nice, it's still wet," Lupe said.

"Please don't ask me such questions."

"Very well." She took the towel off and shook out her long black hair. Without saying a word the girl started to brush it out. "It would be much longer, but *el viejo* says it gets in the food."

"Oh . . . what does *el viejo* do?"

She laughed. "No not that *viejo,* I don't have one of those. Pa Cullington. When I worked for Emma I could wear it any length I wanted."

"You worked in her apartment?"

"Yeah, she needed me then."

"Not now?"

"Depends how it works out for her. Then I had my work cut out for me."

"Such as?"

"Well, I had to phone the psychiatrists to say why she couldn't come, and I had to take her coke in the clinic and get urine samples from the kids around here and tell her father she was at the clinic when she was blacked out on the bed. You know Emma."

"You also had to hold her when she cried?"

"Yeah. Don't worry, it's just holding."

"Why would I be worried?"

"The look on your face when you saw us."

"Was it there?"

"Of course. And why not? I mean, it is a possibility."

"Shall we talk of something else," I said.

The old woman, who again wasn't introduced, came out with two more beers and cut limes and a basket of spiced tortilla chips. She put them down and didn't say anything and went back inside.

"Home-made," Lupe said.

"Really?"

"Yeah, and *House and Garden*'s coming around to do a spread, silly!"

"Why not? I hear conscience is back in this season."

"You don't mind that I called you silly, do you?"

"Lupe, *querida*, I'm as much of an employee as you. Call me whatever you please. It could only sound sweet coming from you."

"You're not too bad yourself, for a gringo."

I could smell clean hair and limes coming from her. My

right hand was still and all my muscles good and tight from the motorbike riding the day before. It was heading in one direction. I watched the girl comb out the hair, and Lupe watched the lot. One of the men who'd been standing by the car came toward us. He was dressed Miami chic and smiled all the way over like someone who at the very least carries a knife.

"*Y Emma?*" he said, still smiling. I was glad, I didn't know what to expect.

"She'll be coming later."

"Good. I heard she was back." From the pocket of his shirt he took a gram of coke and dropped it in my lap. "Here's for while you wait."

"If you insist."

From the same pocket he took a piece of paper with a beeper number written on it. "And if you wouldn't mind giving her this. My old one got hot. Tell her Chihuahua sends all his best."

I took it and he nodded. He chased some of the children playing around, and they all laughed as they scampered. He went back out through the bar. I put the coke in my pocket.

"You putting it away?" Lupe said.

"I'm sorry, I didn't think. You want some?"

"Not here." She nodded at the girl who was combing. She sent her over to play with the other children. We took our beers and walked down the steps and across the lot and through a gap in the brambles into a clearing. We stood outside the crashed-car compound. It was lit like a stadium for a night game, and Lupe walked right over to a hole in the mesh. The entrance was about a quarter of a mile away from us at the other end, and I could see the guards' cabin and two tow trucks waiting to have their cars checked in. Lupe pointed to the right. "Those are the small accidents." She pointed to the left. "Those are the ones no one will come for." We walked toward the write-offs. These had no numbers stuck on their windshields. The burnt-out, mangled shells were stacked in rows—the ones that had landed on their roofs and were caved in and the pole-catchers and the front-impacts.

"A lot of has-beens," Lupe said.

"I guess." I handed her the coke. She said it was already cut, and she stuck a nickel into it and used it as a shovel to bring some to her nose. She handed it back to me, and I used the same method, and we drank at our beers. "*Salud,*" I said.

"*Dinero y amor,*" Lupe said. She snickered, and when she did the ring of coke she'd had on her nostril blew off and floated down and landed like flakes on her damp chest. We walked further between the cars. I walked behind her because it was too narrow. She was looking up at all the buckled shapes when she walked right into one and grazed her leg on a twisted fender. She held her thigh. "*Hijo de su madre!*"

"All right?"

"I think so." She sat on the passenger seat of a doorless car. I knelt down and she lifted her dress to show the cut. It was high on the thigh. On the inside was a bead of blood trying to push out. She kept the dress up longer than I needed to see it. I brushed it with my thumb, and immediately she brought her hand down over mine.

I was shooting pool when Emma charged in a few minutes after eleven. Lupe called to her from behind the bar and pointed to me. "Six out of ten!"

Emma gave a cry of delight. She knocked back the shot that was waiting for her at the bar, took a beer, and came over to me. "Way to go, champ! Poke, poke, poke. One big all-you-can-eat-night at Hojo's."

"What's your secret?"

"A year in the bin. The less you do it, the less you need it. Particularly with some goods thrown in."

"And you don't want to get messy."

"Particularly with you."

"Well, I'll send you a walker from Paris."

"Paris?"

"I'm gone."

"Breathe through the nose and count to ten."

"You're back among your own."

"And ditto, I mean vice versa. This is your country too."

"I've watched you. You don't need me."

"Do I have to?"

"Actually, yes."

"Give me a break, you just haven't caught the thread of the drinks yet."

"You'll find someone else to give you leash."

"You are pissed. Loosen up, man, we'll take the Fairlane and be in Mexico for breakfast. Matamoros, Reynosa, wherever you want. We'll take a chunk of dough and not stop till we hit Belize City or Colombia. Christ, but it's not as if you had anything to rush back to."

"Maybe that's it."

"You're going to force me to do things I don't want to."

"Start here!" I handed her Chihuahua's number. She took it and went to the phone. I went outside and waited in the front lot. Pickups pulled in, and some of the people recognized me from the other night and greeted me. One couple both patted me on the back. The woman pressed a miniature bottle of vodka into my hand. I didn't understand why. The man said, "How about them Astros anyway?" I told him that I hadn't seen the end of the game. They went in.

Chihuahua was fast. When he arrived he honked twice and Emma came out. He kissed her on the cheeks. They caught up on news: who'd OD'd since their last meeting. They laughed about the time she'd punched the narcotics department's phone number into his beeper for him to phone. Then she asked for a hundred dollars' worth of heroin. He said he only had thirty. A real dealer, I thought. Start them low, keep them wanting it, and control it for them, because they're worth a lot more alive than dead. His beeper sounded, and a new buyer's phone number flashed up on the little screen. He knew who it was by the number, and he said that they could wait for him to phone. He handed Emma three ten-dollar envelopes and told her he was going to Vegas for a few days, so if she wanted to score before that she'd have to phone him in the next two days. A real pro. Vegas was probably a lie, but he'd just inserted that tiny note of urgency to assure the second score, the most important one of them all. They hugged, and as he left he hit the nose of his new black car going down from the lot to the roadway. He pulled over and got out. None of the paint was chipped, but the front plate was dented. He said, "*Su puta madre!*" and got back in and drove off.

Emma stood with the three envelopes in her hand. "I'm quite willing to tear and scatter them," she said.

"Time to play chicken."

"Something like that."

"Emma, we've been here before. How could you possibly expect me to help? You should have just stayed away."

"Really? So you wouldn't have me on your conscience?"

"No, because two's a crowd in my book."

"And one is in mine! What the hell do you think is the point of going blotto? Please, Francis, please can't our adventures go on together for a stretch of road? That's all I'm asking."

"No."

She looked down at the packets in her palm and closed them in a fist. All I was going to get now was an "Oh well, there you have it" of cocked eyebrows, which she gave me, and then she went inside.

I didn't have time to start the car when three men surrounded me. "Keys, *compadre,*" the meanest-looking one said.

"Why?"

"Who knows why? To fuck you up, man!"

I gave him the keys. He went into the cantina. A moment later he came out counting bills. I was still in the car. "Nice wheels," he said.

"I know."

"Hope you don't think a taxi's going to come anywhere around here."

". . . ."

They smiled among themselves. "Don't worry, man. I've done work at your *mamita*'s place. We can take you halfway there if that's where you're going." He slapped my back, and I got out of the car and climbed into the back of a pickup with three other men. It was loaded with gardening equipment. We hit our nose coming down onto the roadway. I passed my miniature of vodka around, and it was soon gone. "We'll soon be gringos," one of them said during the drive.

"That's good."

"New immigration law. Me Reyes, *el gringo.*" He beamed and leaned back against a lawnmower. I had to hold on to the sideboards because of the speed. The wind felt good in my face, and I watched stray dogs roam past Circle K's flashing signs. They left me a few blocks from the house. I thanked them, and they pointed me in the right direction. As I walked I could hear hissing all around me. I wasn't sure if it was automatic sprinklers on the lawn or crickets or just the heat. An H.P.D. squad car slowed down to check me out, and a block later a River Oaks Police Department one did the same. They both cruised on without stopping. I was running with sweat by the time I reached the gates and the dogs came up to snarl and bark at me. I pressed the intercom and the security guard told me to stand under the camera.

"What the hell are you doing *standing* there?"

"Just let me in."

"Got to come down for you, bubba. It ain't the dog's feeding time yet."

He drove down and picked me up, and we went up to the house together. In the kitchen the table was covered with dismantled handguns and a case of brushes and oiled cloths and rods. Each clip was loaded and rested beside its pistol. The security guard and Cullington were snapping them in.

"Know about guns, Francis?" Cullington said.

"Not a thing."

"Al here does. Damned sight more than me. Learned it picking off gooks. That right, Al?"

"Sure is, Mr. C."

"Picking off gooks from the shrubbery in the Mekong. Couldn't afford a jammed gun then. Only had to jam once and *bam!* Adios amigos."

Cullington took a tray from a cupboard and loaded all the pistols onto it. "You mind carrying these for me, Francis?"

"No," I said. I followed him out of the kitchen. As we passed the light box, he shoved up all the switches and every light in the house went on. In the library he took two false-back books from a shelf and placed a snub-nose in the space. He replaced the books. He went over to a desk and got down on his hands and knees and placed another on an under-ledge. "The poor bastard that gets this far doesn't know what he's got coming, does he?"

"I'm leaving."

"I figured so. Will she be all right?"

"Not even Lester could bring her back tonight. She'll be all right."

"How much do I owe you?"

"Nothing."

"Whatever."

". . . ."

"I should never have expected you to be in for the long haul."

I put the tray down on the desk and went across to my bungalow. I threw my clothes into the suitcase and left the bottles on top of the fridge. When I got back to the house Cullington was still in the library with a bottle of bourbon and two glasses. He handed me one. "I take it you're going to Paris."

"Yes."

"I just booked you on a flight changing in New York. It

leaves in three hours. I called a taxi, figure you don't want to sit around here."

"Thank you. I don't."

"What options does she have, Francis?"

"I don't know."

He let his eyes wander around the room. They rested on the tray of pistols. "How does a rich woman kill time? That's the big one. She's let it become an unsolvable puzzle."

The guard came in and said that the taxi was coming up the drive. He took my case and we went out onto the front portico. At the top of the stairs I shook hands with Cullington and he tried to hug me, but I turned down the steps before he could. It wasn't about me. It was about last hopes, and I wasn't crying over anyone else's. He went back in, completely undone, and the guard closed the door. I didn't look back as we went down the drive. To see the huge lit-up house with just Cullington and the guard waiting inside for her was not what I needed to see.

The airport was sinister at that hour. I took my case as far as the line of coin-operated TVs. I got behind one. Maintenance men worked on a conveyor belt. They turned it on and boarded it and went in behind the plastic flaps. Then they reversed it and came back out. Across from me on the seats a man slept with a cowboy hat pulled down over his eyes and his boots resting up on his suitcase. There were also cleaning people leaning on their machines and talking.

I took change from my pocket. I didn't have four quarters, and I couldn't turn a TV on. I went through all my change. My hand was shaking. I looked at the change jangling in my hand. I put it back into my pocket. Some coins fell and rolled away until they turned back on themselves and then fell over.

I had only said I was leaving to see where it took us. No second chances, I thought. Not with Emma. You don't get those back, not once they've been said. You can wish all you want, but you don't get those back. Not from Emma. How's this now for your forced play? Now, here, in a deserted concourse, rattling in a bucket seat and blowing town. How is it now? Here. Now. Now, now, now, now what? That's it. That's the big one. Now what?

I gripped the armrest. I was shaking all over now.

PART THREE

CHAPTER 17

Hunger forced me out of bed on the third day. I had been lying with a bandana wrapped around my eyes. The phone cord was leading into a drawer, with the receiver lost and smothered in shirts and the beep announcing disconnection. I put on my bathrobe and went downstairs. The *boulangère* asked me if I was sick. I said slightly and bought three croissants. I walked further down the street to the newspaper booth and bought two papers. When I got back to the house the concierge had already taken up her position sitting in the doorway. She said she hadn't expected me back this soon. The car was still parked in front of the *tabac,* she said. She wondered whether that had been Emma she'd spotted one day. I looked out at the street. It dazzled and was still. I said, No it hadn't been Emma, and I walked back up the stairs.

I was going to give it my best shot. I brewed coffee and put it on a tray with the croissants and the paper. I tried to take it up on the roof, but I couldn't hold things in my sore hand so I had it by the window. The paper said it was the same heat all over Europe. French poultry farmers were having a terrible time, and people had died in Portugal and Spain. What a country! I expected to read someday that French poultry farmers were having a terrible time and then in a small paragraph that three Pershing missiles had blown Central America off the map. I looked up from the paper and out at the buildings and roofs along my street, just for the pleasure of being back.

Then I paced. I leafed through bills. I leafed through my Tintin collection. I opened my dictionary. My eyes scanned the pages:

débâcle: downfall.
déboire: disappointment, setback.
débonder: open the sluice gates (of one's heart).
débouché: outlet, prospects. *Quels débouches a-t'il?* What career prospects does he have?
débusquer: to drive out of cover, to come out of hiding.
décentré: out of center, out of tune.
déchéance: fall from grace, downfall.

I slammed the book shut. It wouldn't take much today, fusewise. Granted, you don't ordinarily just pick up a 2,000-page book and happen on four of them screaming one word at you in two languages: decomposition. No, today it would not take much. In fact, I decided, it would take no more than this. I fell back on the bed.

I soon decided that this would not do either. One day in bed I could put down to jet lag. Three was despair. Three days in bed was enough. If it wasn't going to turn into ten days in bed with the curtains drawn, it had to be stopped right here. This day had to be lived. If only to spite her.

I jumped off the bed. To keep my impetus I cut through the layers of bandage on my right hand. It was filthy. I was happy with what I saw. The knuckles were turning from purple patches to yellow patches, and the swelling had gone down. I knew I had an Ace bandage somewhere, and I would put it on after I showered. I put on a record of Callas singing great lyric arias and dragged the speakers from the sitting room to the door of the bathroom. I filled the sink with steaming water and took a clean washcloth (Bristol Hotel) and let it soak in the sink. I put a new blade in the razor. I wrung out the washcloth and wrapped it around my face to soften the three-day stubble. Today would require some reckless risk taking, I thought. Like the old days, my heart would be set pounding. Boom-boom-boom. I would go out dabbed in my stolen Roger et Gallet, spruced up and ready for action. It would be a day to make me glad again to live in France. I would enjoy some wine and some light and the feel of a good shirt.

I took the washcloth off and soaked it again and wrung it out again and applied it to my face. The mirror had steamed up, and I thought, Aren't I the smoothie after all? Sleaze in the eyes of so many, but aren't I, because of exactly that, the guy who survives whatever the cost? Isn't that the one advantage of this position? Yes, oh yes. Emma, I will squirm out of this one too. Callas trilled. I wiped the mirror clear with a towel and began to lather my face.

The fencing club would be my first stop. In my second year in Paris I had made a special trip to London by night ferry to order a linen fencing suit. I delighted in every piece of it—the plus fours that came up almost to my chest, and the chest cloth that covered the heart against too violent lunges, and the jacket with its high collar. What I enjoyed most, though, was slipping myself glances between bouts. My mask tucked under an arm, the kid glove held in my right hand, and carelessly twirling the big-domed handle of my saber. Erect but not rigid, flushed from a bout, and with a white towel over my neck, being gallant and swapping stories in the mirrored *salle d'armes.*

I reached the club on foot and took my equipment from the locker. The changing room was empty, and I dressed quickly. As I crossed the gymnasium to the fencing hall it was completely silent instead of filled with the usual loud clash of sabers. Inside, the *maître d'armes* was talking with an old man who always came to watch. He stood beautifully, having fenced all his life. "How's *l'Américain?*" the *maître d'armes* said. I told them I'd been in Nice. The old man called me *mon cher* and asked about my hand. I said I'd fallen on the beach. We agreed that the beach in Nice could be chancy. The old man thought this amusing and wondered, in beautiful French, whether the whorehouses of Bangkok still had flaps that one had to drive through so no one could see you alight from the car. A large policeman who'd been on motorcycle escort all day came in cursing the minister of finance for having had him out in the sun all day. The *maître d'armes* gave him a recipe for cucumber soup with yogurt which was just the thing for this heat and to stay svelte. The big man was delighted to note it down.

They talked on, and I avoided seeing myself in any of the mirrors. I wondered why I felt ridiculous. I had loved the old-boy atmosphere in this room. I had loved the resounding grunts of lunges and the sharp voice of the *maître* calling out the positions as he gave a lesson: *Quart! Quint! Première!* I'd loved the courteous rituals of the sport: the unmasked greeting with the sword held straight up across the face, then the fling of the fight and the ritual handshake afterwards. Now my eyes finally did catch themselves in one of the mirrors. I knew it would be a fight all the way. I looked at myself in the mirror, and the only thought I had was, You're a farce.

A guy I particularly disliked came in, but he didn't feel like fencing yet. I watched him talk. When I first had started coming to the club, he had sat around with long hair reading Nietzche. One day he came in and gave everyone a business card which under his name had "Epicurean" as occupation. It was the first time anyone remembered him speaking. Since then we had mainly discussed our Jesuit educations, matching each other bloodbath for bloodbath. Now, with short hair, he explained to us all how well he was doing as a graphic artist and how his shop had been discovered by some big agency, and again how well he was doing in general. I cut him off by asking if he was ready to fight. He said he was, if I insisted. We fought with foils, and he trounced me, and once we'd shaken hands he got back onto his favorite subject—his salvation. "It was so simple. Once I discovered I was a greedy person everything else just fell into place." He seemed ready to continue, but before he could I excused myself and left.

It was getting dark when I came out. I walked up the Boulevard St.-Germain from Maubert. Across from the Flore I stood watching the crowds. There was a time when my favorite thing to do after fencing was to come up here to the terrace of the Deux Magots or the Flore and sip a *citron pressé.* With the excuse of having to retip a foil I would have them with me and leave the bag leaning against the table. I felt debonair. Wet hair combed back, saber handles showing, I could approach any woman. In fact, one of the best blow jobs of my first summer had been administered by a Dutch girl, sporting the Anarchist flag on her lapel, whom I'd first spotted right there watching the mimes in front of the Eglise St.-Germain. I continued along on the far pavement, wondering how it could be possible to live in the same city for even twenty years and have to suffer such memories at every second corner. I turned left to go up to the Luxembourg. I crossed behind the Théâtre de l'Odéon and then over the Rue de Médicis to the rails. The guards were ringing their hand bells, but I managed to get in just before they closed the gates. I thought I'd walk across and leave through the Fleurus gate.

The man who rented the sailboats on the central pond was collecting them all and loading them onto his cart. Some of the children wouldn't give up the bamboo canes they'd used to push the boats off from the banks. I continued on. I saw Lee facing up toward the Observatoire. He was dust-kicking a Frisbee. I watched him throw it at an angle so it bounced up and then landed in the dust. He walked over and picked it up and threw it again. The bells were now ringing all around us, but he didn't seem to notice. A few years before—I couldn't remember when, but certainly since Emma had left—he had stayed with me for several days. I remembered receiving a call from the Aérogare d'Invalides, where the airport shuttle had left him, and he told me whoever it was who had given him my name and asked if he could stay for a night. A couple of hours later, after walking all the way, he stood at my door in T-shirt and torn jeans, with a beat-up suitcase and carrying a bottle of wine as a present. "Man oh man, it sure isn't the outbound at rush hour!" The next morning he jumped on the phone, calling all the other golden boys who were going to make their fortunes modeling here. Bookings were slow. His agent renamed him Chuck because he thought it "just the butchest name for a blond," but even then he wasn't moving. As always, to get him by, his agent introduced him to some older man at a party. He stuck to that for a few months, then switched sides again and began on the blue-rinse set. The same old story. Turning around, he spotted me and threw the Frisbee over.

"Yo! If it isn't fast Franky. How's tricks?"

"Great. You're looking dashing."

"Am I? Momma never stops telling me how good I look in her money also. Float one up and I'll show you a wheelie." I sent the Frisbee up on a soft flight, and he caught it twirling on one finger. He grinned with pleasure. "Just spent a month at Antibes. Hôtel du Cap, *bien sûr.*"

"Anything happening?"

"The usual: AIDS, Lacroix, and who's redoing my pied-à-terre. 'Lacroyee,' as Momma says. I'm gonna get me a Lacroyee! Baby, are you listening? Yes, dear, just get back into the wheelchair!" One of the guards began to blow his whistle furiously at us. The gardens were almost empty. Lee ignored him and threw the Frisbee back to me. "You always call her 'Momma'?" I said.

"Sure. Not to her face, though. Not until she's loaded anyway. She kicked me out last night. Yes sir, this boy been walking."

"Oh."

"Qualms. You know how they get now and then."

"It's the heat."

"Course it is. I'll let her stew for a few more hours. There's a million places I could be, and as far as she's concerned they're all beds."

"That should do it."

"Sure. Then we'll get out of here and go back down to the Côte for the rest of the summer. You know me—have dick, will travel." We had succeeded in getting one of the guards to storm toward us. Lee fingered the Frisbee as if he were going to throw it again. The guard shouted from a distance. "*Monsieur!* You are in a—"

"—*situation irrégulière.* I know, I know."

We walked back to the St.-Michel gate. A guard was holding it for us, and we were the last ones out. He didn't look pleased. "*C'est la vie, ciao bello, adios amigo,*" Lee said and gave him a wave.

"*Saloperie d'étranger,*" one of the guards said to another.

We started down the Boulevard St.-Michel toward the river. "I hate the Boul Mich in the summer," Lee said.

"Boul Mich? You're a regular *titi Parisien,*" I said.

"Getting there, for whatever it's worth. So where have *you* been, Franky?"

"I just came back from Houston."

"Houston! Whatever for?"

"I don't know. I got to see the Astros play a lot."

"The Astros suck. Baseball sucks. If you haven't seen the Lakers in the Forum you don't know what sport is."

"You should get Momma to get you season tickets."

"I should."

"As a sign of affection and all."

"I get those already. This could be our eight-months anniversary present. Yeah, that would really be '*pas mal*' at all. I'd hang out on the beach in Santa Monica and have great tickets to the Lakers. Unfortunately she likes the European life-style. Talking of which, soccer sucks too. Can you believe the scores? One-nothing. I mean, *zzzz!* Want a drink?"

"These places are too crowded. How about buying some Sauternes and going down to the river."

"Cornball city!"

"I know. I'll invite. I really don't want to hang around here with these people."

We had reached the Place St.-André-des-Arts. I couldn't remember the closest Nicolas wine store so I went into an Arab grocery and bought a bottle of Sauternes. They had peaches also, a crate of large ripe ones, and I bought four of those, too. We walked back across the boulevard and through the crowds outside the Greek restaurants and past all the browsers outside Shakespeare and Company. We crossed the Pont au Double and then over to the Ile St.-Louis and went down the steps to the banks of the river. There were plenty of people down there too, but not as many as everywhere else. The few benches were all taken, so we sat on the flagstones with our legs hanging over the sides. The Sauternes was cheap stuff, and the cork was no good so it was easy to push it into the bottle. We each took a peach, and we passed the bottle between us.

"You look like shit," Lee said.

"Thanks."

"No, serious. No shit, deep shit. I wouldn't say it otherwise."

"Maybe I'll leave all this."

"Ah, one of those. I have such fond memories of all the places where I've said that."

"Tell me about it."

"It's not just that, though."

"I just lost something good."

"How good?"

"Like probably those one-in-a-lifetime things."

"Do they exist?"

"Yeah, they do. I really think they do."

"Who?"

"You never knew her. Emma."

"Well, if she's meant to come back, she will."

"I left her."

"What you do that for?"

"I don't know."

"Well, anyway, look at Momma, she knows I'll come back and we'll get together again. Emma will come back."

"And I'll be in the chorus singing oh happy fucking day! It's over, I blew it, and that's it."

"Wow, you got it bad."

"Sorry, it slipped out. Have some more wine."

"Don't be sorry, you're right. It's one big bitch, but so what? Everyone's wise to that much."

We sat there and ate the peaches, which really were good, and drank the wine, which really was warm and bad and only drinkable because of the peaches and because we both wanted a drink. There were lonely-looking old men walking their dogs in the darkness and still some of the tourists who'd come down to the water's edge for pictures. At intervals the tour boats lit us all up as they came down under the bridges, flooding the quays as they passed with the white glow of their stadium lights. If you had one of the apartments around here, I thought, you would spend half your nights trapped in your own house by these lights. That or you had the curtains drawn. It was a bitch, this view, and living behind drawn curtains. Nothing was ever as good as it sounded. We finished the wine.

"Now I'm ready to call Momma," Lee said. We stood up. The quays were now filling with lovers, and I tried not to notice them. We went back up the stone steps to the bridge and then decided to go into the German tavern to get the sweetness of the wine out of our mouths.

Lee drained his mug in one swoop and went to use the phone. He came back smiling. "Told you. She was waiting for me." He ordered another couple of beers. "I'll pay," he said. "I'm back in the money."

"Did you think you might not be?"

"Just for a moment maybe. Maybe that would have been better. In the final analysis, as they say."

"Maybe."

"Would you like to come and meet her?"

"Not at such a poignant moment."

"What I mean is that she's got a couple of girlfriends passing through on their way to the south. It might do you good, you know. A break."

"Thanks, but not tonight."

"As you wish. I'll probably be back in September. I'll give you a call. And don't worry. Go buy a crystal and hang it around your neck. It attracts all those good vibes that float around." We shook hands and he left. He ran because he had to cross the river to Pont-Marie to get to the right Métro line. I ordered another beer, and while the barman poured it I went to use the phone. I called my answering machine. There were no messages, not even hang-ups. I searched my address book and called Lisa. We could at least laugh over the night with Cullington. Her machine said she was in Tunisia for a week's shoot. She gave her agent's phone number. I hung up. I hoped for her sake it wasn't a lie. I began to look up some other numbers, but then suddenly I just closed the book. It was no use. I went back to the bar and drank the new beer and paid and went out. It was completely dark now, and I continued walking.

My chauffeuring lasted five months. Then, as such things go, I'd been lucky to find Matilda. A four-day crash course. She had booked me for two days. We spent them parked in leafy corners drinking Champagne. By the end of the second day we were in the sack. Afterwards she sent me home because she was going out to dinner with friends. It was a crash course in firsts.

The next morning, coming to meet her at a café just up the Rue Royale from Maxim's, I spotted her sitting outside waiting for me. I stopped far enough away so she wouldn't see me. She was dressed as though she'd had hours to put herself together. She had. It was a look I would come to know. It was another first: first picture of primness who—whether I believed it or not—was waiting there for no other reason than to meet me.

Straight on to another first—the first time I was tested. Still sitting at the café she handed me five hundred dollars in unsigned traveler's checks. She told me to sign them once there at the café and then go up and countersign them at Cook's up the street. When I came back she was smiling, delighted even. "Oh good, now we can really do things. You would have been very dumb to consider that enough to cut out with."

This was followed up with another key moment—my first presentable wardrobe: a suit, blazer, flannels, and ties from

Sulka, and everything else bought at the Galeries Lafayette.

That same night the big lesson. Going out dressed up, we stood on the landing of the hotel, waiting for the elevator. Another couple came out of their room and along the corridor toward the elevator. She knew them, but it was too late to escape. There was an exchange of greetings between them. I didn't turn away but just stood there, expecting to be introduced. The elevator wasn't coming, and when she could no longer avoid it she finally introduced me. I got to see for the first time that special hand movement, like leafing through a book, trying to find exactly what title to give me. "This is Francis. He's a . . . a . . . a . . . an artist friend." The elevator arrived, and to avoid dragging this out Matilda suddenly remembered she'd forgotten something in the room and we had to go back. It had only taken those few seconds to tear apart her whole fantasy. It could have been so simple. If I'd had the grace to pretend I just happened to be there waiting for the elevator they would have had the grace to pretend to believe it. I'd forced her hand, the big no-no. I'd been introduced and so made real. If I was real, she suddenly was also, and that was not tolerable. An emaciated screwball with a twenty-four-year-old. That's why one never got caught with one's tricks. In the room she just sat on the bed, silent in her going-out clothes, not even furious, and I left.

I was still walking. From pure habit I had walked all the way to the Place de la Concorde. My turf. I was specter of one square mile, with the Concorde at its center. Ever since Matilda it had become my turf. It had the stores where they shopped and the hotels where they stayed, the Tuileries to stroll, and the river for the view.

Like kissing any girl, the first time was the hardest, and

soon after I got over Matilda I discovered the women like her who came from all over the world for shopping, for gallerying, to take art-history and restoration and cooking classes, and for the period of those visits they became drunk with the city. Here things were as they should be. Gardens gave onto views that gave onto monuments that gave onto more gardens, colonnades, and victory columns. It was elegance à la Française, and for the period of their visits it twinkled across the keys of their souls with all its lightness. No more than a divertimento for the spirit maybe, but they were delighted to be among it all.

I could see it. I had taken to following them. A few paces behind, stopping when they stopped and continuing when they did. A process that could take hours. I would study them going from store to store, not having the courage to make contact and letting them disappear forever into hotels, restaurants, and cabs. And then with time came the courage, and I realized it would just be a logical development to "See Paris Right." With that, I knew I could finally approach them. Boom-boom-boom. I knew I could do it.

The Boulevard de la Grand Armée goes through the center of the Arc de Triomphe, down the center of the Champs-Elysées, through the fountain of the Rond Point and the Obélisque at Concorde, through the golden gates of the Tuileries and the central *allée* of trees and through the carousel to the inner courtyard of the Louvre. This line crossed with the Madeleine, Rue-Royale, Concorde, Chambres des Députés line and the Invalides, Esplanade, Pont Alexandre III, Grand Palais line. And somewhere among all this you are sitting, in a wicker chair maybe, in the comfort of your shopping bags and feeling completely seduced by the city. I appear as an added prop and take my place in the collage of your sensations with a look that you might not tolerate in any other city. I hope that you, so weary from a day's shopping, can allow yourself one more peccadillo and at least entertain the thought.

Because our eyes do meet. Whether it's across a terrace of wicker chairs or across a store, at Angelinas or among post-card stands. They meet, and your eyes immediately scamper. Mine stay. I am no longer embarrassed at keeping a steady gaze on you. It is for you that I do it. It is to get through to you that I dare offend so many. Almost all. Almost.

Your eyes flit back, in the steam of a teacup or in a hand mirror or from the tip of a cigarette you're lighting. My eyes are still there, and yours leave again, this time slower. To what back seats or dormitories, first loves or marriages do you go? Does it make you sad or does it make you daring? Do you realize that carte blanche at couturiers is not enough? Are you sick of Hubby's playing around? Or are you simply tempted by the possibility of a little memory you can stash away all for yourself?

And so we might stroll and let a view or a shade of light set the mood. It's late dusk, the light is right, and I offer my walking tour. A guide, always talking and amusing you, letting the thought that you're being picked up be more seductive than anything I could say. It has to be. There is always so little time for both of us to pretend that it started in complete innocence. And it is at these moments that the mixture of light and props takes time itself and holds it very briefly and very still before giving it back with a slight distance, and it is just in this space, which the city has created for you, that you might look across at me and say yes.

We continue down the Boulevard de l'Opéra in the late dusk, toward the Palais Royal, which waits for us like some secret garden. We might look in the windows of the Grand Véfour, or we might not. The light has almost faded, the treetops wave encouragement, and the pact has to be sealed. You know it too. You turn away to ask encouragement from the city which has gotten you into this. I come up from behind and put my hand softly on your shoulder and you turn and then—God, that first kiss, that fully clothed first kiss when our bodies in each other's arms tremble with delight and anticipation. . . .

I could have continued winding myself in it. I realized it was not long before dawn and I had been walking all night. I was back in the gardens of the Palais Royal. My hand was gripped around one of the metal-back chairs. I could either place it gently in the fountain like some pathetic bouquet in the waves or I could collect every chair in the garden and fling them all in. I did neither.

For five years I'd thought that like some comic-book hero I was always ready for adventure. I thought I lived for those moments of pure vulnerability between walking a few paces behind a woman and talking to her. I thought, Face it, except for the clothes buyer it's been well over a year since you did anything like that. Now you get your work on the phone. I sat on the chair. "I am a callboy," I said out loud. "I have become a callboy." I had long ago made all the mistakes to cringe at. I had picked up many copies of *WWD* from bedside tables and labored through many conversations. I could stick to drivel for hours, talk the season's hemline and food groups, diets, spas, and resorts. I could bluff a tour of the Louvre and get tickets to a sold-out opera. There was more to the curriculum: I came on average three times a night and did not make scenes in public. I was well read and could speak two languages and enough German for impolite conversation when needed. I was adept at the special gymnastic feat of remaining a hard body without being crass enough to remind anyone of what they were doing, and I had every reason to hope for a good position as a traveling companion in my declining years. And even more, I was someone who in about a week robbed drunks, slapped Greeks around, scored for the one woman I loved, who was just out of a clinic, played father against daughter, broke knuckles in anger, joke of jokes felt homesick for America, shrugged at heroin deals, refused to put an arm around a man on the verge of tears, and now to prove I was still a hero I was imagining a woman I had walked with all night. After three days in bed and one day wallowing, that's where I was at in the coming morning.

CHAPTER 18

I walked all the way back to the house. When I opened the door I smelled Emma's perfume. She was asleep at the kitchen table. Before her were a full ashtray, mirror and blade, a half-empty bottle of gin, a camera, and a scrawled note: "You bum! Waited up for you. I wanted to take pictures. Wake me if you dare. I love you." I stood for a moment in the stillness. I walked down the corridor to the sitting room. A Roxy Music record was scratching on the turntable. I lifted the needle and turned all the switches off. I dropped into the beanbag chair. I could hear the pigeons cooing on the ledge outside the window. The next two hours I spent just sitting and staring.

The sound of a chair creaking in the kitchen brought me out of it. I heard a growl and a mumbled, "Oh Jesus," said in pain. I heard her stumble up and the tap turn. A glass was filled and was gulped down. I heard paper being torn, probably the note. She shuffled along the corridor and stopped at the sitting room door. She had sunglasses on. It must have been quite a binge. Her eyes only got raw on serious binges.

"Hi," she said.

"Hello."

"Try and stay around until I get back, will you? This time." She continued toward the bathroom. I heard the shower run for a long time. She came back in my bathrobe, still with her sunglasses on, and got clean clothes out of the tote bag that was by the sofa. She went back to the bathroom to dress and then to the kitchen for her purse. Then she let herself down on the sofa, carefully, not sure what a sudden movement might do.

"Well, this is cozy. You saw the note?"

"The one you tore up."

"One doesn't like to remember one's soppier moments. Anyway, I'm back."

She opened her purse and took out two small envelopes. One pink and one wax paper—heroin and cocaine. She took a small straw from the purse and in turn held each of the packets open and stuck the straw in and took two small measured snorts. She closed the packets carefully and put them back with the straw into the purse.

"And where have you been?" she said.

"Wallowing."

"I've been thinking about you, too."

"What makes you think I was thinking about you?"

"My game leg, Francis, my game leg."

"Well, don't think about me today. Today I intend to remain wallowing. Tomorrow I shall stand on the Place Malesherbes with the Russian Embassy on one side and on the other the Médéric chef's school. Depending on how my breakfast is sitting, I shall either become an exquisite craftsman or a defector."

"Can't you stop being a smart-ass, Francis? Open your eyes. Something has to change!"

"Tell me about it."

"I'm going to."

"Well, I'm sorry, Emma, not with me. I've had it with new beginnings. I really have had it with them. Don't tell me your plans. Just leave. Please, for both of us, just leave."

". . . ."

"I mean it. I really am sorry, but I'm too tired."

"I'm going back to the clinic."

"The clinic?"

"Well, you needn't sound so surprised."

"I'm just trying to keep up."

"I knew only too well where I was headed for in Houston. I'm ready to take the bin seriously now. Really seriously, and I want you to drive me over there."

"If you really mean it, I'm happy for you, but I'm not going."

"Bitterness cramps your style. We'll go, the two of us. We'll fill an ice chest with Champagne and go stoned and bombed through the tree-lined roads. It's the only way. Please, Francis, I've had that image all the way across on the plane. And anyway it's not as if you were completely innocent in all this." She held up her purse for me to fully understand her point.

"Sure, sure, a week ago you were your father's sob story right on the sofa there, and now you're this week's cause."

"Is that what I am?"

"Of course not."

"And you *will* take me, won't you?"

"Yes, Emma. If you think I can do any good, I'll do it."

"One thing though, could you carry my purse for me?"

". . . ."

"It's crossing a border that makes me nervous. Airports are cool."

"I can't drive you to a drug clinic and carry your drugs for you."

"You know I'll never go if I don't have them. It's only to get me through the first few days."

"They don't check you at the clinic?"

"I've blown up too many urine analyses."

"They don't throw you out?"

"But that's what we're there for."

". . . ."

She held out the purse to me. "Go on, think of it as Machiavellian."

"Jesus, what is it about you that reminds me of someone who always phones the ambulance before gobbling the sleeping pills?"

"Touché, buster, and while we're at it, exactly who is it that *you're* trying to save?"

"Oh, forget it, just get your stuff." I took the purse and opened it and took all the envelopes and the straw and put them in the pocket of my jacket. I clasped the purse shut and threw it back to her on the sofa.

We headed out of the city. The traffic was blocked up all the way to the Porte de Clignancourt and the périphérique and even on the Autoroute de l'Est until we got past all the satellite cities. We were drinking beer, and our brand-new ice chest was in the back loaded with Champagne. Emma was knocking the beers down fast since we left. I had a towel over the back of my seat. Emma had a map of France folded open to the area of our route. As we went she filled it in with a blue ballpoint. It looked like a blue worm curved around Paris and facing out toward the plains of the Ile de France. She kept her elbow on the open window, and the warm wind blew her hair about her face. She looked out at the flat country as we passed. It would be flat all the way to the Jura and the foothills of the Alps. In the wheat fields teams of combine harvesters and trucks were working. They would work all night, keeping ahead of the summer storms. The trucks drove alongside the harvesters, and the evening light mixed in with clouds of chaff. Soon the cars coming toward us began to put their headlights on.

In the early night we pulled into a gas station. At the diesel pumps there was a line of the harvesting teams. The drivers were all talking grouped around the pump island. I checked the oil and water, and Emma stretched her legs. Then I went to pay, and when I came back she was over with the drivers cracking open the Champagne. There was nothing better, she told them, when you had had a day's worth of chaff and dust in your mouth. Half of the first bottle spewed out on the steps of a tractor cabin, and she delegated the opening of the rest. The attendant joined in, bringing a stack of cups from the coffee machine. Between us all we emptied the eight bottles. I took the ice chest to the water station and emptied it over the grate. We got a fond send-off. Back on the road Emma resumed her position at the window, with the map on her lap and looking out at the now dark land. "What a picture back there. That has to go down for the album."

We stopped to eat at a truck stop up in the Jura Mountains. The rigs were parked all around the restaurant. They kept their engines turning over for their refrigerated compartments. It was no cooler than on the plain. We walked across the lot toward the lights. Inside, the room was very loud, with all the truck drivers cheery before a night on the road. The fare was chalked up on a board: *Asperges vinaigrette. Steak, frites, vin, pain, fromage. 38 francs, service non compris.* The only available table still had the empty dishes of its last clients. We took our places, and a heavy, aproned woman came over to us. *"Bonsoir, les jeunes."* She took away the plates and glasses and took up the used paper tablecloth and put down a new one. She slapped down a basket of cut baguette and two glasses and a bottle of red wine. *"Deux du jour?"*

"Oui," Emma said. The waitress wrote it down on the tablecloth and circled the total. I poured a glass for Emma and then for myself. Emma looked around. Up behind the bar a television blared, and the drivers around us talked routes and speed traps and knocked back Cognacs. The waitress yelled an order into the kitchen and came back to us carrying four plates in one hand and six in a row on her other arm. She got an order mixed up and someone cracked a joke. One of the drivers said something about the size of her breasts. She heard it and put her arms akimbo and stared them down until they cowered and almost giggled.

"You look perky," I said.

"It won't be like this in the straitjacket tomorrow." She picked up an asparagus with two fingers and rolled it in vinaigrette. The moment she lifted it up her mouth closed. She dropped the asparagus, and her chin fell down to her breast. She lifted a finger slightly from the table to tell me just to sit it out for a moment. Long enough to let the smack fan out in whatever way it wanted. In a few seconds she was back. She put the asparagus back on the plate. "Give me the stuff, will you?" she said. I took the heroin from my jacket pocket and handed it to her. She went into the bathroom.

Back on the road she rested her head on my shoulder and watched the lights coming toward us. I took my bandaged hand from the wheel and stroked her cheek. She closed her eyes and kept her head on my shoulder. "Even up here it's so hot," she said.

"It's nice at night. It feels different," I said.

"God only knows what impulses it will bring out in the good Swiss burghers."

"Animal instincts."

"When I get out of the bin what will we do?"

"Celebrate."

"With Perrier? Let's get away. Let's buy a goat farm in the Auvergne and retire."

"The winters are too cold. Let's stow away to the Orient and be completely untraceable because of our lack of credit cards."

"Who would trace you? I asked first."

"That'll get you a zero for sportsmanship."

"I'm sorry. What's wrong with cold?"

"Cold what?"

"Cold winters in the Auvergne."

"Nothing."

"Cold brings out the good girl in me. Well, not really cold but wool. Soft wool, like lambswool. Maybe I should just keep a lambswool cardigan around me at all times. I feel snug and cozy. I just want to stay home and putter around the house. Why can't I do it, damn it? I swear I become possessed. It's not as if it had anything to do with having fun anymore. I just want action, a buzz, input, sensation, call it what you will. Some people obviously call it having your marbles loose."

She kept her head on my shoulder, and we continued winding our way further up the mountains. After a while I passed a reflecting sign for a rest zone. I took the feeder that led to it. Hearing the gears shifting down, she lifted her head and opened her eyes. Across from the toilets there were campers and trucks parked for the night. The plates were from Germany and Scandinavia and England, and the tail-lights reflected my headlights as we moved between them. When I pulled in we sat still for a moment, recovering from the motion of the car. "Umm, smell those pines," Emma said.

"Let's take a walk," I said.

We got out of the car and walked along the pavement. One of the campers was lit up, and an elderly couple sat out under the camping light. The man read over a picnic table, and beside him the woman was doing needlework. "Warm night," Emma said.

"I'll say, luv," the man said. "Where you heading then?"

"Switzerland."

"Oh, that's close. We're going to Lake Como. Whole of bleeding Europe seems to be on the road tonight, don't it?"

"Yes. We're trying to keep awake."

"We thought we'd take a breather too. But now we can't sleep with the heat, can we?"

"Want a cupatea then?" the woman said.

"No, thank you. That's very kind of you," Emma said.

"It will only take a jiffy. My eyes won't take this needle-work any longer."

"No really, thank you."

"Well, bye now then," the man said.

"Bye."

We walked further along the row of parked cars until we were beyond them all. We slid down an embankment of pine needles and fallen cones to a picnic site. There was a trestle table and two benches made from pinewood. Through the trees we could see the lights moving up along the road. Emma walked to the ledge and looked down into the valley. I came up from behind and put my hand under her shirt, resting it on the small of her back. She didn't turn. I lowered a finger into a belt loop and pulled gently, and she leaned back onto me. I could feel her warmth. I brought my hand around and rested it on her belly.

"Wasn't that a nice-looking couple," she said.

"Yes."

"I bet they've been married for years and years."

". . . ."

"I think I could manage the needlework part."

I undid the top button of her jeans, and she bolted. "Shit!"

"What?"

"Don't be a jerk." She turned back and walked past the picnic table toward the embankment.

She didn't reach it before I had her pinned down on the pine needles. "I can't take it, Emma, I swear I can't take it."

"I told you if I needed a fix it would be quick and incognito. Christ, you of all people must know what I mean!"

I let her go and stood up and walked back to the ledge. She came up behind me. "Sorry, I only meant I don't ball friends."

"Since when?"

"Since it became fishing off the company pier. No, sorry, low blow. We are friends now, Francis, and that's good."

"Damn 'friends'! I don't want to be your friend. I love you!"

"I'll drive. Let's go."

"Don't bother."

"Well, you might not be so hysterical when you wake up, that's what I mean."

"Get lost! Go with the Brits, catch a bus, Nanny's taking the day off!"

She slipped once climbing the embankment. "Now are you happy?" she shouted from the top. "Now are you happy, you lousy bastard? Now that you've spoiled it all, are you happy now?" She turned, and it was silent again. I sat on a boulder and looked way down to the roofs of the boarded-up ski resorts and the lights coming up along the road and their reflection on the sky. When I walked toward the car I saw she'd accepted the cup of tea from the English couple. I didn't know whether she'd decided to continue on with them. I got in the car and sat there. I repeated, "You don't care," three times to myself and started the engine. Then I saw Emma running toward me. I thought it was just the drugs that she wanted, but she opened the door and got in. We drove on without saying anything.

We got to the border point before daylight, but there already was a line of cars waiting to go through. The French waved us through. The Swiss made us pull over onto the shoulder. The guard asked for our passports. We gave them to him and he began to study them. Beside us they'd pulled over a rig loaded with bales of hay. Two guards were on top pushing long metal spikes through the load. On the ground another pushed his spike crossways. The truck driver stood at a distance until they decided that there was nothing hidden.

The guard who'd stopped us was done with Emma's passport and had almost finished with mine. I would be glad to get out of the place. I understood why she didn't like to cross borders with anything on her.

"Suspicious car, huh?" Emma said. The guard had been ready to hand our passports back. He smiled. "No, not suspicious. You are American?"

I pressed Emma's knee with mine so she wouldn't say anything.

"Yes, officer."

"On holidays?"

"Yes, holidays. Just love to come here on holidays."

"And where is it that you're going to spend your holidays?"

"In a spa, officer."

"Ah a spa, that's good. But at your age?"

"You know how it is, get revitalized and all."

"I see." He held the passports out. I was stretching across Emma to take them through her window when she suddenly took her face in her hands and cried, "Caught!" The passports were held back.

"Caught, mademoiselle?"

"Yes, caught. I've really come for an illegal dishwashing job and to be one more Social Security leech. I've come for some of that famous Swiss sense of fun. I've come to climb the goddamned Matterhorn. Are you going to let us in or aren't you?"

The guard told us to drive across to one of the official buildings. It was a garage. Two guards in gray mechanics' suits were smoking and waiting for someone to be sent in. One of them motioned to me to drive over a repair pit. They told us to stand behind a brightly painted yellow line. One of them climbed into the pit and began tapping the engine and shining his torch into possible hiding places. The other took all the luggage out and then with a flashlight also began on the interior.

"Next comes the body search," Emma said. "Get out of this one, Nanny."

When they started on the luggage I took my chance and stepped toward them. "Try not to mess up the clothes all the same."

"Get back behind the line please, monsieur."

"Sure I'll get back, just don't mess with them."

"His livelihood depends on them," Emma pitched in.

"We are being as careful as possible."

"Thank you," I said. With my back turned to them I put my hand in my jacket pocket and grabbed all of Emma's little envelopes and the straw. I stood back behind the yellow line, but now right beside a drum full of drained engine oil. With a loud cough I dropped all the envelopes into it. They didn't make a sound. It took them a few nerve-wracking moments to absorb the oil—they were just floating there on the surface—and then they sank.

After all that, they didn't even ask us into the stripping booths. She waved at the guards as we left. The road now began to curve downward toward Nyon. We could see Lake Geneva below us, and the first sun came through the pine trees in long fingers slapped across the oiled road.

"Oh, for God's sake don't pout," Emma said.

"I can't believe you'd do that on purpose."

"The little scene up on the mountain, of course, was completely normal."

"No, but I said I was sorry."

"No, you didn't say you were sorry."

"Well, sorry."

"Well, now we're even."

"Okay, we're even. Where's this clinic?"

"The clinic's in Vevey, but we're going to Geneva first to score a little something. You can blame yourself. I told you I wasn't going into that place without something to get me through the first days."

I didn't even argue. "How can you keep on and on, Emma? Just tell me that."

"Curiosity," she said.

In Geneva Emma directed me through the center of the city and out to a housing project. We stopped in front of a small Turkish tea hall. Inside there were two old men. One smoked a hookah pipe and the other read a Turkish newspaper. Emma greeted them without stopping, and we walked right through into a courtyard. A young Arab in Bermudas and a tank top was having a fight with a couple in *charcutiers'* aprons. The Arab was screaming, "*Raciste!*" and the *charcutier* brandished a block of lard to keep him from getting too close. The *charcutier*'s wife was almost crying because the clients could hear it all through the back door of their store. She was right. From the courtyard I could see all the clients peering in at us from between shelves of pâtés.

"Shalom, there," Emma said, and the Arab turned around.

"Well, shalom, shalom." He left his opponent in mid-sentence and came toward us.

"What is it you're celebrating, Mustapha?" Emma said.

"Oh, nothing. I was bored. There's nothing like giving

these people a hard time, is there? As if I cared whether he left his pork pots out here."

"Shall we go upstairs?"

"*Certainement.*" He turned around and told the couple that the argument was far from over. He led us up a concrete stairway and along a concrete walkway with the doors painted different colors. We went into his apartment, and he motioned us to two naugahyde chairs.

"Well, what do you have for me?" Emma said.

"Don't be in such a hurry, Emma. Have a mint tea, relax, introduce your friend."

"Introduce yourselves. I want smack, coke, and hash if you have it." The Arab rolled his eyes at me and said, "Yes, Emma."

"You have it?"

"*Quel appétit,* Emma. You catch me at a bad time. I'll give you what I have."

"Of course."

He shook his head at her, then got up and walked over to a dresser. He kept his back to us, and Emma didn't bother to go and look over his shoulder into the drawer. He gave her heroin in two waxed-paper envelopes and cocaine wrapped in aluminum foil. She took some of the cocaine immediately. Then she did a quick calculation and paid him in dollars.

"I'm sorry, Emma, but that's all there is. If anyone comes from the clinic I'll send some back with them. We can trust each other."

"Why does that sound wrong in a Turk's mouth?" Emma said, smiling.

"Ah, Emma, Emma, same old Emma. It's good to see you."

"You're getting to look more like a terrorist every day."

"That's why I hardly leave the house anymore. They think I'm Abu Nidal. Imagine being all by myself in this heat. The thoughts I get."

"Tell me about it. I've got a six-month stretch to look forward to now."

"Well, come and see me, we can discuss it."

"I might."

He put on a Michael Jackson tape and showed us his moonwalk. Emma watched him and smiled. I knew I'd never ask her how well she knew him. I'd never even ask why she had to flirt with him in front of me. I didn't want a fight now. Now we were heading for Vevey and the clinic, and she could do anything she damned well wanted as long as we kept on going there. We left him still practicing his steps and having completely forgotten his fight. In the courtyard I saw that the wife had gone back to serving the customers but the man was still waiting. The heat was getting to the block of lard in his hand. I saw it had a sheen.

We drove along Lake Geneva on the highway. Emma pointed out all the towns down by the edge of the lake, and because it was so clear even across it in France. One of the towns we could see was Thonon-les-Bains, she said and the other was Evian. She said that much better than the mineral water there was the casino. It was a very smart casino, and she said she liked to escape for a day or two in season to go and play the tables there. Both towns were backed into the Alps, and from across the lake the peaks gave off a clear blue glare I thought must have been snow.

We drove into Vevey and parked in the central square. It was full of banks and tea parlors and souvenir stores. When she got out of the car she pointed up at the mountain behind us so I could see the sloping roof of the clinic. Far above the roof, near the peaks, there were still patches of snow between the ridges. We walked down toward the promenade on the lakefront. On all the benches along the path people were sitting looking out at the water with the blank stare of people looking out to sea just to rest their eyes. A light breeze lifted off the lake, and it felt very good as we walked. We walked up and down the promenade for a while.

We reached the statue commemorating Charlie Chaplin's residence in the town, and we stopped to look at it. In its cast likeness he seemed to have joined everyone else in gazing across the lake. We crossed the grass behind him and sat at a terrace and had a drink. There was a canvas awning down over our table, and it felt much better to be in the shade. We watched the joggers and the dog walkers and those who just watched the lake. Emma went into the bathroom and took her purse. I thought, I'll do absolutely anything to help her over this. When she came back out I got up and put my arm around her and like that we walked back toward the car. I felt that finally there was nothing else to say, and she must have also, because we didn't say anything, and when we reached the car we just got in and drove out of the town and up toward the mountain road.

CHAPTER 19

There was a good view from the head psychiatrist's office. His secretary had welcomed Emma with kisses and asked us to wait inside for Dr. Amudsen. The French windows were open, and we stood at them looking out. Below us, on the terrace of the cafeteria, patients sat in groups talking or looking across the overhang to the lake. Four patients in romping suits played croquet on the flattest part of the lawn. Way below us on the lower slopes I could see what looked like strips of vineyards. Below that, houses and the town. A ferry left its wharf in Vevey, and a half-dozen speedboats broke the calm surface of the lake.

Other patients passed below us, crossing the lawn toward vegetable patches. They pushed wheelbarrows loaded with bags of fertilizer and carried rakes and spades over their shoulders. From our window each plot looked like it was a different style. Some were rows of flowers, others were vegetable patches, and others were like a vicar's garden—cultivated wildness. An old woman and a youth passed below us. They carried their gardening tools in baskets. They both looked up and saw us at the window. "Hello, dear!" the woman said.

"Hey, buddies!" Emma said.

"That was quick," the youth said. "How did it go?"

"Terrific."

"Just dying to hear all about it," the woman said. "But now we have a lot of weeding to do. We're working on our self-discipline this week. Ehehehe!" They waved and continued toward their plots.

"That's Mrs. Carter," Emma said to me. "Quite the A list of the Palm Beach Stoli rocks set. She loves it here. The only person she could get to come and confront her was her Cuban houseman. You should have seen *that* session. She had to threaten to fire him on the spot before he would say anything. Under her warm wing is Mohammed, *vieux* Beirut, lived for three months in Claridge's, I think before he almost OD'd and they flew him over here. His family flew him, though maybe Claridge's pitched in."

"Thanks for filling me in on all that."

"Welcome to nut land, Francis."

"Quite a place."

"Hiking, gardening, finger painting, a real Club Med for the delirious."

"It doesn't look too trying."

"You look surprised."

"I suppose I just didn't know what to expect."

"Not quite this casual though, huh? See, there are loony bins and then there are holding pens. The first is paid by concerned relatives and the second by us or by trust funds or by our lawyers. Makes all the difference in the world, because we're the only ones they have to keep happy. Amudsen's going to love me. It's the best thing for renewed enrollments to have someone come back so soon. Proof that it really is a tough place out there and that they're better off up here after all. We're happy, we cry a bit for them and give them back their jargon, and they're happy."

"I see."

"Oh, poor baby, don't sound so disappointed. I'm still going to get better. It's just a question of comfort."

"You're sure he's not going to give you a hard time?"

"But the payments on his villa in Capri depend on me. I've even seen the pictures."

There was a sound behind us and the door opened and the doctor came in.

Emma continued, "Isn't that so, Herr Doktor?"

"Emma, how nice to see you."

"And you too, so soon. This is Francis Buchanan. He's convinced me to come back." We shook hands, and he motioned for us to sit down on the other side of his teak desk. I had expected someone in a white coat. He was well dressed in a white voile shirt and a pressed blue linen suit. His face was healthy and jolly, like a peasant who has just gotten a good price for his cows.

"So, you're back, Emma."

"For the sequel."

"Ah, same old Emma." He crossed his fingers and swiveled on his chair, the way doctors tend to do. "You do remember my saying that you weren't ready for more than two or three days' leave."

"And boy, were you right, Doctor, so let's skip it. I'm back, and I want Francis to get a good room in the guest quarters. He'll be coming to confrontation."

"Aha, so you're ready to treat this seriously."

"Yes, Doctor. I think, well . . ."

"Yes, Emma?"

"Well, I think I finally faced complete defeat. Faced up to it, I should say."

Amudsen looked thoughtful and now not only swiveled and knotted his fingers but brought his hands up to rest on his lips. "I see, I see. Good. Well, you'll have to wait a week for confrontation. We don't want to rush it."

"A week! What will I do?" I said.

"Oh, we'll think of something," Emma said. "He might as well use his time here simply as a detox for himself, don't you think, Doctor?"

"Certainly. We have been known to perform that service." He actually winked at me. "I'll have to see about the cabin, though. We're all full up with the medal ceremony."

"What medal ceremony?" I said.

"The one for our old patients who've had a year's sobriety. Maybe next time Emma comes back it will be to receive hers."

"That would be nice. Wouldn't it, Francis?"

"Yes. It would be very good."

He undid his fingers and turned on his chair. His eyes wandered out the windows and down the drive. "Oh no," he said. I turned to see. A black Mercedes was coming up the drive. We watched it as it came to a stop and a chauffeur opened the door for a beautifully dressed Arab woman.

"Mohammed's mother. She's still here?" Emma said.

"She moved down to the Trois Couronnes but comes up every day." He sighed. "But Doctor, I see very little improvement since yesterday!" he mimicked a thick Lebanese accent.

"I told you Herr Doktor was a sport," Emma said.

"Good, very good, Emma. Go on, consider yourself readmitted. I have too many problems today. The medal ceremony, and now this woman."

We shook hands and left him at his desk, waiting for his next meeting. She was already talking with the secretary outside. There was also a nurse waiting for Emma. Emma asked her to wait a moment, and we walked down the corridor.

"You didn't tell me about confrontation," I said.

"Oh, it's nothing. Just be yourself."

"I don't want to be myself in front of twenty people."

"Twelve. Five nuts, five family, and two counselors. It's not as pompous as it sounds. The only bores are the counselors, who're all ex-dipsos and, you know, have the answer. But anyway, let's face it—all they can do is dredge the stuff up and leave us to deal with it. They're home reading the paper in their slippers while we're still dealing with it."

"Is that how it works?"

"Yes, and anyway you're here for me and not for you. You will come?"

"Yes. Has anyone ever been cured here, just as a question of interest?"

"The medal ceremony speaks for itself, doesn't it?"

"Yes, it does. I suppose I was sort of shocked by Amudsen."

"He's fine. He's a gangster."

"He would have been glad to see you spend years here without doing anything."

"But now it's all different. I've zoomed in on my own answer."

"Which is?"

"That being spaced out gets to be as boring as being sober once was. That everyone, everywhere, is the same—bored.

And that I love you for having brought me here."

"And I love you for having come."

I had full use of the facilities. Amudsen's secretary found a bungalow for me, and I changed into one of the terry-cloth bathrobes and walked back to the center through an underground passage. It probably was necessary in the winter. The walls of the passageway were lined with glass showcases for jewelers and *chocolatiers* down in Vevey.

I was massaged in a glass box overhanging the lake. The whole room jutted out from the side of the building, and the couch was positioned so I was facing straight out. I felt like I was floating, and the closest objects I could see were a herd of brown cows, and they were way below me and looked very small. When the masseur was done with kneading and pounding me, I walked into the next room on the corridor, where I was asked to sit down and a young nurse wrapped pneumatic leggings on me. They came up to my thighs. She turned them on and they slowly inflated until they held my legs very tightly. They stayed like that for a few minutes and then began to deflate and all the blood rushed back in. Then they began the process again. A bearded man was plumped in a seat beside me. He faced straight out to the lake. Across from me an extremely gaunt woman in a caftan stared at a cover of *Paris-Match.* Her nurse had a manicure set in her lap and was doing the woman's nails. The woman suddenly began to mumble, "I didn't do it, really I didn't do it, I didn't." The man paid no attention; the nurse patted her hand and continued filing.

I called over to the nurse who'd plugged me in and was now working on a newcomer. "I think I've had enough," I said.

"But you're not half there," she said.

"That'll be all right."

"You might as well wait, the water-jet baths are all taken."

"I don't want a water-jet bath either."

"But—"

"Just get them off, please."

She took them off and I walked further along the subterranean corridor toward the pool. At least this was in the daylight. The waiters moved between the Scrabble and backgammon players with trays of mineral waters and teas. It could have been an ordinary hotel except for a sign over the pool which said that it was out of bounds except when a member of the staff was present. Mrs. Carter, the woman who had greeted Emma, had finished with gardening for the day and was now lapping the pool. When she reached the Plexiglas that separated the outside from the inside she ducked underneath it and continued in the brilliant sunshine. She rested her elbows on the ledge of the pool and smiled up at me. I smiled back. "You're new?" she said.

"No, I'm with someone."

"Problem yourself?"

"Not even a tiny one."

"Myself, I just open the fridge and everything screams, Eat me! I open the bar and it screams, Drink me! Among others."

"You should work on your self-discipline, Mrs. Carter."

"I am." Her smile broadened. "Emma is the only one who doesn't guss up to Amudsen, you know? I saw you with her too. You shouldn't have made her come back."

"I didn't."

"Well, she sure didn't."

"Yes she did."

"Wow!"

"I know."

"Well, don't lie about it when the time comes."

"What's that?"

"Emma. She doesn't know what she is, but she wants to take the easy way out. Don't let her believe it—she's no ding-dong. I've burnt many bridges; it has been excruciating!" She brought the conversation to a close by sinking her head below the water and pushing off toward the other end.

I walked back into the pool building and went over to the bar. I asked for a grapefruit juice. There was no charge. I took it away from the pool and across the lawn and behind the vegetable patches. I put my bathrobe down on the lawn and lay on it to take the sun. I was right where the steepness of the downgrade began, and without lifting my head I could see the lake dazzling with sun below me. Then I closed my eyes.

I hadn't been there ten minutes when I heard a man's voice calling. I didn't think it was for me, and I didn't lift my head. A moment later I heard it again and it was right over me. It was a concerned voice. "Are you all right?"

I opened my eyes. I couldn't see anything with the sun in my face. I shielded my eyes, and I could see a white coat against the sun and the face of a large man. "Are you all right?" he said.

"Sure I'm all right."

"Have you just arrived?"

"Yes, I mean no. I'm not a . . . I'm a visitor."

"Family member."

"Yes."

"You're sure you're not here?"

"I know I'm not here."

"The first day of tranquilizers can be disconcerting, particularly in this heat."

"Look, am I out of bounds or what?" I took the keys to my chalet from the pocket of the bathrobe and showed them to him.

"Who are you with?" he asked.

"Emma Cullington," I said.

"Ah Emma, Emma. Is she back?"

"Yes, she's back."

"Well, please stay as you are. I do have to check. You do understand?"

"Of course."

Soon after he left, the ants started. I found them in my grapefruit juice and then moving across my chest. I stood up and shook out my bathrobe and put it on and walked over to my bungalow. All these guest houses were like miniature Tyrolean chalets. They had steeply sloping roofs to distribute the weight of snow in winter. There were two rows of them, looking somewhat military. Inside mine there were two beds, a bathroom, and a television up in a corner that slanted down toward the bed so it could be watched comfortably with your head on the pillow, like in a hospital ward. Between the beds was a small library, with books in French, English, and German on addiction. I showered and dressed. I read the laminated poem on the desk. "Don't walk before me, I will not follow. Don't walk behind me, I will not lead. Walk beside me and be my friend." I put it back down. I lay on the bed and switched through the channels. I got the midday news in three languages. A plane crash. It was only midday. I had another week of this before I could do anything for Emma. And then what? What could *I* confront anyone with? I needed a drink.

There was only one other building near us. I could see the roof from the gates of the clinic. There was a small sign on it, and I could just make out "Hôtel Bellevue." I walked down the road toward it. The banks of dry grass on either side of the roadway hummed with heat and clouds of gnats. I came down to the level of the hotel. It was a large old building. There was a cattle guard at the gate, and I crossed it and walked down the drive. The parking lot was full, and I crossed it and went up the steps to the foyer of the hotel. The bar was in the back of the building and opened onto a very large balcony that looked down to the lake. It was very crowded. All the tables were covered in mineral waters and teas, and I thought that all the people around were probably the ones that the sobriety ceremony was for. There was a large buffet at the end of the bar and beyond that a dining room. A sign posted outside the door said that they only served eight-hundred-calorie lunches. I walked out to the balcony to see if there was a free table. I couldn't see any. There was a group of children looking through a viewfinder and arguing whether the town in their sights was Lausanne or Montreux. One said that it couldn't be Montreux because it would be to our left and the viewfinder was pointing to our right along the lake toward Geneva. Up next to the handrail to the balcony I saw a table with only one person at it. It was Cullington. He was looking straight out across the lake. I stayed completely still so he wouldn't see me. He was under a canopy, with his jacket and tie off and his shirt opened. He wore sunglasses and fanned himself with a copy of the *Wall Street Journal.* His garment bag and briefcase were on a chair beside him, and there was an empty tumbler before him. He took a handkerchief from his pocket and mopped his forehead. He suddenly turned to call a passing waiter and saw me and stopped fanning himself. He grinned and waved me over.

"Well, well," he said.

"Look, Cullington, get this straight. She ran away from you."

"So she did, so she did." He sounded quite drunk.

"Yeah, she did."

"Yeah, to here. She ran to here."

"But this time it's going to do her some good. What the hell do you have to arrive on the scene for?"

"Oh shut up. What do you know about it? Sit down, have a drink."

". . . ."

"You might as well. I'm not going anywhere." I sat down. Cullington continued, "Yep, I've been having a couple of drinks here to see if I can't work it up to go over and join y'all and get this sorted out for once."

The waiter came over to take my order, and Cullington said, "You might as well make it a double. I'm on doubles. You probably need a few yourself." I ordered gin and Cullington ordered bourbon, and the waiter left. "Well, don't you see me now? Drinking up the courage to get up and cross that road. I'll tell you, boy, it was worse than ever once you'd gone."

"How'd you know she was here?"

"Told you that you knew nothing. I called Amudsen, that's

how. He told me she was here with you and I told him it would be worth his time to make sure she stayed until I arrived. I got to Geneva this morning."

"I didn't think you knew Amudsen."

"Only by phone, but I sure know his type, and that's all I have to know."

"So you didn't just think you'd get this in because there was an OPEC meeting in the neighborhood."

"You're a jerk."

"Look, Cullington, I only mean she's got a better chance without you than with you. She's the one who matters."

"Wouldn't you agree that it's my right to decide who she's better off with?"

"Of course it is, so decide it, for Chrissakes!" I shouted this, and it stopped the conversations at the tables around us. It stopped our waiter dead in his tracks as he approached with his tray. When he saw the table wasn't going to go over he started toward us again. First he put two doilies down and then two glasses with two ice cubes each and then he poured the gin and the bourbon from bottles on his tray. He poured tonic until I told him to stop, and he left the bottle on the table. Cullington didn't want water. I thought it was a strange moment to appreciate a correctly poured drink. Cullington said, "Put it on the tab," to the waiter and then turned back to me. "They still do all that confrontation bullshit?"

"Yeah. I'm booked for next week."

"Sort of thing would get a boy down, I imagine."

"If you go over, you're going to have to do it."

"I know, and I'll do it, too. I'm going to go up that road, and whatever it takes this time I'm going to do it. This is my final attempt. They want me to stay, I'll stay. I'll put up right here and stay as long as they goddamned want. I'm going up there and I'll do anything they want. She can tear me apart if that'll do any good. She can scream at me whatever it is I'm guilty of. This is the showdown."

"It is?"

"Yes, it is. It's the hardest thing I've ever said, but I don't want any part of her second wasted decade. I get mad if I lose a day. She's wiped out from seventeen to twenty-seven, and she's heading into her second decade in just the same way."

"And if you're wrong?"

"Do I look like someone who's wrong? . . . What do you mean?"

"That she doesn't agree that this is the showdown. You need two for a showdown."

"If I'm wrong I have one final offer."

"As in deal?"

"Yes, as in deal, smart-ass. As in you're a deal, I'm a deal, hospitals and shrinks are deals, and lawyers and Daddy's wills and codicils and blocked trust funds and toeing the line are all deals. How much d'you think it would take to get Amudsen to testify on a non-compos-mentis deal? Don't you think that would go halfway toward slowing her down? Or maybe you think she might be tempted to go and starve in that little love nest of yours again? It's actions, boy, actions that count, wake up!"

". . . ."

"I'm sorry, Coach."

"It's the heat."

"Yeah. Let's drink up and go."

We went back up the road together. Between the heat and the garment bag, Cullington looked like he was about to collapse. He sat down on one of the banks of dry grass to catch his breath. He faced the lake with his hands on his knees and tried to breathe in deep. There wasn't the slightest breeze. I stood beside him. When he got up I carried his garment bag the rest of the way.

There were groups of people all over the garden now. We walked through more standing in the hallway and outside Amudsen's office also. His secretary wasn't at her desk, and we waited. I put the garment bag down and sat on one of the chairs. Cullington paced and studied the people, who were standing in a group talking. They spoke English and seemed to be catching each other up on news, so I thought they were here for the ceremonies. Cullington sat down beside me and whispered, "They're all so much older than Emma."

The secretary arrived, flustered and carrying sheaves of paper. Cullington introduced himself and asked for Amudsen. The secretary said that he was probably out in the garden with all the old patients and that it was a very hectic day with the ceremonies. Cullington wanted to know what the ceremonies were for, and she told him they were for the people who'd lived a year of sobriety. We left the garment bag and the briefcase with the secretary. As we went out to the garden, Cullington said, "Did you hear that?"

"What?"

"A year's sobriety. Isn't it great?"

"Yes, it is," I said.

The first group we passed were current patients. They were grouped around a woman with notebooks and charcoal sticks. I passed them, but Cullington called me back because he wanted to listen. The teacher was saying, "So keep it fairly simple. Those mountains are only geometric forms, so just try the wash work to describe the volume of their positions in space. Later we'll get to more interpretive use of the medium." Cullington looked at me blankly, and we continued across the lawn.

We found Amudsen beside the vegetable patches. He was sitting on a blanket with a small group. He waved at me as we crossed toward him, and then he must have realized who Cullington was and he stood up. "Dr. Amudsen," Cullington said.

"Mr. Cullington."

"I'm glad you managed to keep her."

"We have Francis to thank for that."

"Whatever. How is she?"

"Working at the moment, I believe."

"Working?"

"They do light duties."

"Of what kind?"

"Emma's on kitchen duties. It slows them down slightly, when they first come in. Most arrive here, as you can imagine, in a certain state of excitement."

"Full throttle, you mean. It might take more than kitchen duties to slow that girl down when she's on full throttle. Anyway, is the confrontation afterwards?"

"It's good to see your enthusiasm, Mr. Cullington, but no, it is too soon. I could, I suppose, rush the process and put her in a group by tomorrow."

"That would be good. No, no it wouldn't. Don't rush it. I don't want anything to go wrong. Just do it the way that the people getting their medals tonight did it."

"Why don't you both come to that, in fact. It will be good for you to see. It will be starting shortly."

"Yes, of course. So, how long before confrontation? I'm sorry, I only have to know to call my office and my pilots. They're waiting in Geneva."

"I think in all honesty that there is no danger in starting tomorrow. Emma has done the prep work long enough. She always refused the confrontation part. Maybe we should just throw her in the deep end."

"You shouldn't blame her about the confrontation. I never offered before, did I?"

"How many people know her well enough to confront her?"

"Me . . . him . . . the people at my house."

"Maybe the two of you can talk about things before tomorrow. You're going to have to share the bungalow. Tonight I don't think there's a free bed for five miles around."

"Well, whatever. Can I see Emma?"

"Yes. Let's go to the kitchen before the patients' dinner begins."

"Yes, let's go, let's go."

We crossed back across the lawn, and Amudsen led us around the outbuildings to the kitchen. The door was open. We could see Emma at the stove. She wore an apron and held the handle of a large frying pan. She was sautéing baby potatoes. Amudsen was going in the door, but Cullington put a hand on his shoulder. Amudsen stopped, and Cullington said he just wanted to watch a moment. Emma had two cup measures beside her on the counter. One was full of chopped onion and the other of chopped parsley. She was talking in Spanish with two old women. They looked as if they were kitchen workers, not patients. They were laughing at whatever Emma was telling them. Emma drained the potatoes in a colander so they wouldn't have too much grease, then she put them back in the pan and threw in the onion. After sautéing these she threw in the parsley and tossed it all together and then emptied the pan into an earthenware bowl, and one of the patients who was on serving duty took it into the dining room.

"Doesn't she look better already?" Amudsen said.

"I suppose. I've never seen her like this before," Cullington said.

"Are you ready?" Amudsen said.

"Yes, let's go."

We walked into the kitchen just as Emma turned around for a cloth to wipe the pan with. "Lordy lord, they hunt in packs!" she said.

"Hi, baby, surprised?" Cullington said. He was smiling as best he could.

"Answer a terrifying question for me, Daddy. Do you think that I might be even the slightest bit insane?"

"Of course not."

"Then what am I?"

"Special."

"Oh come on, that sounds even more retarded. What am I really?"

"Isn't that what we're here for baby, to find out?"

"Francis and I are. I don't know what you're here for."

"To help, baby, to help if I can."

"Fax it, Daddy! Fax your help from the office! Sitting in circles makes you nervous anyway."

"Give me a chance, baby. I'm sorry for everything, but give me a chance. What do you think, Doctor?"

"What does he have to do with it?" Emma said.

"About what exactly?" Amudsen said.

"About therapy, about my going."

"I think it's a conducive environment. That's all one can expect. It happens so rarely, but—"

"But what, Doctor? Get to the point," Cullington said.

"But I've seen more people than you would imagine, Mr. Cullington, come out of sessions having finally said what they meant."

"And what is it we're going to say that we mean? That if I hadn't been born my mother would still be alive."

"Emma!" Cullington cried.

"That you always wanted a son, blah, blah, blah. We know all that! We all know everyone's problems boil down to very little."

"Well, if everything is so simple then what are you doing back here?" Cullington said.

"Christ, everything does have to be explained to you. I'm saved from myself. If I leave now and it all goes wrong again, what then, big boy? Where would I stop then?" Emma was in tears. One of the Spanish women who'd been washing dishes came over and patted her on the shoulder. Emma gripped the woman's hand. Cullington didn't move. The kitchen noises continued all around us. I went out the back door, and Cullington followed me.

There were three banners hanging over the stage where the medal ceremonies were being held. One read "Life is not a dress rehearsal." Another read "God give me the courage to change the things I can, to accept the things I can't, and the strength to know the difference." The third, hanging right over the central podium, said "The way we are living will have been our life." There were five people up on the rostrum. They were not introduced, but they kept on spotting people in the crowd and waving to them, so I thought they had to be counselors. Amudsen took the stage to applause and stood behind a table loaded with velvet pouches, each one holding a medal. He had introduced Cullington and me to two teenagers, a boy and a girl, who'd come from South Africa with their mother for her acceptance, and we sat beside them.

The mother was the first one up. Amudsen handed her the medal and kissed her on both cheeks. She went over to the counselors and hugged each of them in turn. There was much applause, and she stood by the microphone fingering her medal and with tears in her eyes. She spoke haltingly. "I'd just like to thank Dr. Amudsen and all of you who helped so much, and God, I know I was a tough nut to crack, but more than anything I want to thank my two children for having seen me through so much and having kept their faith in me. Well, just that they had faith that someday I'd do it." The whole room began wild clapping. The mother came down from the podium. Beside me the daughter was dabbing at her eyes, and I could see the boy's hands were shaking. Cullington was watching the woman clutching her medal and walking toward us. Both of the children hugged their mother, and Amudsen let the applause die down by itself before calling out the next name.

I watched four. They all made short speeches and thanked their friends and family. I left between the fourth and the fifth and told Cullington I'd be at the bungalow. He said he wanted to stay to the end. I walked back down the corridor to the kitchen. Dinner was over, and they were cleaning up. Emma was back with the Spanish women, who were now working in the steam and rumble of the huge dishwashers. While they loaded plates on the rotating saucers Emma scraped cooking sheets. She introduced me to them all, and they smiled. She took a clean plate and filled it for me with meat loaf and spinach and some of the potatoes she'd cooked. She took me into a pantry to eat. She brought up a stool for me and a bottle of mineral water, and she leaned against the counter while I ate.

"How's last year's class doing over there?"

"Fine. It's quite moving."

"And rightly so."

"For sure."

She scratched herself—a smack itch. "Jesus, that Mustapha gave me some heavy stuff. It's so pure, I mean wow!"

"You'll still have it tomorrow?"

"Just a couple more days. Just snipping at it, don't worry."

"Don't worry? I feel sick knowing you're on that stuff in here."

"It's better than not being here at all."

"Is it?"

"Oh, baby, please don't. I won't have it much longer. It got me here. You got me here."

"Yeah, but now it's just one more joke."

"Go on, eat up. Someday I'll get my medal, don't worry." I finished all the food on the plate and drank the bottle of mineral water. She took the plate back to the kitchen and came back to the pantry. "I'll walk you . . . I'll www . . ." She stood trying to talk for a moment, and then her chin fell back onto her breast and her eyes closed. I shook her arm. It was completely loose. I closed the door of the pantry so no one would see her. I shook her again, and she was still loose. By the time I'd gotten her to sit on the stool she was coming out of it. She smiled up at me.

"Emma, why don't you tell them you're on it?"

"For what? Let me. I'm an old hand, aren't I? And don't you go getting ideas either. Not now."

"Well stay sitting for a while."

"Oh, for god's sake!" she jumped up off the stool and slapped her sides. "I'm fine, see? I don't think I'll walk you to the cottage, though. I'll need all my strength tomorrow."

"We all will."

"I love you, Francis. Will you always remember that?"

"Yes."

She opened the door. "Let's go." As we came out of the pantry the Spanish women were all smiling at us. They probably thought we'd been kissing.

I was in bed leafing through *The Addictive Personality* when Cullington came back from the ceremony. He said he'd stayed to the end and had met some of the people and congratulated them. Most had gone back down to the Bellevue for dinner. He sat down on his bed and called the hotel in Geneva where his pilots were staying. He told them he was going to stay for a week or ten days and that they should stick around for a few days to see if they couldn't get themselves chartered back to the States. He started to make a joke about there being no more free rides with the price of oil being what it was but he stopped himself from laughing. He knew he shouldn't be laughing. The pilots must have asked him if he was all right.

He said, "Yeah, sure, just a little blown away, boys. Let's talk tomorrow."

I watched him take his nightshirt and his toilet bag from his garment bag. He put them down on the desk. He picked up the laminated poem and read it and put it down. He took an *Oil and Gas* magazine from his briefcase and put that down without opening it. He took *Theories on Addiction* from the cabinet between the beds and read the blurb and put it down on his bed to read later. He was as uneasy as I was.

"Want a cigar?" he said. "I only have one, but we can share it."

"I'll keep to cigarettes."

"It doesn't bother you, does it?"

"No."

I had the windows open, and he walked over to them and looked down at the collar of lights around the lake and lit his cigar. He kept on looking out at the lake while he smoked. "I just can't understand it," he said after a few minutes.

"Understand what?"

"Drugs, her, her on drugs, her need. And you can't expect me to."

"I don't."

"So what is it exactly? I mean, what's so great about drugs anyway? I mean, explain it to me. What's so appealing about walking around with your brain all messed up anyway?"

"Who knows?"

"Come on, Francis. I have to understand something before tomorrow."

"Well, for her it's like . . . making up her own movie as she goes."

"Movie?"

"She picks and mixes as she goes, and she waits to see what comes out."

"Picks and mixes what? Where is it she's going 'as she goes'?"

"Tripping, Cullington, tripping. She mixes everything, whatever is to hand. Temperatures and sensations and people and crowds and memories."

"And then?"

"Then they all melt into each other."

"And that's a trip?"

"That's what stokes a trip, her trips."

"And then?"

"Then you watch it as it fades, and you glow inside."

"Well, why doesn't she just drink a bottle of Latour? At least that doesn't kill you."

"I don't know."

"You know better than I do."

"She would if there was nothing else at hand. She prefers a heroin and cocaine and gin cocktail, but if that's not around of course she'd take the wine, and if that weren't around a Walkman and crowded streets would do. If you like tripping, you like tripping."

"Well, if it's tripping that she wants and not drugs, what the hell is she doing here?"

"Oh, forget it."

"Come on, you have to explain it to me."

"I didn't say she didn't like drugs. What is there to like about them? She likes what they do. Isn't it a bit late to be putting all this effort in?"

"For you, yes. I would say for you, yes."

"Meaning?"

"That if you've known this all along and known Emma for so long I would definitely say that it's very late to be concerned."

"You, of course, are completely innocent."

"What do you want me to do, Francis? Scream it from the rooftops that I've screwed up. You think that doesn't hurt, to know that I've done it all wrong with her? You have a child, you do what you think is best for it, and if it blows up in your face, then that's just bum luck."

"If she'd never met me, then she wouldn't have turned out like this, is that what you mean?"

"Not at all, Francis. You were something that was just waiting to happen in her life, and I'm glad that when it did happen it was you. I know you did try, and probably your best, and I know it's draining. In a way, I've always meant to thank you. I knew that at least she was with someone who loved her."

". . . ."

"Jesus, listen to me. Am I nervous or what? It's only eight o'clock! What time do you think reveille is around here? Listen, when this is all over I'll treat the three of us to a couple of weeks in Italy. How about that? We'll get out of this damned place and have a good time. How about it?"

"Sure."

"We'll just run around in that car of yours and have a couple of laughs. I think we all need a couple of those."

". . . ."

"Christ, it's only eight o'clock. Are you nervous?"

"Yes."

"Are you tired?"

"No."

"Why don't we go and have a drink at the Bellevue? Why don't we go and see Emma and then you and I go and have a drink."

"I'll wait here. You go and see Emma."

"Okay, you're right. Thank you."

"What is it you're going to say?"

"I just want to say something to her before the shit hits the fan tomorrow. I want to tell her about the medal ceremony we saw. I want to tell her that I love her."

"I hope they don't mind family going over at this hour."

"For what they charge I should at least not have to worry about what they think, right?"

"That sums it up."

I hadn't finished dressing when I heard his heavy footsteps running back across the gravel and up the wooden steps. He threw the door open. "She's not there!"

"What?"

"She's not in her room. They buzzed it and went up and she's not there."

"The kitchen?"

"No."

"Maybe she's visiting with someone, it's still early."

"Amudsen's checking. Chances are she's at the Bellevue having a drink herself." He turned and ran back across the gravel and started up the driveway to the road. I took the car and caught up with him at the gate. It was bolted and he pulled it open, and I drove out and he shut the gate behind me. We sped down the road to the Bellevue. It was all lit up, and the parking lot was full. I left the car running at the front door and we ran in. At the bar the ceremony people were taking up every table. The glass partitions to the terrace were still open, and all the tables out there were taken also. Cullington went from table to table, and I went to the barman. I described Emma, but I didn't have to, he knew her by name. Yes, she'd been there only an hour before. She'd used the phone. The operator would know. I called Cullington over and told him, and we went out into the foyer. The operator was in a room behind the concierge's desk. We could see her console was jammed with wires, as though everyone in the hotel was using the phone at the same time. Cullington called to her, and she signaled to him to look at her console. She kept on talking into her mouthpiece. The concierge asked if he could help. Cullington said no, he wanted to ask the operator a question. He shouted in if she'd put a call in for a young woman an hour before and where it had been to. The operator didn't answer. Cullington lifted the flap and went into the room. The concierge followed him. The operator said this was the height of rudeness and yes she'd put a call through for a taxi to Geneva and yes she was sure it was Geneva because the first company had not wanted to go that far.

We ran back out and got into the car and drove back up to the clinic. Cullington had to get out to open the gate again. Amudsen was standing at the front door of the clinic waiting for us. Cullington got out. "What sort of damned place is this anyway? They just come and go as they please?" Amudsen handed Cullington a sheet of paper.

"This was on her bed. You mustn't have seen it. Good-bye, Mr. Cullington." Amudsen turned back into the building.

Cullington read the note, handed it to me, and ran toward the bungalow. "I'm getting my stuff!" he said.

I read the note. "Francis, this has been the messiest move of all. The end of something had better be nigh. I'm going to Paris."

CHAPTER 20

We sped back down the mountain and through Vevey and onto the highway to Geneva. Cullington sat silent, listening to the engine. I had to be careful that it didn't overheat. I could hear the pistons slam through their revolutions at their highest speed. We were coming into the outskirts of Geneva before he spoke. "If only we can find her . . . before she has time to . . . start on something else, I suppose."

"Train or plane first?" I said.

"Train. She might be afraid of meeting my guys at the airport."

We ran up the steps of the train station. Two Turks were pushing polishing machines around the floor, but otherwise it was empty. All the stores in the foyer had their signs switched off and their metal shutters rolled down. The departure board confirmed that the last train of the day had left. I could see people moving around in the waiting room, and I walked across to it. It was crowded and hot inside. Along one wall some backpackers lay asleep on their packs. Beside them another group was sitting on their packs. They spoke American and raised liter bottles of beer to me in drunken greeting. Beside them a Turkish family sat on cardboard cases that were held together with rope. The grandfather and father each held a child, and a woman was spreading cheese triangles on a loaf of bread. Beyond them was a group of local bums slapping each other and beside them a soldier sleeping with his leg through the strap of his duffel bag. There was no Emma. I turned back toward the door, but I saw I couldn't leave. A police patrol had blocked the doorway, and two of them moved along the benches hitting their nightsticks against them and shouting, "Réveillez-vous!"

We all had to show our papers before being let out. The bums were the first out. One shuffled around trying to find his feet. The cops looked at him, amused for a moment. One of the younger ones then grabbed him and threw him out into the hallway, where his friends were waiting. Next up was the family of Turks. The grandfather now carried the two sleeping children. The father fumbled in an old carryall, and the head guard rolled his eyes and told them to stand to the side until he'd finished with everyone else. The backpacker who'd raised his bottle of beer to me was in front of me. He was still drinking from the bottle and had his American passport and Eurail card ready to show. He turned around to me. "Just look at how they treat these people." I didn't feel like talking to him. I looked beyond the cops to the concourse. Cullington was waiting for me beside the group of bums, who had started an arm-in-arm dance.

"I said, Just look at how they treat these people," he repeated.

"They're used to it."

"What difference does that make?"

"All the difference."

"You're a fine one."

I had reached the doorway, and I handed the head cop my passport. He didn't even open it. He said American passports looked like they had a new format and gave it back to me.

We walked back outside to the car. Cullington sat in the passenger seat with the door open, and I sat on the running board with my feet on the roadway. "Well, fuck a duck, fuck a fucking duck," Cullington said. "What are we going to do now?"

". . . ."

"I'll call my pilots at the hotel. Leave this thing here and we'll go by plane."

"You go by plane."

"I'll buy the damned car off you."

"No."

"You can even come back sometime and pick it up."

"That's it, let's strike a deal."

"I'll pay more than it's worth."

"If I wanted to sell to you it sure as hell would be for more than it's worth."

"I see."

"No, you don't see. You don't see that I've had it. You don't see that all deals are off, that I'm sick of deals, and that I'm not in a rush because I'm not chasing your daughter anymore. I'm simply going back to Paris."

"Call it whatever makes you happy, but of course you're still chasing her."

"Look, Cullington, if you can't do it alone, drive with me. You can pay for the gas." I looked across the lawn. The drunk backpackers were having it out with the police patrol. They had laid their sleeping bags under some bushes between a statue and the street, and the police were shining their flashlights in their faces and telling them to move. The backpackers rolled up their sleeping bags as slowly as possible, but the cops didn't move. With their packs on, they came back across the lawn.

"How about a lift somewhere, Mr. Civil Liberties?" the one who'd spoken to me in the waiting room said.

"Get lost," I said.

They continued on past us and then suddenly turned and threw the beer bottles at us. One hit Cullington in the leg, and the other landed on the roof of the car. We both ran across to them.

"What's with throwing bottles?" Cullington said to the leader. "You think you're bad or something, you little motherfucker?"

"Yeah, matter of fact I—"

Cullington hit him in the mouth and sent him to the ground. He picked him up and threw him against a car. The other one who'd decided to fight swung at me with a full beer bottle but missed, and his whole weight was off and he fell between the grass and the roadway. I kicked him hard in the stomach. It wasn't relief, but it was enough. A third one who hadn't moved was shouting for the cops to come. I watched them start out across the lawn toward us. They came very slowly. Cullington's adversary was now shielding his face. A copy of a guidebook had fallen from his pack and with the seam side down Cullington was whipping him with it. The cops separated them.

"He insulted my sister," I said to the head cop. "You understand?"

"Of course," he said. Then he whispered, "It should be we

who thank you." He slapped Cullington fondly on the back. "*Pas mal* for an old fellow. Not bad at all."

"You're damned right it's not bad at all. They broke the mold when they made me."

This I couldn't translate, and the cops followed the backpackers all the way down the street. Cullington turned to me. "God, I feel better," he said.

I walked over to a faucet on the outside wall of the station. I twisted the key and it started flowing, and I bent down to let it flow over my head. I kept my head underneath it for a long time. It felt good, and I knew just how hot I had been. Some of the water ran down my back inside my shirt, and I washed it around in my mouth also. I didn't bother drying my head with my shirt. It would be dry soon enough, and until then while I drove it would keep me cool.

Cullington called his pilots from a phone booth to tell them to meet him in Paris. We drove out through Geneva, looking for directions to the border points. We were stopped on both sides, but this time only long enough for the guards to peer in at our faces and check our passports and then they waved us through.

Every hour or so I had to stop to let the engine cool. Then I had to wait another fifteen minutes before I dared take the cap off the water tank. At every night station I got out, and while I waited I jumped and squatted to keep awake. Cullington kept himself going on laced coffee. I watched him at bar rails when there was one and coffee machines when there wasn't. In pidgin French he got into conversation with anyone around, pumping them for details as if they'd help him keep awake or at least keep his mind off whatever was coming. From a barman: the favorite drink of all night drivers. To combine harvester drivers: the route the wheat took from the field to the loaf. From cops: the car that most often broke the speed limit and what sort of driver. Back on the road, he kept his eyes open for long stretches.

I hardly had to change gears. I kept my left elbow on the open window and my bandaged hand on the wheel. I watched the dark countryside. Every house in France seemed to have its windows open also. While we were still in the mountains the large stone farmhouses had theirs open, and then also when we came down to the plain and had to drive through villages looking for all-night stations. The upstairs windows on the main street of every village were open, and every village and town looked the same. I had driven through several before I realized that the next day was Bastille Day and there would be dancing in every village in France. That's why they all looked the same. There were cords of paper tricolors between the lampposts and bandstands in the Place d'Armes and viewing podiums in the promenade of plane trees in front of every town hall.

I had a vision of Emma the first summer we'd been together. We had gone on a two-day trip to Burgundy. We had driven through many of these villages—villages full of *gendarmes* on bicycles and old men in straw hats bent over their tomato plants and runner beans. Emma held the vineyard map, and as we drove she pointed out Chambertin and the Clos de Bèze and Romanée-Conti and the Clos de la Roche. Then we just lay on a blanket pulled into a quiet shady corner away from the road. We just lay on the blanket and took out packages from our picnic basket and drank a bottle of wine. Then we just lay on the blanket, glowing with the wine, and the grapes were bloating in the sun beside us, and we were glad the sun hadn't come around yet and we were still in the shade. Then we just lay on the blanket, and all we could hear were the swallows that swooped over the vines, and Emma rolled over on top of me and I could feel her breasts on my chest and behind them the *boom-boom-boom* of her heart, and then our clothes were on the blanket and she was lowering herself onto me and she was smiling now, so far away, and then bent over, covering my face with kisses and stiffled cries.

I remembered more. Afterwards, driving further on the shoulder of the hill of the Côte d'Or until we reached Meursault. We pulled into a courtyard full of geese. The winemaker, because I knew the owner of a restaurant in Paris that he sold to, invited us into the house for a tasting. I remembered a moment: while he went down to the cellar for a bottle we sat on a caved-in sofa. Emma kept her head against me, the sun was setting behind some bell tower, there was a swarm of gnats in the window and the pounding of a barrelmaker's mallet. I remembered more of that moment: the curious goose looking in from the courtyard, the lace curtains swelling into the room, the cat walking across the table and arching its back, and Emma's head now held back, drunkenly laughing at it all. I remembered thinking, She is happy because of me.

Cullington's voice brought me back. "I'm going to lock that girl up. Believe me, I can play hardball too. I'll lock her away in a hut in South Texas fifty miles from the nearest gas pump. That should do it."

"So you're awake," I said.

"And thinking, Coach, and thinking. The thing is that absolutely anything that comes down the chute seems completely normal to her. She'll find a way to enjoy almost anything. That's her gift and her problem."

We still had two hours to go before Paris.

CHAPTER 21

We got into Paris late in the morning. We came off the loop and into the city through the Porte de Clignancourt. There were flags and balloons out along the street. The cafés on either side of the street had all their tables out, and all the awnings were pulled down. The terraces were crowded, and I thought people were going to go down to the Champs-Elysées later to watch the procession. We got behind a street-cleaning truck and I couldn't pass. The truck sent jets of water along the gutter and then followed with all its huge brushes turning. I didn't remember there being any procession on this street, but it looked like they were going to leave it all clean anyway. I stayed behind the truck all the way down the street; there were cars coming from the other direction, and it was just as easy to stay behind it. I didn't know where we were going either.

Chances were she was on a binge. In this heat and being Bastille Day, and she knew the streets would be teeming all night, yes, chances were that she had taken up the challenge. Chances were she was well into it by now too, a serious one this time, not just topping off like she'd been doing in Switzerland.

"'Where are you going?" Cullington said.

"'Anywhere," I said.

"'Let's go to the Meurillon. It's our best chance."

"'Is it?"

"'Where else?"

"'I doubt she'd waste a trip around the Meurillon."

"'Trip, trip, what makes you think she's tripping?"

"'Spare me, Cullington."

"'Well, then, where?"

"'Let's go and wait at my place. She has a key to it."

"'Wait? I'm not waiting."

"'You're going to comb Paris?"

"'Why your place?"

"'Because it's the closest thing to a 'can' neighborhood, that's why!"

We didn't have to wait. From just inside the apartment we heard her sniffle. We walked down the corridor to the bedroom. The door was open and the window was also and there was a slight cross-current. We stood at the doorway. She was holding the sheet up to her neck and faced straight up toward the ceiling with her eyes closed. It had been a binge. Her breathing was quite rapid. The fan was fully extended on its stand and was slanted down toward the bed and locked in that position. Its soft whirr sent ripples along the sheet. She was naked underneath. Her face and arms were wet, and the sheet was wet and stuck to her breasts and the dip of her navel and the mound of her pubis. One leg hung outside the bed so her thighs wouldn't touch. Bolt tight she lay. The beads of sweat on her forehead joined together and pushed themselves down her temples and down the taut ridges of her neck and down into the cleft of her collarbones.

Cullington moved forward from the door and knelt down beside her. He picked a corner of sheet up off the floor and moved to mop her face. She whipped her head away from him. He let the sheet drop. She brought her head back around and looked at us. The huge bulges below her eyes were the texture of leaking balloons. There was hammering on a nearby roof, and the whirr of the fan locked on its axis, and she sniffled again. It was a parched face. A face to hold a cup of water toward. Cullington picked up the sheet again and tried to mop it, and again she pulled away.

Her lips parted, bursting the threads of mucus that bound them. "Don't touch me!" she hissed. Her voice was garbled in hoarseness and phlegm. Cullington let go of the sheet and stood up and took a step backward toward the door.

She brought one of her hands out from under the sheet and dragged it along under the bed, grasping for something that should have been there. She leaned over the side of the bed to look and brought a jar of honey from under it. She stuck her tongue into the jar and, using it as a valve, let the honey flow down slowly between her lips. She put it back down. She took her purse from a chair beside the bed and emptied it on the sheet. The aluminum foil Mustapha had put the coke in was empty when she opened it out. She shook her head and licked the inside of the wrapper. The straw she'd been using she nipped with her teeth and tore open and licked clean of anything it could have on it. With her hand shaking she opened the jar of aspirin onto the palm of her hand and looked at all the pills. She flung them across the room. Her clothes were in a pile by the bed, and she went through every pocket and in turn flung them to our feet. "Not even a lousy little line of coke to start the engines!" She screamed at me. It was as if she couldn't even see her father.

"Instead of looking so fucking tender, how about going out to score!"

I didn't answer.

Cullington went back out to the corridor, and I followed him. "Can I have the keys to the car?" he said.

"It's open," I said.

"I'll take my bag." He turned around and left. I went back into the bedroom.

"Please, please go out and get something, then I'll be nice," she said.

"Emma, it's time to stop."

"No, baby, not now. Go get something, then we can talk, then I'll be nice, then I'll stop. Don't leave me like this now, don't let me down now, please, please go out and get something to get me through. Don't let me down now, if you love me."

I did two things. I tried not to run, and I tried not to think. I walked downstairs. Cullington was gone. I walked up to a square where dealers sometimes hung around on the benches. There were none there. I took an alley into a street of cheap hotels for Arab workers. All along the street they were sitting out in front of the buildings. My eyes scanned both pavements as I walked. I thought there might be a dealer I knew among them. All along the street the groups were relaxed because there'd be no swoops for I.D. controls today. There was no dealer. I stopped at a corner outside a bar. If I just stayed still I thought something might happen. I saw the barman was checking me out through the glass front, and then he nodded to a man who was playing a video game. This man turned around and looked at me. He handed his game over to someone else to finish and came out to the street, smiling. He wore platform shoes and green bell-bottoms. He wasn't dark enough to be African; he was probably from the Caribbean, I thought.

"You look like you really need something," he said.

"Smack."

"Don't know what it is."

"Shall we take a walk anyway?"

"Shall we?"

"Come on, let's go."

"Du calme, du calme."

"Okay, okay. *Du calme.* Let's go."

He led me down an even narrower street. Women were leaning out their windows chatting to each other over our heads. There were groups sitting outside the buildings here, too. We stopped beside one of the groups. They were all watching a television that rested on the roof of a car. It was powered by long cables coming down from a first-floor window. The procession had already started. My dealer called to one of the men, and he stood up and came strolling over to us. He looked at me from my shoes to my eyes and stayed there.

"What do you want?" he said.

"Smack."

"How much?"

"Two fifty. And also two fifty coke."

"I stood up for that?"

"Okay, five hundred of each."

"I thought you only wanted smack."

"Don't break my balls, pal. You have it or you don't."

"I won't break your balls. Not for five hundred francs." The dealer who'd brought me thought this very funny and began to laugh. The one who was selling smiled also and told me to wait. They both went into the building. I watched the television. The Champs-Elysées was teeming. The president was taking review standing by the Arc de Triomphe. He stood under a huge, limp tricolor. In a close-up I saw that he too sprouted beads of sweat on his hairline. I saw a soldier faint in front of him. He crumbled to his knees and tried to hold himself up on his rifle. No one broke ranks to help him, and after a moment on his knees he just stood up again. The dealer in bell-bottoms called me into the hallway. It was bare inside and much cooler. He sat on the first step with a newspaper folded underneath him so as not to stain his trousers with the wormwood dust. I couldn't see his friend, and I walked toward him. Suddenly I was grabbed by someone behind the door and thrown across the hall. I heard my face crack as I landed against the wall. The second dealer was now holding me against the wall and grinning in my face. The one in bell-bottoms stood up from the stoop and walked across to me. "Well, if you want smack, first we're going to have to see the tracks on your arms, won't we?" I heard a knife flick open; it was in his hand. He slit both my sleeves to the elbow. Quite expertly too, the knife not even grazing me. "So, where are they?"

"I snort it," I said.

He began to frisk me while the other one held on to me, still grinning. He took my wallet and my passport. He began to laugh when he opened the passport. "*Un Américain!* This is exotic!" He put my passport back into my jacket. He said, "*Voilà, monsieur,*" as if he were a customs agent, and began on the wallet. I wasn't too worried about him. The one that was holding me and grinning in my face looked crazy. I thought of screaming but didn't. A young woman came down the stairs with a child and walked right past us as if we weren't there. No one would come if I screamed, and I didn't want to get the two of them angry. I thought of fighting. At best I would escape, at worst I'd get a knife in me; no, that wasn't the worst, the worst was getting a dirty needle stuck into me. I didn't want to find out whether heroin dealers carried things like that around. Maybe they did. It would keep cops at bay much more than a knife. The best I could hope for was that they'd make me prove I snorted it. I'd be vomiting all day afterwards, but that would be all.

The one who was going through my wallet had taken all the money out. He put the wallet back in my jacket. "What do you think?" he said to the one who was holding me.

"What do I think?" his grin widened. "I think our American friend deserves a . . . pardon, because it's Bastille Day. Yeah, I'll pardon him because it's Bastille Day. I'll show—what's the word?—magnanimity." He released the pressure on me and then let his hands drop. I thought of running then, but I wasn't going to leave after that with nothing to show for it. The man in bell-bottoms sat back down on the newspaper and began counting out pink heroin envelopes and handed them to me with a small Zip-Lock bag of cocaine. "There's something funny about you all the same, *Monsieur l'Américain*," he said.

Now I ran. All the way down and through the alley and past all the groups in front of the hotels. Seeing me coming, some of the men ran into the buildings because they thought it was a raid. And I did think now, as I ran back toward the house.

I thought, No, no, no, please no, no, please. I am not doing this. Please. No. Run. The sooner you get there the sooner you won't be doing it. Run, faster, run faster. She'll feel better. She's got to feel better. God, no. Just run.

She grabbed the envelopes off me and cut a line of each on a record cover, the heroin line shorter than the cocaine one. She took the ink cartridge from a ballpoint and in two quick sweeps with the barrel to her nose she made them disappear. She tapped the pen over the record cover for anything that might be left behind and then wet a finger and brought it across the surface and rubbed her top gum with it. Then she shuddered and closed her eyes as the first wallop arrived. After a moment she opened them and smiled. "Lordy lord, did I ever need that."

"Don't talk to me. I can't talk," I said.

"About what?"

"I just can't talk."

"So we won't talk. Thank you, anyway."

"Don't *ever* thank me for *that.*"

"Sorry, sorry."

". . . ."

"I think at some stage last night I was doing an inventory of the house."

". . . ."

"What I mean, Francis, is that . . . we're going to need some stuff for the house."

"Like what?"

"Like pots and pans and some more furniture and a washing machine. You know I can't bear the launderette."

"Wait a minute, wait a minute. 'We'?"

"What else?"

". . . ."

"I thought you'd be happier to hear it."

"What the hell made you think that?"

"I shouldn't have?"

I stood up and walked down the corridor to the kitchen. I sat at the table and put my head in my hands and closed my eyes. I had to close something behind me. I just needed a moment of keeping everything out. It was all happening too fast. All coming at me at once. For a moment I thought I'd fallen asleep at the wheel and I was dodging oncoming traffic. Then I opened my eyes. It was blurred, but there was no traffic. I'd driven too long. I should have let Cullington drive some of the way. I had to be much fresher for this. I had to think, and I had to be lucid. I closed my eyes again. It was all still coming at me, but I knew it wasn't traffic and I knew I hadn't crashed over any dividing lines. Why were my eyes blurred when I opened them? It wasn't tears. I knew I wasn't crying. I felt my forehead. It was streaming with sweat. It must have been from running back to the house. I shouldn't have run, I should have walked. What the hell difference did it make? It was streaming into my eyes. It stung. I tore the sleeve off my shirt where it had been cut, and I mopped my forehead with it. My eyes were still blurred. It was exhaustion. I couldn't remember when I'd last eaten. I thought it was the cellar in Houston. I couldn't remember when that was. I couldn't remember when I'd last slept. I'd walked one night, driven to Switzerland on another, and driven back the night before. And then the heat. It was just like Emma had said in Houston—it was like being under water. Like still and green water. Water. I could hear the shower running. I could hear the fan in the bedroom still running. I could still hear the shower. I'd been hearing the shower a long time now. She'd spent a long time in the shower. She'd spent much too long in the shower, much too long to take a shower.

I ran down the corridor and knocked on the bathroom door and called her name. There was no answer. I called her again through the door and there was no answer. I grabbed the doorknob. My hand was dripping, and I couldn't turn it. I thought it was locked. I thought I was going to have to break it down. I grabbed it with both hands and it opened easily. I ran through the steam and pulled the shower curtain. She had a bar of soap in her hand and had her back to the faucet and the water was running down her head and back. She looked up at me. "What is it?" she said.

"I thought . . ."

"What?"

"Nothing."

"Nothing?"

"Well, I should have been glad when you told me you were moving in."

"Oh, you thought that I might have . . ."

"Yes."

"I told you, didn't I? That's the one payoff of being a smack head, you don't go that way."

". . . ."

"Come on, Francis, snap out of this. I'm almost ready. We'll go out."

I went back out. Now I didn't want to sit down and I didn't want to close anything behind me. I took the sheets off the bed and put them into the pillowcases and threw them into a corner. I swept up the aluminum foil and the aspirins that Emma had thrown and I put the lid on the honey jar. I took out clean sheets and put them on the bed. I was finished when Emma came out wrapped in towels. She'd left all her clothes in Switzerland, and while she dried her hair I found some of her old clothes in the crates and gave them to her. While she dressed I took a quick shower and changed my own clothes, and then when we were both ready we went out to shop.

We walked. Emma had her smile on. Everyone in the neighborhood was taking advantage of Bastille Day sales. We walked on a street that was closed off from traffic and was lined with bolts of material and clothes bins. I watched Emma search through a bin of rayon blouses. She thought the colors were wonderful and held them up for me to see. We looked at stacked pots and tested the blades on cooking knives. We went up and down the street on either side. We bought three checked vinyl tablecloths and three aprons that were also in checks. We bought a brown Pyrex dinner set and three dusters made of fluorescent feathers. We also bought a reading lamp in the shape of the Eiffel Tower. Emma wanted to keep on buying, but I said we couldn't carry any more. We decided the washing machine could wait, and on the way home we bought three bottles of wine.

Walking back to the house we saw that people had already started to dance on the street. In front of the building next door they had a ghetto blaster out and were playing a reggae tape. There was a group forming already, because the girls who were dancing danced very well. We watched them for a moment and then continued on. Emma's head was still moving to the rhythm as we went up the stairs with our arms loaded.

In the house she threw one of the new tablecloths over the sitting room table. Then she found a reggae album and put it on. I opened one of the bottles of wine and poured two glasses. She sipped at it and put it down. She took one of the feather dusters in each hand and began to bounce around the room, dusting and laughing to the beat. I sat looking out, with the windows thrown open to the evening. I could see the sun setting in the windows of the building across the street. I heard Emma snort behind me; she'd stopped her dusting. I didn't turn around. Then I heard her start to dance again. I was alone on this one, I knew. If I had asked, "What are we to do?" she would have answered, "Dance."

When the record finished she put on the other side. She came over to me and sat in my lap and leaned back. We watched the last rays of sunlight. "It's your time of day, Francis," she said.

"I know."

"Mmm! I feel so good. My man's just got back from a hard day's work. The food is ready somewhere, piping hot. We'll use the red-checked tablecloth tonight. I'll wear the red-checked apron, too. Don't you think?"

"Whatever you want. Today is your day."

The phone was ringing. I let it. The answering machine clicked in. It was the Greek. "Hello, *chéri!* I'm in town, completely by chance. I'm going to a ball tonight. I'd just love to go out on the town with you afterwards. I'm at the Meurillon until eightish. *A bien toto,* kissy-kiss!"

Emma hadn't even heard it. She was leaning back into me, with her eyes closed. "I do love smack," she said. "It's as if your body and your spirit drift apart. You're light and without a care. It's all beautifully clear, and you can watch your body and your spirit just drift away from each other. One day I suppose they drift just the tiniest bit too far apart and you can't get them back together. Your body has floated off without you. Pouf! You're a goner. I suppose that's how it happens."

"That's how it will happen," I said.

"I suppose. It seems to happen often enough."

"It could happen to you."

"What can I tell you except that even knowing that, it's still too wonderful to give up."

She stood up off my lap and took the coke I'd bought over to the table and began to cut it on a mirror. It would be all ready for the night ahead. It was almost dark, and I could see her reflection in the window.

Do it now, I thought. She won't know. If you can't do it, just turn around and look at her. You've been here before, haven't you? Emma on heroin and you just happy to have her. Turn around and look at her—she's even wearing her old clothes. This could be three years ago. Oh, she's happy now, that's for sure. You've come through for her now. Now maybe she'll love you, is that it? She's smiling now, and it's because of you and because she's feeling all that stuff running through her system. Look at her one last time, because you know you're going to call Cullington. You've got to call Cullington. You have to just do it, now that she doesn't suspect. Now you can do it, now move, move, move, move! Because if you keep on looking at her you'll never do it.

I left her cutting coke and listening to reggae. I locked myself in the kitchen. The music was very loud. If she walked down the corridor I wouldn't hear her coming. She could be right outside listening. What would it matter then?

I called the operator, but no one picked it up. On top of the fridge was a bowl full of matchboxes of hotels and restaurants. I found one from the Meurillon and I called it. I asked if Cullington had checked in. I was told that he had. I asked to be put through. It rang for a minute before it was picked up. His voice was weak and very far away. "Yes?" he said.

"It's Francis."

"Yes?"

". . . ."

"What? She hasn't—"

"No. I want you to give me your word of honor."

"Word of honor? What are you talking about?"

"You've got to come and take her."

"What?"

"But I want a few hours."

"I'll come right now."

"She won't go now."

"Why not? . . . I suppose I can figure."

"Cullington?"

"I'm here."

"We'll be at the Café Dakar sometime around four or five. The place where we met."

"I remember."

"And don't come before then."

"No, kid, I won't. You've got the next few hours. You'll deliver?"

". . . ."

"You'll deliver?"

"Yes."

I put the phone down and redialled the Meurillon. I asked for the Greek. "Hello, it's me," I said.

"*Chéri!* You got my message."

"Yes, I'm just in the door. It's nice to hear from you."

"Oh, you're sweet. It's just completely by accident that I'm in town."

"I'm very glad you're here."

"When can we meet?"

"Tomorrow."

"Not tonight? After my ball. Yes, meet me at midnight, *chéri,* masked, on the Pont des Arts."

"I'd love to tomorrow, anything you want tomorrow. I really do want to see you."

"You really do?"

"I really do."

"Really, really?"

"Really, really, and I really want to do to you every little thing you really, really want me to do. Tomorrow."

"So you can really really wait."

"I didn't know you were coming."

"I know, *chéri,* I know. You know the way I get."

"That I do."

"Oh, you're naughty, *méchant.* Tomorrow, then, but let's make it romantic."

"How about the Tuileries at dawn. We'll have it to ourselves."

"Can I wake up?"

"Of course you can. Six in the morning. It'll be romantic. I'll give you a dawn ride in the car."

"You've convinced me."

"I can't wait."

"Before you go . . . say something bad to me before I go out."

"Baby . . ."

"Yes, yes."

"This time tomorrow you'll be squealing on the carpet and I'll be whispering filth into those little ears of yours."

"Ummhumm! You are bad. Now I can go out."

"Goodnight."

"*A demain, à demain.* Kissy-kiss."

I needn't have worried about Emma. She was still at the table cutting the cocaine. I lay down on the sofa. She came over and lay beside me. I brought my arms around her and clasped my hands in front of her. Just like the old days. I buried my face in her hair. She must have heard me.

"Don't cry, champ, don't."

With my knees inside hers our bodies fitted snug into each other, and we held each other, together like skid marks.

CHAPTER 22

Arm in arm we strolled down to the Boulevard de Clichy. It was crowded with out-of-town gazers, German tour buses, and the dazzle and flash of all the neon. We walked past a group of elderly Scandinavians chuckling and prodding each other as they filed into the Moulin Rouge. Then past crowded game halls and men in cheap pinstripes handing out passes to strip joints and past couscous halls with greased-up mirrors and windows stacked with oozing pastries. We crossed over to one of the shooting galleries in the center of the boulevard. We watched men take aim and fire and then hand their girls gifts like pink fluffy rabbits to put on top of their dressers. I paid the attendant, and he gave me one of the air rifles and five pellets. I managed to drop a lead ball, but the prize for that was a handful of candies. Emma laughed and took the gun and five more pellets. When she lifted the gun she couldn't hold still enough to fire. Even when she rested her elbows on the zinc her hands shook, and she gave the gun back to the attendant. The couple beside us got our pellets and the candy, and we continued down the center of the boulevard.

We reached a place where an accordionist sat up on a tarpaulin-covered platform. The old people of the neighborhood moved about in the clearing below him. To his *"Moi, j'aime Paris . . ."* they sang their response together, "La Boulevard des Italiens, la Porte de St.-Denis!" We joined them in the dance. It was an arm-in-arm one, and we fumbled through it. From the other side of the podium the concierge called to us. She was dancing with her husband. She said, *"Bonjour, Emma,"* and Emma smiled and said they'd have time to catch up on news.

We danced to two songs and then we got off the Boulevard de Clichy and started to walk back to the house. The closer we got the better everything looked, as if the heat and the darkness combined to show off the war-zone look. Coming through the streets we could already hear the concentrated pulse of our own block party, and the closer we got the more crowded it was until we were walking between women frying snacks in oil and children chasing each other between the dancers. It looked like everyone had come for this from all the surrounding blocks, as well as all the people who lived in the hotels. Up on the stage there were three black drummers and a singer, and below them the dark wet foreheads and arms moved like a slick of bilge oil on warm waters. Emma stayed looking at it all. Her smile said, "Here is fuel." I knew tonight I was being cast in the role of Lester's son. Maybe I always had been? It didn't matter now. Emma pulled me into the middle of the pulsing crowd, and we danced.

When the dancing broke up, I let Emma suggest that we continue on at the Café Dakar. Even the alleys on the way there were crowded with other strollers and impromptu dancing groups. At the door of the café we were frisked and then handed the red paper hats worn for the storming of the Bastille, with their red, white, and blue rosettes pinned to their sides. Abadou was hot in white patent leather shoes, a purple dress shirt with a ruffled front, and a lamé jacket. He was up on stage trying to figure out the wiring for Les Rois du Voodoo. Beside their steel drums and electric organ was a fortress of papier-mâché blocks with a hand-painted "La Bastille" sign hanging over it. We managed to get to the bar and order beers. Emma took up her saloon stance and smiled out at it all. "Oh, I'm so happy. We're lost, Francis. Lost in the back room of a bar in the back streets of the back streets of the City of Light. And I'm with my favorite man forever."

She didn't bother to go to the bathroom to snort. She just bent down as if she had dropped something and snorted below the bar. Not that it mattered, but Abadou would not have liked it.

I watched the drummers on stage. Two of them sat beside the organ with their drums between their knees. They had the tip of every finger bandaged with masking tape, and the moment they began to play Emma set off across the dance floor, dancing faster and faster as the tempo increased.

I stayed at the bar and watched her. She took Abadou off in a sultry tango. She broke up other dancing couples and made threesomes. They didn't mind her antics—they smiled kindly, almost encouraging her. Some of the women let her take their men off across the dance floor, and the men just laughed, like the ones at the cantina. Their smiles were orange from constant cocoa-bean chewing. She came dancing back toward me at the bar, now with her eyes open and now with them closed. She was a berserk princess, and yes we were lost, and yes it was delicious. She was right about how wonderful it was to be lost. I got to thinking watching her that it was as if troubles couldn't reach us here. That's how I had to think, watching her dance, I had to forget what was coming, I had to forget what I'd done, I just had to think that for the time this would last we were out of the reach of any troubles, as if we'd been granted a period of grace. I watched her dance backward into the crowds, weaving now among the other dancers, her hips among all the others, swaying like palm tops in the breeze of some tropical port.

An hour must have passed this way before it was time for the storming of the Bastille. Only women were allowed to take part. With a mike in his hand, Abadou asked them all to line up across the dance floor. It was to be a very correct storming—they had to wear their red caps, and they were all given empty bottles for the destroying part of it. When they were ready, Abadou lowered his hand and shouted, *"Aux armes, citoyennes!"* and they ran across the dance floor yelping, with the bottles held over their heads. When they reached the stage they scaled it and then began to pummel the soft castle.

Abadou had been generous with the presents he'd hidden. Any woman who found two had to give one away. There were chocolates, perfume, and silk stockings. Emma found costume jewelry earrings, but another woman found the main present, a sash that read "Miss Liberté." While she held it up for everyone to see, Emma grabbed it and offered her the earrings. Neither one was letting go of the sash. Abadou rushed over. "Don't spoil the fun now," he said. "You're my Miss Liberté." I was at the foot of the stage and offered Emma my hand so she could get down. She took it and hopped back down to the dance floor, and the music began again.

She put her arms over my shoulders and we danced slowly now, completely out of rhythm with the music.

"We should have gone away, Emma. We should have gone

away years ago." She kept on dancing with her head on my shoulder but didn't answer, as if she were thinking about this. "Away where?" she said.

"Anywhere, out of Paris for a start."

"It would have been nice then. A type of elopement. Or you could have been a knight and you could sure count on me to be in distress. You could have been a *bandolero* and just grabbed me off my feet. That would have been your best chance to take me."

"And now . . ."

"Now it doesn't matter, Francis. It's too late for us now. We didn't do it together, and now you've got to save yourself alone, my love." She spoke with a peaceful expression on her face. As though she had not said anything that was new to her. As if she'd been waiting for the moment to say it.

"I know it's time. I love you," I said.

"And I love you, but this will have to do. For the time being we're at a little cabin down by some beach, away from all woes. All around us are the villagers, and I suppose I'll have to be the girl who escaped from the mansion on the hill for the night. Don't be sad for me, it's enough. All I can hear now are the waves breaking on the beach outside. That's all I can hear. They break soft and dark in the moonlight, and they wash over everything."

I drew her closer and felt the slight arch of her back give. It was far from clear to me how much time passed while we were like that. Then I saw Cullington standing in the doorway with his pilots. His eyes were nestled between all the other smiling eyes and copper lips. The bouncer put a hand on Cullington's shoulder and one of the pilots immediately slapped it off. The calypso music stopped, and the three men walked toward the dance floor, in a wedge, expecting the worst.

I signaled to Emma with my eyes, but she didn't have to turn, she just gave an "Oh well, there you have it" with her eyebrows. She walked across to the bar and picked up a beer and waited for him to come. He was standing behind her when she turned around.

"You couldn't let me leave my way, could you?"

"Leave?"

"I was ready to leave, I was going to leave, and I was going to do it all by myself."

"You might have been talking, baby, but tomorrow morning you'd be sober. You'll never leave by yourself."

"How can you dare to presume that I—"

"Calm down, baby."

"Calm down, he says. Lawdy lawd, with the load I have inside me tonight, that's a lot to ask."

"Why don't you just come with us?"

"Why, why, why everything? Because I love this buzz too much. Right here is everything I'll ever need, right in this room, no more complicated than that."

"Enough talk," Cullington said. "Let's go." He grabbed her elbow, and she swung out of it.

"Hands off, jerk! Francis, help me!"

Cullington grabbed her again—by the elbow with one hand and by the hair with the other. She looked at him, quite startled by the force he was using. "Francis, help me! Help me!"

This is it, I thought. This is it. Five seconds more and it's over.

"Francis! Help me!"

I looked down at my knuckles. They were white gripping the bar rail. I didn't move.

"Well, fuck you all!" Emma said. She tried to pull away from Cullington, but he held on. She lurched toward the bar rail to get away, but she tripped. Cullington didn't let go, and he fell down with her. He steadied himself over her and grabbed her by the ears with both hands. She pulled away, and he screamed, "Stop it, baby!" She pulled again, and he began to drag her across the sawdust by the ears. The dancers parted before him. He was pounding her head against the dance floor as he went and screaming, "Stop it, baby! Stop it! Stop it! Stop it!" When he reached the stage a microphone wire got tangled in his arm and brought the stand down over his back, and only then did he stop. He let her head down gently in the sawdust.

His men were still beside me at the bar, not moving until called for. I walked across the dance floor to Cullington, and they followed me. He was bent over her, whimpering. His shirt was wet through, and all the dancers in their red caps were standing around him. Emma had a trickle of blood running down her right temple. I went back to the bar to get some wet paper napkins. I brought them back and gave them to Cullington. He dabbed some of the blood off her face. Then he picked her up and the crowd parted to let us out.

We drove. Emma was slumped in the back seat. Cullington and I were on either side. The pilots rode in front. The bleeding had stopped, and one of the napkins was stuck to her forehead with a large scarlet stain, and the hairs of her bangs were matted into a spike.

At the Meurillon the night doorman came out to open the car door. When he saw Emma he made a move to lift her out.

She sat up and nodded that it wasn't necessary. The whole night shift looked at us cross the foyer. A concierge and two bellhops and an old maintenance man up on a ladder cleaning a chandelier with spray and rags hooked onto his belt. Cullington asked for his key and a first-aid kit. The pilots came up to the room with us. In the room she dropped onto the bed. Cullington opened the tin box and wet a swab of cotton wool with peroxide and dabbed at the cut. He then dabbed it with Mercurochrome.

Emma opened her eyes from the sting. She was startled by the light. Her eyes swept over us all and then rested on her father. "Oops. Daddy!"

"A real oops, baby."

"Who the hell am I kidding? I'm going to blow up, Daddy, I'm going to blow up!"

"You're not, baby, you're not now, not now."

"I'm sorry to have disappointed you, Daddy."

"Don't, baby, don't. You didn't. You don't. We'll get by." She put her arms around him and then they loosened and fell back down and she was out. Cullington got off the bed and walked into the sitting room. The pilots and I followed. Suddenly he turned and swiped me across the face with the back of his hand. It sent me to the floor.

"I'm sorry. I just had to do that," he said.

"He deserved it," one of the pilots said.

"Shut up," Cullington said.

"He's right," I said.

"Whatever."

The ring on Cullington's hand had gashed my cheek and it was bleeding. He went back into the bedroom for the first-aid kit and handed it to me. I dabbed some Mercurochrome on the cut. Cullington told one of the pilots to phone the concierge and get a doctor to come and check Emma, then to get a nurses' agency to send a nurse for the flight. They would also need some kind of bed with wheels. He should then call the house and tell them to get it ready for Emma's arrival. He also wanted a certain doctor in Houston to be ready and their own takeoff time confirmed as soon as possible.

My face had stopped bleeding, and I put the swabs I'd used into the wastepaper basket. I stood up. "Good luck," I said to Cullington.

"Thanks, Coach. If I can ever—"

"Don't bother."

"Give me your word that you won't contact her."

"For what?"

"Yeah, for what?"

This time we did hug, and I walked out. The pilot who wasn't on the phone escorted me all the way to the front door.

Outside, the sky was dark blue and still held back day. I walked between the statues of the Tuileries to the river. Leaning over the Pont des Arts I watched a barge come toward me. It moved quickly through the water. Its open decks were loaded with coal. The captain and I were the only people around, so we waved to each other. His dog ran around the deck and barked up at me. They disappeared under the bridge and then continued down toward Notre-Dame.

An hour later I had walked as far as the Ile St.-Louis, and I began walking back toward the Tuileries. I went in through the Louvre entrance just to savor the view up through the *allée* once again. I spotted the Greek. She was sitting under a chestnut tree and must have asked the kitchen for breadcrumbs. She held a paper bag in her lap and sprinkled out the crumbs the way a sower sprinkles seeds. The pigeons fluttered down toward her and caught the first sunlight in the angles of their wings. I walked around the fountain from her and sat on one of the chairs. We had plenty of time to watch each other through the spurting water. She pointed at the cut on my face and I motioned that it was nothing. She pointed at my bandaged hand and I made the same motion. Then I started to laugh. It was not a moment to laugh, but it just came over me. It was over now. Seeing me laugh, she too began to laugh. I was in my rumpled suit, leaning back as if the night before had never ended. She was under the leaves, and the sun now dappled across her stockings and skirt and swinging hand. When I didn't stop laughing maybe she understood. With a hand full of bread crumbs she waved me over and I shook my head. She waved me over again and I stayed sitting. She was not laughing now. I stood up. I straightened myself and walked back around the fountain and across toward the trees and the gate. She didn't take her eyes off me. I was still grinning as I passed her.

"You're only a lousy bum on the make!" was the only thing she could think of screaming after me.

When I reached the gate I looked back. She was still watching me go, but suddenly with no more anger, as if she were somehow glad for me. I turned toward the gate. It was on the grapevine.

I continued out across the Place de la Concorde. The pavement was strewn with confetti and spent crackers, and the city mechanics were already unlocking the metal barricades around the square and loading them back onto their trucks. I remembered as a boy diving off rocks and hugging the seabed until my lungs were empty. Then facing up toward the sunlight dazzling on the surface above me and pushing off the sand in a sprint to reach it. I remembered the frantic moment, thrashing in the shafts of light, when I thought I might not make it, and now, as I crossed Concorde, I shuddered as I always did then in those last blinding seconds, just before I burst through the surface with my lips blowing open for air.

TITLES OF THE AVAILABLE PRESS
in order of publication

THE CENTAUR IN THE GARDEN, a novel by Moacyr Scliar*
EL ANGEL'S LAST CONQUEST, a novel by Elvira Orphée
A STRANGE VIRUS OF UNKNOWN ORIGIN, a study by Dr. Jacques Leibowitch
THE TALES OF PATRICK MERLA, short stories by Patrick Merla
ELSEWHERE, a novel by Jonathan Strong*
THE AVAILABLE PRESS/PEN SHORT STORY COLLECTION
CAUGHT, a novel by Jane Schwartz*
THE ONE-MAN ARMY, a novel by Moacyr Scliar
THE CARNIVAL OF THE ANIMALS, short stories by Moacyr Scliar
LAST WORDS AND OTHER POEMS, poetry by Antler
O'CLOCK, short stories by Quim Monzó
MURDER BY REMOTE CONTROL, a novel in pictures by Janwillem van de Wetering and Paul Kirchner
VIC HOLYFIELD AND THE CLASS OF 1957, a novel by William Heyen*
AIR, a novel by Michael Upchurch
THE GODS OF RAQUEL, a novel by Moacyr Scliar*
SUTERISMS, pictures by David Suter
DOCTOR WOOREDDY'S PRESCRIPTION FOR ENDURING THE END OF THE WORLD, a novel by Colin Johnson
THE CHESTNUT RAIN, a poem by William Heyen
THE MAN IN THE MONKEY SUIT, a novel by Oswaldo França Júnior
KIDDO, a novel by David Handler*
COD STREUTH, a novel by Bamber Gascoigne
LUNACY & CAPRICE, a novel by Henry Van Dyke
HE DIED WITH HIS EYES OPEN, a mystery by Derek Raymond*
DUSTSHIP GLORY, a novel by Andreas Schroeder
FOR LOVE, ONLY FOR LOVE, a novel by Pasquale Festa Campanile
'BUCKINGHAM PALACE,' DISTRICT SIX, a novel by Richard Rive
THE SONG OF THE FOREST, a novel by Colin Mackay*
BE-BOP, RE-BOP, a novel by Xam Wilson Cartier
THE DEVIL'S HOME ON LEAVE, a mystery by Derek Raymond*
THE BALLAD OF THE FALSE MESSIAH, a novel by Moacyr Scliar
little pictures, short stories by andrew ramer
THE IMMIGRANT: A Hamilton County Album, a play by Mark Harelik
HOW THE DEAD LIVE, a mystery by Derek Raymond*
BOSS, a novel by David Handler*
THE TUNNEL, a novel by Ernesto Sábato
THE FOREIGN STUDENT, a novel by Philippe Labro, translated by William R. Byron
ARLISS, a novel by Llyla Allen
THE CHINESE WESTERN: Short Fiction From Today's China, translated by Zhu Hong
THE VOLUNTEERS, a novel by Moacyr Scliar
LOST SOULS, a novel by Anthony Schmitz
SEESAW MILLIONS, a novel by Janwillem van de Wetering
SWEET DIAMOND DUST, a novel by Rosario Ferré
SMOKEHOUSE JAM, a novel by Lloyd Little
THE ENIGMATIC EYE, short stories by Moacyr Scliar
THE WAY IT HAPPENS IN NOVELS, a novel by Kathleen O'Connor
THE FLAME FOREST, a novel by Michael Upchurch
FAMOUS QUESTIONS, a novel by Fanny Howe
SON OF TWO WORLDS, a novel by Haydn Middleton
WITHOUT A FARMHOUSE NEAR, by Deborah Rawson
THE RATTLESNAKE MASTER, by Beaufort Cranford
BENEATH THE WATERS, by Oswaldo França Júnior
AN AVAILABLE MAN, by Patric Kuh

*Available in a Ballantine Mass Market Edition.